DEAD POOL

THE HARRY STARKE NOVELS
BOOK 21

BLAIR HOWARD

Printed Cleveland, TN 2023
ISBN-13: 979-8-9891031-1-9
Library of Congress Control Number: Pending

For Jo, as always.

1

Victoria Blue wasn't exactly anti-social. Not in the sense that she stayed inside with the curtains drawn and the phones unplugged. But if she was pressed, she'd have to admit she was at least uninterested in being social. Kind of a funny change, really. As a girl she'd been the typical, almost stereotypical chatty, pigtailed, rope-skipping kid who didn't stop talking until she fell asleep. And even then, if the stories were true, she kept up the grinning and muttering during happy dreams.

It wasn't that anything particularly bad had happened to her either, driving her into her shell and making her keep the rest of the world at arm's length. No, it was more of a steady, consistent, only mildly irritating experience with people that had led her to slowly keeping her guard up.

She hit the button on the one-cup coffee machine in her kitchen, thinking, hardly for the first time, that Hilden Heights was not quite what she'd been led to believe. Sure, it was wealthy. One of the wealthiest neighborhoods in the area. But as the saying goes, money can't buy class.

Maybe that was too harsh. But as much as she hated to admit it, there was a glaring difference between old money and new money, and if anyone doubted that, all they had to do was drive around a few of the neighborhood streets and take a look at what new money could do. Pools, intricate landscaping, and too many cars to even fit in the multicar garages. Boats left out in driveways. It was funny; in a lot of ways, the new money wasn't entirely unlike neighborhoods with no money at all. The only difference was the cost of the items left out in the elements.

But that wasn't her concern. She knew very well that she was extremely fortunate to be born into the family she was and that it was through no effort of her own that she ended up in such a comfortable position. Even with her work, which she was proud to say supported her lifestyle without any of dad's, or grandma's, or great-grandpa's money, she would be doing just fine. Maybe that was just another blessing of wealth, though. Not every kid grew up with a computer, let alone multiple ones, and it had surely given her a jumpstart when she'd taken an interest in software engineering.

She was a quick study and had put the hours in, so sure, maybe she'd picked the Heights to be in what seemed like a familiar position, socio-economically speaking, but she also liked being able to just hunker down at home, do her work, create her programs, and be left alone for the most part. No harm, no foul, as her dad would've said.

You'll never get a man like that, her mom would've muttered.

But who needed a man when you could take care of yourself? And besides, she had Dipper.

She patted her thigh softly and the little black and brown

Yorkshire Terrier stood up in his dog bed, stretching his front legs before trotting over to where she stood at the kitchen island.

Victoria pulled a thin rawhide chew from a bag in one of the cupboards and tucked it in her back pocket. Dipper immediately sat, attentive but not overly rambunctious, another thing she knew she had to be thankful for. Yorkies weren't known for their calm demeanor, but she'd hit the lottery with Dip.

The coffee maker let out its final gurgle and whoosh, and grabbing her laptop from the marble island, she took her work and her dog and stepped out through the sliding glass door into a screened-in porch, then onto a concrete patio. Off to her right, a small pool glittered in the morning light, the pool jets sending quiet arcs of water out to keep the salt and chlorine mixing. To her left was her workspace, at least on days like this. A solid roofed pergola, complete with an outdoor couch and round concrete table, awaited her.

Dipper skipped along at her side, eyeing the treat in her pocket as she walked over and set down her things. The sun was warm, though not hot enough to prevent her from getting a few hours of work done before she headed in for lunch. She handed the rawhide to Dip, who took it gingerly in his jaws and then circled the table a few times before finding what was apparently the perfect spot for snacking.

Maybe a ranch would've been wiser, she thought, glancing at the fence around her backyard. A lot more work, and Dip wouldn't be able to run quite so free—she'd heard more than one story about owls and hawks making a meal of small breeds like this—but it would at least give her a place she felt like she could relax. Here, the neighbors' roofs and windows were visible, despite the required extravagant space between homes, and even with her thick curtains, she always felt like she was just too exposed.

The feeling was only confirmed when she realized the

bubbling of the deck jets wasn't the only water she could hear. A shape moved on the other side of the fence, casting a shadow through the slats and sending misty sprays of water into the air.

"Gotta get those flowers, don'tcha, Nel?" Victoria said under her breath just as a head poked up over the fence between her and her nearest neighbor's yard.

"Good morning, Vickie!" Nel Modesto called. "I thought I heard you out here."

Heard, or saw? Victoria thought. The situation was only made worse by the fact that she could see the woman, which only meant one thing. Nel Modesto was standing on one of the landscaping structures. Most of the homes, Victoria had noticed when house-shopping, had backyards that were more concrete than grass. Not that she had any right to complain, she supposed. But the Modestos had built themselves a kind of brick and concrete bench all around the perimeter of their backyard, then packed in enough potting soil and flowers to make God rethink the Garden of Eden. The fact it also allowed Nel to "unobtrusively" glance over her fence whenever she felt like it was certainly just a coincidence. Heavens no, folks in the Heights would never be that snoopy. Lordamercy.

"Morning, Nel," Victoria called, deciding it was pointless to request that Nel stop using the diminutive. "Vickie" made it sound like they were friends, good neighbors, confidants. If that's how Nel wanted folks to view them, well, it wasn't exactly Victoria's problem. "Thirsty flowers today?"

"Oh, these passion flowers," the woman said, stepping back down and out of sight, though her voice carried just fine, even with all the running water. "You'd never guess they were wildflowers with all the attention they demand. You know—"

Victoria groaned inwardly.

"This is actually one of two state flowers. Quite the fuss

over it a while back. Most folks wanted the lily, but here we are."

Victoria mouthed the last four words along with Nel. She'd heard the story at least half a dozen times, and all she really wanted to do was get down to work. But, she supposed she couldn't fault the woman for trying to be friendly. It wasn't Nel's fault Victoria preferred Dipper to any human companion she'd ever had.

"The weather's been cool in the evenings yet," Victoria said, hoping to wind things up. "I'm sure you'll get it figured out. You've always got the perfect concoction to make them grow."

"Oh," Victoria heard Nel say. "You're flattering me. Mostly it's just water and sun, but now that you mention it, I do have a new plant food I've been wanting to tell you about. Let me see if I can find it in the garage."

Victoria watched the shadow move through the fence slats back toward the house. It was a childish move, but she also knew this was her chance to get back inside and avoid wasting a good forty-five minutes talking about soil nutrients with a woman she was only truly slightly acquainted with. Victoria closed her laptop and picked up her coffee, looking around for the dog.

At some point, he'd apparently given up the rawhide, an unusual choice for her little guy. Instead, he was standing over at the corner of the fence, stock-still, his attention rapt on something.

"Dip," she said, her voice barely above a whisper. She supposed she could leave him out, but Nel would be just as likely to come grab the dog and bring him to Victoria's door as anything. Just being a good neighbor and all, of course.

When the dog ignored her completely, Victoria put down her things and walked over to the fence. The lots on this side of the Heights were offset, meaning that while she and Nel shared a fence line, the home behind them actually was split down the middle, half butting up on Victoria's side and the other half on Nel's. Dipper, for his part, was staring right through the corner of the fence, meaning whatever had his attention was happening in Hattie Baker's backyard.

What that could be, however, was beyond Victoria. Hattie hadn't even reached thirty yet, and she was enjoying all the things that youth and new money could bring. Her favorite of which seemed to be sleeping until at least noon every day. But that didn't mean a partygoer hadn't decided to sleep in a lounger by the pool, or more likely, food had been left out on one of Hattie's garishly expensive platters.

Silver platters but not land, or stocks, or literally anything else, Victoria thought. Grandma would roll over in her grave.

She walked over to the dog and, fully aware that she was doing exactly what she'd just been irked by Nel for, Victoria tried to peek through the wooden slats and see what had Dipper so attentive.

At first it looked like nothing. Hattie's backyard was empty besides the overflow of pool furniture. The house looked dark; its curtains drawn. Then, just beyond the edge of her little slit of vision, she thought she saw it. Someone was in the pool. Early morning floats weren't exactly Hattie's style, but as she'd been keen to let everyone know, despite the ridiculous size of the pool, it was heated and could be used "even on the most frigid Tennessee evening; it's practically a giant hot tub!"

Victoria almost dismissed it and turned back inside, but something in her brain registered the scene as being off, just a little wonky, as her dad would've said. Like a state having two state flowers, as Nel would be saying shortly if Victoria didn't get back inside.

But still, she couldn't help but be curious, and before she realized she was doing it, she'd pulled a chair over and stepped up on it, trying to keep her head low while at least figuring out what exactly was going on in Hattie's yard. The woman always played music when she was out, and she was rarely out alone. And again, it was barely the crack of ten AM.

Victoria's eyes widened as she took in the pool, and then she quietly, albeit shakily, stepped down from the chair and scooped up her dog. The work could wait. Nel could wait indefinitely. Victoria needed to make a phone call. This was entirely not the thing she was anxious about getting involved in when she'd first moved to the Heights, but it certainly did nothing to cancel out her concerns about being too close to people. Now she'd be involved. There'd be more questions. Interviews. Gossip. More than anything, gossip.

But, she thought, an anonymous call might at least buy her some time. If nothing else, it would keep the cops from showing up at her door at the same time they did Hattie's. At least, she hoped so.

Whatever her own concerns were, she couldn't in good conscience just go back inside and wait. Hattie Baker, even if she did sleep in and did listen to music too loud and did buy platters instead of real estate, didn't deserve to have her dead body floating in the pool until someone happened by in the next who knew how many hours.

Victoria slipped back through the porch and pulled the sliding door closed behind her, Dipper in the crook of her arm and her coffee and laptop still out on the table. She took a deep breath. How to even begin? "I'd like to report a death"?

2

June 10, 2022
Friday, Four Weeks Later

There are certain days in life that, as much as you don't want to, you realize you've just kind of cast them off. When I was a cop, it was Tuesday afternoons. Nobody's doing anything interesting on Tuesdays, though I suppose it's just a matter of time before people start figuring that out and everything shifts. But Friday nights, Saturdays especially, when your real troublemakers are still half-cocked from the night before, those are days to look out for. Tuesdays though... Just about the only time less interesting than Tuesday was Friday afternoon.

Fridays, you know trouble might be looming, but you're so close to the inciting incident, as they say, that it's strangely calm. You always had your day-drinkers, but they were usually alcoholics who we'd seen so many times in and out of rehab and drug court and the drunk tank that they'd greet us by name when we pulled them over. After I got out of it, I'll admit I was a little surprised to see that things changed.

When you're a private detective, you're not waiting for someone to come over the police radio and let you know about a crime in progress; you're waiting for someone to come knock on the door of your office, or hunt you down on Google. Usually a good long time after either their conscience or their nagging doubt has gotten to them. And even then, as much as I hate to be a guy who takes money for moral retribution, we don't come cheap. My staff, my office, to be fair, my skill set, cost me a pretty penny, and I've gotta cover it some way or another.

The thing is, though, I'm human. And on this Friday afternoon, when the phones were quiet and the staff were all off chasing down their own tail-ends about cheating wives and missing savings, I was sitting at my desk, for once, a little bored again.

Maybe it's one of those things you don't appreciate until it's taken from you. I'd been through the wringer with a lot of cases since I'd gone freelance, and more than one of them had involved bullets coming at me. But that also meant on the days when there were no bullets, my adrenaline was keyed up with nothing to focus on. Thank goodness for Amanda. And Jade. Refocusing had been a thing I'd struggled with. One of the things Amanda had almost not married me because of. But time passes and old cops turn into old detectives, and sooner or later, no matter how many bullets you fire, miles you run, or cases you solve, you realize those things pass. Family is the thing that sticks around.

If I'd learned anything from the people who came into my office with their life savings and a hope that I could help them, it's that family sticks around.

Depending on the family, I suppose.

Either way, it was late, I was bored—if we're being honest— and in the very Family Man way I'd been trying to take on, Amanda and I had accidentally started a tradition. I say accidentally because it was more out of my own laziness than anything and Jade was far too young to get the idea of a habit. But, hey, you do what you can.

So, for us, Friday was pizza night. Amanda had gotten to the point where she could work when and how she wanted, and my job didn't exactly come with a punch-clock, so we sort of fell into it. And it was good for me to not spend every other night in a beat-up car outside of a motel, sort of hoping and sort of not hoping a guy would show up with a wedding ring in his back pocket.

I texted Amanda just to double-check, something we'd fallen into more for her sake than mine. You spend a lot of years bolting out the door only concerned about your gun and it's tough to adjust to the idea of texting "be home soon honey" and double-checking her pizza preference.

But she was worth it.

Amanda texted me back "yes!" like it was the first time we'd done it and I didn't have her order written down in the notebook I kept of important things. Pizza orders maybe don't count as important to most folks, but I like to know. It's her, after all.

I sent her some nonsense about anchovies and pineapple, jokes I knew were tired but also part of the Tradition, and started gathering up my things. With any luck, it was going to be a calm weekend. Amanda and I were even considering just hitting the road for a few hours. Jade was still probably too young for most of the fun parks, but nobody really gets hurt by spending an afternoon in the mountains. Especially if you're in a baby-carrier on your dad's back.

I grabbed the last few files and shoved them in my collapsible folder, figuring the worst-case scenario would be me reading on the back porch over a cup of coffee and then just passing the underwhelming news on to Jacque, Heather, and the rest come Monday.

But Jacque, as she tends to do, and not that it's her fault—at least not entirely—apparently had other plans. Just as I zipped up my laptop bag and stood up from the chair, she popped her head around the open door and, quite unnecessarily, knocked on the frame.

"Got a minute, boss? You might like this one."

You might like this one from Jacque was the most ephemeral phrase there could be. Sometimes it meant a real brain buster, and sometimes it meant a bag marked "Free Money." Shoot, sometimes it was a joke.

I raised an eyebrow and looked at her. "How so?"

"How so," she said, strutting into the office with a folder in her hand, "depends on how involved you want to be. If you want my opinion, there's not a lot here. But you know how people like to have Harry Starke working for them. So I'm passing this one up the ladder. See if you learned anything in your Business Ethics classes."

"That bad?" I said.

"I don't know if I'd charge for it." She sat down in the chair across the desk from me, and I sat as well. "But I'm not running this show. You get the hard questions."

"What is it?"

"Accidental death."

I sighed and shook my head. These were the worst. Some sad guy or girl comes in, unable to cope with the fact that sometimes life, and death, just happen, and they're ready to throw money at you all day long just to help it make sense to them. There's always another path to track down, another person to interview. And in the end, it turns out your brother or husband or girlfriend was cleaning his gun or hit his head on the side of the pool or didn't follow the instructions on the side of the medication bottle. The ethics behind them was gray, especially if you were a guy who was in it for the money, but I'd told my staff to bring me the gray ones every time. We aren't hucksters and we aren't looking to drain your bank account before we tell you what you couldn't quite yet admit to yourself. But, and I know this is selfish, it was throwing off pizza night. My family counts too, after all.

"Was this a call or an email?" I asked, not bothering to open the folder she set on my desk. I can find out quicker by asking.

"Neither."

I groaned. "He's out there, isn't he?"

She nodded. "I know you hate accidentals. If it helps, I'll stick around. We'll talk him out of it together. Sometimes it helps to, you know..." She shrugged.

"Have someone with a little more 'mom' in them? Yes, I know."

"I don't know if I would've put it quite that way, but yes. More opinions concurring, more validation to the argument."

I glanced at the write up in the file and then back at her. I knew I'd done the right thing, but I was reminded weekly, if not daily, how accidentally lucky I'd been. "All right," I said. "No time like the present."

Jacque smiled one of her trademark quiet smiles and stepped out of my office. I had time to pull a notepad out of my center desk drawer, get a pen, and at least arrange myself in a way that didn't look like I was gunning to get out of Dodge in the next few minutes, before she appeared in the door again, an arm out to usher in my next consultation.

I stood up and held out a hand. "Harry Starke."

"Mason Willis," the young man said, his eyes just barely flitting between Jacque and me. "Is this a private meeting?"

I sat back down and gestured for the two of them to do the same. "If you're looking for help, I'm not exaggerating in any way when I say this young woman might offer you more than I even can myself."

Willis glanced over at her and then back at me again, as if to verify what I was saying. Jacque in no way looked like a private detective, but then again, you say those two words to most people and they think of Humphrey Bogart. Shoot, I don't even look like Bogey.

"Well," Willis looked down. "I s'pose it doesn't matter who helps. I heard you were the best, and if you trust her, then she must be the best, too... right?" He glanced back and forth again.

"I don't mess around, Mr. Willis," I said. "My associate tells me you're here about your girlfriend? An accidental death?"

He paused for just half a beat, and I knew. He wanted to see me, and he got Jacque, and he adapted. This wasn't going to be a quick consultation.

"Well." He rubbed the back of his neck. "The thing is, that's what they say. The cops I mean. But, no. It wasn't an accident. She was murdered."

3

I shot a glance at Jacque. Not because it was her fault. These guys come in with all kinds of stories and we're not exactly in New York City. A black woman in the South just doesn't get the same response a white man does. It's nothing I'm excited about, but it's a fact. Thankfully, she knows that as well as I do, and she understood my look for what it meant. *Record this.*

I saw her reach into her pants pocket and pull out a cell phone. With almost the same kind of ESP, she looked at Mason and he shrugged.

"Not like it's any secret at this point," he said.

I knew if we were going to do this right, I needed to cut in. "This is the point where you tell us whatever you think, whatever you know, and you don't get the two confused, all right?"

He nodded.

"And you don't care who hears it, because you asked for our help."

He nodded again.

"All right." I settled back in my chair, thinking Fridays were the new Tuesdays. "Start at the beginning, go slow, and don't get hung up if we ask you something. We aren't cops. We're just trying to help."

"Yeah." He laughed slightly. It was an uncomfortable sound, part apologetic, but I didn't know if he was apologizing to the police or me. "Look." He ran a hand through his hair. "This isn't something..." He took a deep breath and then just... sat.

I looked at Jacque and she gave me the briefest of shoulder shrugs. *Let him get on with it when he's ready.*

"This isn't something I'm bringing to y'all lightly." He pinched the bridge of his nose, then rephrased. "This isn't something that I'm bringing to you lightly. I know I don't come across as your typical client." He gestured at himself.

The young man had on brown khaki pants, probably Dickies. They were stained with paint, caulk, mud, and who knew what all else. The thing is, when you show up with your name stitched on your shirt, it's not terribly difficult to tell where you fall in the job pyramid.

"Mason," I said. "You could be a plumber or a ditch-digger or a millionaire in disguise; it doesn't change what's gotten you in here. For what it's worth," I said and took a wild guess, "carpenter?"

He laughed, the tension visibly easing from his shoulders. "HVAC."

"That's the way to do it," I said. "Minus the whole, you know..."

He laughed. "Every job has crappy parts."

"So they say." At least he was relaxing. If he couldn't trust Jacque, which no one tends to do (who trusts the first person you meet?), he was at least seeming more comfortable.

"It's really not that bad," he said. "Nine times out of ten, we go out and hook up a few pipes, sit around and literally watch glue dry. It's not a bad deal, man..." He trailed off, apparently realizing he was postponing the inevitable. "You probably wanna just do this, huh?"

"It helps," Jacque said. "But we're used to the long way around the barn. This isn't really the place most people figure they'll end up. We aren't the neighborhood grocery store."

Mason laughed again and looked at her. "You remind me of her a little bit." He looked at me. "I don't mean to be rude, but, she keeps you in line, I bet."

Jacque and I both laughed at that, genuinely.

"More than you know," she said, and I couldn't do much else but tilt my head in agreement.

"All right." Mason rubbed a hand across his forehead and, almost as if the gesture did it for him, his face became sincere again. "You get who I am. I'm just another kid from the Chat who got a job outta high school. Nothing wrong with that."

I nodded, thinking about how many kids from the Chat didn't do that exact thing and ended up as the perps in cases I'd taken.

"Look." He laughed. "I'm not a gold-digger, all right?"

I held my hands out as if to say it wasn't my call to make.

"I know how it is," he said, rubbing the back of his neck. "Some blue-collar kid with some girl from the Heights. It's like a Disney movie. Except when it's the guy who's poor... well, I guess I'm the tramp and she's the lady." He laughed uncomfortably, and something about his candor actually made me believe him a little more. "Hattie and I had been together for almost five years. It wasn't a fling. And if I was after her money, you'd think I'd have pulled the trigger by now, right?" His eyes widened. "Walked her down the aisle is what I mean."

Jacque gave him one of her smiles, the one that always calms folks down, despite how rare she can make it be. "It's all right. This must be hard."

"It's..." He looked up at the ceiling and I could see his eyes glisten with tears he didn't want us to notice. "It's... Frustrating. Tragic. Awful. I had every intention of marrying her years ago, but..." he said and gestured to himself. "Girls from the Heights, or maybe the parents of girls from the Heights, aren't too keen if you come home with dirt under your nails." He paused. "That's unfair. But true."

"I think we get it," Jacque said. "You had intentions but no blessing. It's admirable."

"That's exactly it," he said, looking over at her. "I would've married that girl in a heartbeat. I asked her father more than once." He tossed his hands in the air.

"That's hard," she said, giving me a side glance that let me know to stay out of the conversation for a bit. It's not uncommon; she can be rough around the edges, but she can also be the person who makes you feel more comfortable than you've ever been. It's not the only reason I hired her, but it's up there. "So I think, though, what brought you in isn't necessarily that you were struggling. It's that something else is bothering you. Is that right?"

He laughed a little. "You're good at this."

"It's my job," she said. "Same as you. Learn the skills and use them."

He paused for a second and then nodded. "I appreciate that, miss. I really do. But yes, you're right. Whatever was going on between her folks and me is my own problem. The reason I came here is..." He rubbed his neck again. "It just feels..."

"Hinky?" she said.

He looked out the window. "I s'pose that's about as good a word for it as any. And I know this looks a whole lot like some guy grasping at straws and dragging things out, but..." he said, then steepled his hands and thought for a moment. "Okay." He glanced between the two of us. "Let's say one of you walked in one morning and the other one was missing. And you found out the reason that person was missing was because... I don't know, like they had a crack cocaine addiction. Or they got picked up for human trafficking. Or they were, like, secretly a mafioso who'd been living under a secret name. Ridiculous, right?"

I held in a laugh and nodded.

"That's the feeling I had when they told me Hattie got drunk and fell in the pool. Yeah, sure, she drank. Just not often. I told you we dated for five years. I saw her take maybe three drinks in that time. She's not against it; don't get me wrong. It's just not her thing. A glass of champagne at a wedding, sure. But blackout drunk in her own backyard... that's not Hattie. If anything, when she gets stressed, she hits the treadmill."

I knew the feeling, though I preferred outdoors in whatever weather. Treadmills are a little too close to banging your head against a wall. Literally and figuratively.

"Coroner's reports are pretty straightforward," I said. "If the tox screen came back with high alcohol, the question is more of why than anything. But if it's there, it's there."

"I know." He sighed, looking out the window again. "And I feel ridiculous even asking this, but I loved this woman. I know that probably makes me sound even more desperate and illogical—"

Jacque jumped in. "You're making a valid point. If the circumstances of death are unusual for the circumstances of life, like you said, it would be like Harry showing up high. I'd question it. You're doing the same thing I would."

He looked at her, the thankfulness clear in his eyes.

"I mean, it's the Heights." He laughed sadly. "It's unladylike to get drunk. Especially in the morning. And what did she have to get away from, really? Obviously her dad would say me, but we were good. Great really. And she's got her shops..."

A tear spilled, perhaps because he realized he'd used the

present tense, something that no one would be doing with Hattie anymore.

I spoke up. "Tell you what. How about we spend some time looking into this and we'll give you a call. No more than a couple days. That sound all right?"

He looked up at me, partially embarrassed for showing emotion, I'm sure, but partially thankful for having someone listen to him without immediately blowing him off.

"I'd really appreciate that. I told your... partner," he said and glanced at Jacque, "I emailed all the information to you already. I know it isn't much. Just names and dates, really. But anything you need, just call. My number and email and address are all in there. I just..." He caught the hitch in his chest almost before it came out. "I just know that, if this is the last thing I can do for Hattie, I'm going to do it. I know I'm just a grunt, but seriously, whatever the cost, I'll pay. It was... well, let's just say I had it socked away."

I stood up, hoping to restore a bit of the standard, emotionless business setting for his sake as much as anyone else's. "We'll be in touch soon."

"Thank you."

He shook my hand, shook Jacque's as well, and stepped out of the office.

Once I heard the front door close, I looked at her. "Have you checked it out? Who was the officer on scene?"

She swiped her phone and looked down. "Tobin Henry."

I rubbed my face. I've never wanted to hear someone say "Kate" so badly. If it was Kate, this would be a sad moment, but a quick one. I'd never heard of Tobin in my life. "You know anything about him?"

She shook her head. "First time I'm seeing the name."

I sighed. So much for pizza night. "So that's where we start then, I suppose?"

"I'll track him down."

"All right," I said. "And listen, you bring the full Jacque on this. If he's some rookie who's letting things slide, you don't let him get away with it. If it's legit, then... well, Mason seemed to take a shine to you. I may need you back in here when we tell him the worst news wasn't quite over yet."

She nodded and walked back toward her office.

I pulled out my phone to text Amanda. We might be able to salvage pizza, but she deserved to know I was going to have a bit on my mind.

4

AMANDA MADE IT THROUGH DINNER, THROUGH THE bedtime routine, and through me cleaning up our dishes. I walked in from stuffing the pizza box in the trash can in the garage to find her perched on the counter in the kitchen. She was still in her workout clothes, a pair of neon yellow shorts and a hot pink tank, from when Jade had napped earlier that day. Usually, if she has the time, Amanda is a shower addict. But today had been hectic at the office and at the house as well, so, as she said, "You're just gonna have to deal with stinky Amanda."

I laughed when I walked back in. "Still stinky, huh?"

"You can't send me a text like you did and expect me to just let it roll off my back. What's the story?"

I sighed and leaned on the kitchen island, shaking my head. "The Heights."

"What?" She almost leapt over to me. "That place is like a prison! Or, no, sorry. It's like a prison you want to be in. They keep secrets we couldn't even figure out."

Her past as a news reporter, and a darn fine one, despite

how well she'd done her piece on me before we'd settled down, was always just under the surface.

"It seems pretty cut and dried," I said. "Socialite drinks too much, falls in her pool, bangs her head." I shrugged. "Things happen. You know that as well as anyone else."

"Sure, 'things' happen." She gave me sarcastic air quotes. "But when things happen in the Heights, they're Things, with a capital T."

I laughed. "Always after a story, aren't you?"

She hunched up a shoulder and hopped down from the counter. "I can't help it. And neither can you. You aren't just a little bit curious about what happened to the uber-rich?"

"I—" I started.

"Oh, I forgot. You *are* the uber-rich. Well, excuse me while us peons get back to scrubbin' dishes and cleanin' diapers."

I nodded toward the sink.

"Okay. You did the dishes." She laughed. "But I did do more diapers than you today. So either give me a story or camp out by the crib."

I shook my head and laughed. "That's the whole story. I don't know what more you want."

"Well, why's it on your desk, for one. Why is the client so concerned, for two. Who were the closest acquaintances? What was the financial situation? Ooooh." She looked at me, eyes wide. "Who's the family? 'A body in the Heights' is a story, but you've got to spill some details here. This could be a serious story."

"All right, all right." I took her by the shoulders. "You know the Heights. What do you think?"

"Well." She spun away from me and looked up at the ceiling. This was her thinking mode, and one of my favorite things to watch. She ticked off points on her fingers as she paced the kitchen. "One, they've got more than they know what to do with. That includes money, freedom, and maybe, most importantly, attention. The balance on that neighborhood is about fifty-fifty."

"Meaning?"

"Meaning some of them aren't as bad as you actually think. You gonna give me a name?"

I exhaled. She always knew what I did, so why not? "Hattie —" was all the further I made it.

"No!"

"Yes. They've been keeping it out of the papers. Makes the family look bad, I guess. Maybe a fair enough statement."

"I bought this top at her store!" She plucked the tank out from her chest.

"I heard she had some businesses around."

"That's like saying McDonald's sells hamburgers. How do you not know this?"

I glanced down at myself and back at her. Sure, I came from money. I'm not so blinded to admit it. But it also didn't mean I thought about it all the time. Half the things I owned came from online orders because a nice dress shirt that fits is a nice dress shirt that fits. Find one that works and run with it. I had other things on my plate.

"Of course." She laughed. "But the point is, Hattie Baker is basically the Paris of Chattanooga. I..." She looked down, trying to correct herself though I knew her well enough to catch it. "People wait to see what she says about clothes, and then they, or we, or whatever, pay attention." She ran her hands through her hair, a gesture that could mean anything from frustration to excitement but always looked wonderful. "You've gotta take this, Harry."

"Because they're rich or because it's valid?"

"Because they're people, honey." She moved across the room and hooked an arm around my neck. "I know we both spent a lot of time telling stories about things that just happened, but that doesn't make it any less real. If you want to do this, I'm one hundred percent on your side. And if you don't," she said and grinned, "I'm ninety-nine percent on your side. But you can't tell me this isn't worth looking into."

I gripped the island behind me and looked at her. "Okay. Here's the story." And I told her. I knew well enough she'd already made up her mind that I should take the case, and to be honest, I had as well, but I was seeing more and more that Amanda's consensus was something that I looked for. Jaque and Heather were amazing. There was no better IT guy than Tim. My staff was the top of the line. But sometimes you need a person who knows you.

So when she sat back, hitched up on the sink and looked at her nails in the way that meant she was really thinking hard, I knew I was in.

"I know I said it already," Amanda said, "but you've gotta do it. If only for the boyfriend. That guy needs somebody on his side."

I thought for a minute. It wasn't my typical justification, to be sure. But she had a point. This man was breaking his back for a person he loved.

I nodded. "I'll look into it."

She arched an eyebrow. "Seriously?"

"Seriously I'll look into it or seriously you're irritated?"

"You know."

I walked over and picked her up by the waist, reminding myself to be thankful for these moments. "Seriously I'll look into it. For all we know," I added and gave her a squeeze, "we may wanna move soon."

"You wanna move Jade?" She laughed. "Be my guest. Diapers are finally on you."

5

"THIS ONE'S ON YOU," JACQUE SAID, "BUT I NEED YOU TO commit."

I looked at her. I hadn't even taken my bag off my shoulder yet, but Jacque caught me when I got to the office door. "What do you mean?"

"I mean, we've got some questions to answer, and your name is the one on the door."

"All right."

I gestured toward my office and Jacque followed along.

"Questions," I said. "How many are you looking at?"

"More than one." She sat down and pulled out her phone. I wondered if I was ever going to get used to this kind of work. "First, how did this woman get this drunk? You know I enjoy a night out with the ladies when I need one, but don't for a second believe I've been stumbly, stuttery drunk. Let alone fall in the pool drunk. Maybe she slipped. Maybe she hit her head. But two maybes in a row makes me wonder."

I nodded. It wasn't exactly Sherlock Holmes' logic, but it held water.

"Second, even if she was that drunk, why so early? Or, I guess, so late? We'll have to check the coroner's report. You know I respect the dead, but when a body gets pulled out of a pool, you have to respect the time that takes place."

"I think I see where you're going," I said.

"I think you probably do. And the thing is, I like the guy, but there isn't any way you can sit there and tell me Mason isn't at the top of your list for this. And don't do what I know you're about to do."

"Which is?"

"Ask me what the motive would be. I know it's shaky."

"Shaky?" I ran a hand through my hair. "It's right next door to non-existent. The man came in here himself and said they couldn't get married. Take that how you will, but it pretty well cuts him out of the The Spouse Did It category."

"What about life insurance? What if he's the beneficiary? And since Hattie wouldn't marry him, he got her money another way?"

"We'll have Tim look into that. But I doubt it. The kind of people who live in the Heights don't think of leaving their money to anyone other than family. If she wanted him to have her money, she would have married him."

Jacque chewed her bottom lip. It was either a good sign or a bad one, depending on when it happened. What it meant, regardless, was she was thinking hard on what she was about to say.

"What if..." she started.

I held out my hands.

"What if it wasn't about getting something so much as... taking something?"

I thought about this for a moment. I knew where she was going, but I also knew she was struggling to express it. "Like if he can't have her then nobody could?"

She scrunched up her brows. "Kind of? That doesn't feel right. I mean, you saw him. And you know how hard it is to pretend to cry. But you have to admit he's about as close as we're gonna get to a number one suspect. Maybe she didn't drink, but he did. Maybe they didn't drink that often, and he blacked out. I know it's a stretch, but you can't deny there's a possibility."

"You're contradicting yourself," I said. "If you think he got so drunk he doesn't remember knocking his future wife over the head, that's one thing. I'm not sure if that is even a possibility. If you're saying he murdered her and then came in here asking us to solve it, that's a whole different story."

"Would it be that strange?"

I knew what she was thinking of. Plenty of guys—and let's be honest—they are almost always guys, go on killing jags and then realize the true kicker is to have people running around trying to figure out how clever you are. Son of Sam as good as admitted it. Zodiac might've been the only one with enough sense to get out while the getting was good. The cold fact is, there are only a few types of murders. If Jacque really thought Mason was a fame killer, that meant he was either smart or stupid. The smart ones, as much as you hate to admit it, don't get caught. They enjoy watching the dogs run, but they don't pop in to say hello. And even Zodiac got on thin ice there.

"I'm not saying it's impossible," I said. "But let's put that on a list of unlikely options. He's got no real motive and, while I'll give you that he had every opportunity, or at least we have to assume he did after a relationship that long, what would've made him snap all of a sudden? No previous calls about domestic abuse, no previous complaints from neighbors."

"It's the Heights." She shrugged. "Rich people don't like to admit they have problems. It makes them feel like poor folk."

Her accent kicked in hard on the last two words.

"Maybe," I said. "I'll tell you what. I'll look into it. If there's even a hint of a possibility of foul play, you know I'll go all in. But this one is tricky, Jacque. You might just have a guy on your hands who's had bad luck for a good long time."

She shrugged. "Everybody deserves a fair shake."

"All right. How about I call Doc Sheddon?"

Jacque grinned, knowing I was giving in as much as I could really do. "It's been a while. I'm sure he'd be happy to hear from you."

"We'll see."

"That's what we're here for," she said, standing up and strutting out of the office like she'd just won a major battle. The truth is, as much as Amanda wanted me to take the case, places like the Heights are like asking to get burned. When you start sticking your nose in other people's business, things are always going to be tough. When you start sticking your nose in the business of the rich and powerful, you may as well just go ahead and expect big trouble. But, if Doc came up with something, I'd at least have science on my side, and that was a tough opponent to argue with.

I sat in my chair for a moment, thinking, and then had an idea. If Jacque and Amanda were sold on the idea, that was just fine with me. But I had an ace in the hole. Someone who had a law enforcement and psychology background. And she had an office down the hall.

I grabbed my phone and walked down to Heather's space. She was sitting at her desk, back to the door, both computer screens on and a pile of folders on her desk. Amazingly, if anybody could keep track of that many things at once, it was her.

"Hey, boss," she said without looking up. "Almost done with the last case report and I was just getting ready to send you the financials from it."

"I don't ever worry about it with you," I said. "But let me

pick your brain for a second. Have you heard about this Hattie Baker situation?"

She turned toward me and her expression told me a lot, though, interestingly, not everything.

"Some," she said.

"But not from Jacque."

"No, just what was on the news sites."

"And your thoughts?"

"Well, to be honest, I had no thoughts originally. Rich lady gets drunk and falls in the pool. I don't mean to sound cold-hearted, but I feel like that's how the story goes pretty often. I mean, shoot, if she hadn't died, how many people do you think have the same story? Alcohol and pools are always together, despite the fact they don't mix. And if you slip and fall in, nine times out of ten people just laugh and pull you out. The fact that you're sitting here asking about it though... that seems like a different situation."

"Schrödinger's cat, then."

She gave me a small grin. "Pretty much."

"All right." I leaned back in the chair across from her. I could get Jacque started on finding close acquaintances, have her make a list of folks who had seen the woman last. Tim could dig into her online situation and financials. Shoot, if we were really going to do this, there was a good chance we could get the woman's computer. If it was an accidental death, nothing would be locked down by the police. We might have a bit of a hitch with whoever was left in charge of her estate, but those were solved easily enough.

I glanced over at the pile of folders and then back at Heather. "You feel like going to see Doc?"

She looked at me and the stack of work in front of her. "I mean... you're the boss, so I can't really say no. But you see what I've got here."

I shrugged and stood up. "We aren't really office people to begin with."

"Thank goodness someone knows that around here." She laughed. "Your car or mine?"

6

I HAD HEATHER CALL DOC SHEDDON ON THE WAY OVER. Even if he hadn't done the autopsy, he knew plenty of people and plenty of ways to get ahold of it. The form itself was boiler-plate, but it always helped to have someone who knew someone. Worst case scenario, he'd tell us Tobin Henry was just another cop and we'd have to accept that the job was done properly and without incident. But it never hurt to ask.

We pulled into the parking lot and walked inside. The staff was used enough to seeing us, which said good things about business and bad things about morals.

"Welcome, welcome," Doc said as we stepped into his office. "I was just reading things through here. Hilden Heights, I see. You're moving up in the world." He chuckled a bit.

"I don't know if I'd go that far," I said. "This one is more of a favor at the moment. Boyfriend of the deceased seems to think the drinking is a little suspicious."

"Ah." Doc rolled the cursor on his mouse and reviewed the file, though he and I both knew there was very little that escaped his bear trap of a mind. It was why he was the only one

I worked with. "He's not claiming she didn't drink prior to the incident, I assume? There's really no debating that."

"He said it was out of character."

"I see..."

"Before we get into some of our other questions, what was time of death?" I said.

"The estimate is between nine at night and three the following morning," Doc said.

"That's quite the range. What do you make of that?"

"TOD would be difficult to determine because the body was in the water which would affect body temperature greatly; stomach contents, too," Doc said. "It isn't due to a lack of expertise on the ME's part," he added with a smirk.

Heather and I watched as Doc scrolled up and down in the document for a moment. "Well... hm..."

I exchanged a glance with Heather.

"'Hm' is usually intriguing," she said, trying to draw him back to reality.

"As they say, the most exciting phrase to hear in science is not eureka, but 'that's funny.' As they say at least. Though I suppose this isn't a particularly funny place to work."

Heather looked at me out of the corner of her eye.

"So what's the funny thing they're talking about here?" I asked.

"Well, as I mentioned," Doc said, "it's not that alcohol wasn't a factor in things. I suppose there are ways her tox could've come back like this without her drinking, but I'll be the first to say, if it walks like a duck and sounds like a duck..."

"You're on a roll today."

He shrugged. "Efficiency. The point being, alcohol was in her system. If she didn't drink it, someone went to great lengths to make it look like she did. I don't mean to burst any balloons here, but by great lengths, I mean, extravagant ones. Don't pay any attention to what you see on TV. This woman drank, or we should all back away slowly and get a bigger office involved."

"Okay," I said. "I don't have any horse in this race. So she drank and then... what? How do we get from the martini glass to the pool?"

"Oh, it could've been anything," he said. "Tox screens don't discriminate between mimosas and Long Islands. Though I suppose if it helped, and you gave me some time, I could parse it out."

"Alcohol's alcohol," Heather jumped in. "We just need to know if there's more to it."

Doc leaned back in his chair and laced his fingers behind his head. "That's the rub, I suppose. Alcohol is a tricky character. Not knowing this woman, I can't say what her tolerance was. And having never seen her, if you'll pardon the crassness of it, I don't know what her body was capable of handling. Higher body fat, higher alcohol tolerance. But..." He clicked on the screen. "She seems like she'd be..." He glanced at Heather. "Well, in your category."

"I'll take that as a good thing," she said.

"A very good thing. Miss Baker, from all I can see here, was a very healthy, fit young woman. There can be all kinds of mitigating factors, but if we're looking solely at alcohol, then I think the biggest culprit here would be accident."

"Meaning?"

"Meaning, when you look at the rest of the autopsy, it notes that her only other injury was a blow to the side of the head. If she was drinking, if she was by a pool..." He looked back at us. "It's not an uncommon thing."

"Wet concrete and an unfortunate slip," Heather said.

"Or wet concrete and an unfortunate relationship," Doc replied. "You know I don't have any say in how you all go about your job, but if we're being entirely frank with one another, all I can tell you for certain is that this woman had drunk a bit, suffered a blow to her left occipital, and not too terribly long after, drowned in a swimming pool. Or at least a body of water with similar chemical makeup."

I rubbed my jaw. I came to Doc because, usually at least, he made things cut and dried. Today, he seemed to be walking a fine line. Just the facts, ma'am, so to speak. "Let's say you weren't being so scientific," I said. "Let's say you're just a guy who hears a story about a lady and happens to know a thing or two about autopsies. Talk to us like we're your poker buddies."

He laughed. "Those have gone the way of the buffalo. You show one person you know how to second deal... but that's neither here nor there. If you want to know what I find interesting about this whole situation, it's not so much that the unfortunate Ms. Baker appears to have slipped, hit her head, and drowned, it's that the women of Hilden Heights apparently have a tendency to do just that."

"What do you mean?" Heather asked.

"I mean just what I said," Doc responded. "So maybe be glad you aren't so affluent to have ended up in that neighborhood. It was just... oh, less than a year ago, nearly the exact same case came across my desk. And that one I did indeed do the autopsy for. Young lady, pretty, wealthy, prime of life, all that type of thing. Too much to drink, drowned in the pool. Though, to be fair, this woman... Laughlin... Latter..." He looked up at the ceiling. "Loftis. Beatrice Loftis. High BAC but injuries indicated she'd unfortunately dove into the shallow end of her pool. Or fallen, I suppose, now that you've brought it to my attention. That's not the neighborhood to go swimming in."

"Have you seen more of these?" Heather asked before I could get the words out. "Not necessarily exactly the same thing, but close enough to seem odd."

Doc looked up at the ceiling, then down at his hands. "I'd

40

have to think about it. Let me look through some things. I mean, to be completely honest, Hilden Heights is one of those places where things just align. Young folks, alcohol, pools." He shrugged. "I'm not saying it's right or wrong, but to a certain extent, it's math. I'll go through my files and send you an email. Unless you need to know immediately."

"No," I said. "We appreciate what you've told us already. Just thought we'd stop in and say hello."

"Always happy to see you," Doc said. "Don't wait around for dismal circumstances to drop by. I deal with those all day. It's nice to have a pleasant face." He glanced at Heather for half a beat, but enough for both she and I to catch it. Heather is never one to fawn to flattery, but Doc's genial, gentlemanly admiration always got a blush from her. Perhaps mostly because as soon as she did, he did as well.

"We'll try to not be such strangers," she said.

"I'll be in touch." He waved.

As we walked back out to the car, Heather looked over at me. "So what do you think? Open and shut? Just a guy who doesn't want to let it go?"

"Doc or the boyfriend?"

She rolled her eyes.

"I think Doc was doing two things he always does," I said. "One was appreciating good people, the other was accidentally noticing strange circumstances. When we get back to the office, let's have Tim look into the Heights a little more. Specifically, folks who've died in the Heights. And, as much as I hate to say it, specifically folks who've drowned in the Heights. Like Doc said, maybe it's just the math, but I feel like if something catches his eye, it ought to catch ours."

She walked across the lot quietly beside me.

"You have a different opinion?" I asked.

"I don't have any opinion at all yet," she said. "I was trained to not form them, if you recall."

This time I rolled my eyes.

"What I think is this," she continued. "The bruise on Hattie's head could be anything. We didn't see it. Doc didn't see it. But the fact remains something happened. Now, if that means she got hit, or if that means she slipped and hit her own head... well, I'm reserving judgment on that."

"Until?"

"Until?" she mocked, laughing. "What do you think? You can't drag me down here and then not expect me to be thorough. Until we go over to that house and see what the pool looks like. And we find out if she had any guests right before she drowned."

I stopped at the car door. Accidental death wasn't homicide, which was something it always took me a moment to adjust to. Technically, the house was just a house where something unfortunate had happened. "It's not a crime scene," I said.

"Not at the moment, anyway." She opened her door and climbed into the car. "Besides, don't you wanna go see how the upper echelon lives? Oh, wait..." She looked over at me and grinned mischievously.

"My parents are rich," I said. "I'm just—"

"A regular fella," she put on her thickest accent. "Oh, I know."

"Whenever you're done with your routine," I said, "there is one more thing I thought you might find interesting about this."

"Let's hear it."

"The call that came in to report the body," I started.

"I was gonna ask. Wasn't it the boyfriend?"

"No," I said.

"Neighbor?"

"That's the working theory." I backed the car out of the lot.

42

"Meaning?"

"Meaning nobody's quite tracked that down yet. It wasn't a blocked number or anything, but no one seems to have taken an interest in it. Just an anonymous tip. Cops didn't see any foul play. It gets filed."

"But you don't buy it?"

"I'm not saying I do or I don't. All I'm thinking about at the moment is we should take a good long look at who can see into Hattie's backyard and who can't."

Heather nodded and pulled up the address on her phone, already looking for angles.

"I REALLY SHOULDN'T BE DOING THIS," THE MAN SAID. HE
was beefy but in decent shape. The rent-a-cop shirt was tight on
his arms and across his chest. "Rules are there for a reason, after
all. And like I said, without a specific invitation or a warrant,
nobody's supposed to get through this gate."

We'd been arguing the finer points of his position for almost
twenty minutes before he finally seemed to agree that, considering we were hired by a person he was familiar with to investigate a person who technically died on his watch, the rules could
be slightly bent.

Still, he was reluctant, and it took us almost another ten
minutes to get him to open the gate to Hattie's community. I
waved as we drove slowly ahead, Heather giving me directions
from her phone. I'd been to the Heights a time or two, but each
visit reminded me of how vast the economic gap can be. These
people weren't just well-to-do; there wasn't a home we drove by
that didn't cost over a million dollars. The roads were pristine,
the grass in the yards all trimmed to perfection. Even the few
folks we saw out jogging or exercising looked like their workout
clothes certainly had designer labels stitched into them.

Heather directed us up to Hattie's former residence and we parked in the driveway. "It's a strange setup here, isn't it?" she asked.

"What do you mean?"

"Well, usually when people spend this much money, they invest at least some of it in the yard. Y'know, put some space between them and everyone else. But when they built these, it's like everyone had the same idea."

"Put the house far back from the road."

"Right. But when you do that, the backs of them are a lot closer than you'd think."

"That might be something that works in our favor," I said. "Because not much seems to be happening today." I gestured toward the keypad for the electric lock on the door. "Call Jacque and see if she can track down the boyfriend, Mason. Something tells me we've gotten as much help as we're going to from the fellow at the front gate. Without the code, we're going to be peeking in windows."

While Heather got in touch with Jacque, who shortly after got in contact with Mason, we walked toward the back of the house.

"She said he's on his way over," Heather said. "Twenty minutes or so."

I nodded, coming around the corner of what was unarguably a mansion and opening a low wooden gate. Hattie had apparently put a little more foresight into her design, or paid a little more for it, as her backyard was vast. The pool, which could've fit any regular Joe's apartment easily inside, took up one side of the area. The rest was dominated by a large, brick outdoor cooking space and seating for at least twenty people at small and large tables, lounge chairs, and stone benches.

Heather looked around, soaking it all in.

"Are you thinking you've got a new goal in life?" I said with a grin.

"Honestly?" She turned to me, folding her arms over her chest. "The place is a little creepy, if you want to know the truth."

I'd been getting the same feeling. "Kind of Stepford Wives, isn't it?"

"That and, it's just... off. Like, we've been wandering around for a quarter-hour now and I haven't even heard a dog bark, let alone seen a curious neighbor."

"It is odd," I admitted. "But then again, any dog lucky enough to live here probably has his own room inside."

"And his own staff as well." She laughed.

"It wouldn't surprise me in the least."

She looked like she was going to say something else, most likely ask me about my own family, who was none too short on funds either, when her phone dinged. She glanced down. "Mason's out front."

"Let's go find that dog room."

He was already punching in the code when we made our way back around to the porch, where I introduced Heather and Mason to each other.

"Sorry I didn't think to tell you this sooner," he said. "Things have been..." He trailed off.

"It's a hard situation to be in," Heather said.

"And it doesn't get any easier," he said. "I know it's only been a few months, and it's not like I expected this to be something I got over quickly. But I still keep grabbing my phone to text her, y'know?"

I patted him on the shoulder as we stepped inside. "I think you're right where you ought to be. Don't beat yourself up over it."

He shrugged. "Maybe it's silly to be spending so much

money on this. You probably feel like I'm wasting your time, but I just feel like I need to be doing something."

"Not wasting our time at all," Heather said. "Our job is to help people. That can be done in a lot of different ways."

"I want you to know I appreciate it," he said, closing the door. "But, since you're here, let me go grab her laptops. I think there's a file upstairs as well with her passwords and information like that inside. Feel free to look around."

He walked off up the winding staircase that led to the second and third floors.

"Laptops," Heather said. "Plural."

"Probably one for every room," I said.

"Listen, while we've got a minute," she said, her voice lowered. "I know this sounds a little silly, but just so we're covering our bases, you don't think he could've possibly had something to do with it, do you?"

I smiled. She had a good head on her shoulders. "I've thought about that myself as well. But, you see where we are, you see what he's doing. Do you think he'd go out of his way to help us if he knew the path led back to him?"

"It certainly doesn't seem like it. But then again, people do weird things all the time. Could be he's so convinced we won't figure it out that this is just kind of a game for him. Plus, even with all the help he's giving us, we don't know what things he might not be bringing to the table. It'd take days to search this place and he's got a four-week head start."

"It never hurts to be wary," I said, glancing up as Mason passed from one wing to the other on the landing above us. "But until we find something concrete, I say we take him at face value. Besides, everyone slips up sooner or later."

She nodded and wandered around the room a bit, looking at the floor-to-ceiling bookshelf on one wall and examining a few of the knickknacks sitting around on the coffee tables. "Makes the foyer at my house seem a little underwhelming."

"Mine as well," I said. "But would you really want all this? I know it seems like it'd be a life of luxury, but all I see here is a lot of things that could be stolen, a lot of money invested in stuff for the sake of stuff. And besides, look where it got her."

Just then, Mason came back down the stairs, two laptop bags slung over his shoulder and a manila folder in his hand. "There are a couple of tablets in these two," he said, gesturing to the bags, "and the passwords to everything, from opening them up to her email and everything else, are in here." He held up the folder. "I don't know what I'm hoping you'll find, but this seems like as good a place to start as any. The security isn't anything too crazy. At least not that I know of, and we didn't really keep any secrets from one another. After five years, it would've been almost impossible to."

Heather took the folder and glanced briefly inside. "People can be complicated," she said. "And I don't intend to say anything impertinent here, but I have to ask about the alcohol. I know you told Harry that she didn't drink, but the tox screen says otherwise."

Mason ran a hand through his hair, clearly frustrated at having to answer the same questions over and over, but also looking like he knew he'd brought this on himself.

"All I can tell you is what I saw with my own eyes, and that was that Hattie almost never drank. Not when I was around, anyway. I guess she could've done it behind closed doors, but she was almost always with me."

"It's a big place," I said. "And alcoholics are notoriously good at hiding it. Or at least convincing themselves they're hiding it."

"It's something, isn't it?" Mason said, looking up the

winding stairs. "Kind of a waste really. We were almost always at my place."

"Why's that?" Heather asked.

He looked down and shuffled his feet. "I know it sounds like sour grapes, but I never liked it here. The people, the women especially, have this way of prying into your business. Or looking down their noses at you. I went to a few dinner parties with Hattie early on, but it didn't take long before I politely declined most invitations."

"Like the popular kids in high school," Heather said.

"Almost exactly like that. Which is crazy. I mean, we're adults. But all they wanted to talk about was why I didn't get a better job. Why I wasn't making more money. I don't know about you guys, but I was raised to not poke into people's lives like that. Besides, and I know this sounds a little conceited, but I don't do too bad for myself. At least not in my opinion. I made just over 200K last year, but to these people, I may as well be working behind the counter at a fast food place. I wouldn't even be able to rent a room here for that price."

I could tell this wasn't something he was comfortable discussing, and I couldn't blame the man. Wealthy people have a way of demeaning others, often without even realizing they're doing it. But it's evident in all the small things, the expensive bottled water, the monogrammed towels. Comments like "I don't even know what it's like to not spend the Fourth of July on a boat; what do people even do?" I know I, for one, certainly don't miss rubbing elbows with the type. Too much ego-stroking over accomplishments that are too often unearned by the person doing the bragging.

I decided to change the subject and casually asked, "When you were up here, did you ever meet Beatrice Loftis?"

Mason's eyes widened as he looked at me. "I wondered if you were aware of that. I know it sounds crazy, but that was the first thing I thought of after... Hattie's accident. Do you think there's a killer in the neighborhood?"

I looked around the room. "It seems to me it would be pretty difficult to force someone to dive into the shallow end of the pool. And the ME who did the autopsy is a man I trust more than almost anyone. He said the alcohol in Ms. Loftis was clearly to blame."

"But it's weird, though, don't you think?" he asked. "I mean, two women, same neighborhood, both supposedly drunk and both drowning in their own pools."

"Probably not as uncommon as you'd think. These two women just happened to be very high-profile. I can't imagine what the stats are for backyard drownings in a year, especially with alcohol involved."

"Well, since we're here," he said, "do you want to see the back? I'm not sure what good it'll do, but I don't plan on making it a habit of being here."

Heather glanced at me and I spoke quickly, letting her follow my lead. "Probably would be a good idea," I said. "It always helps us to see everything we can."

Mason led us out through a set of French doors to the back. I looked at the things he wanted to point out, but mostly I was waiting to ask a casual, off-handed question. When we made our way over to the pool, I started with an easy question to not make it obvious.

"That's a lot of pool. How often is the pool company out to maintain it?"

Mason stood a little taller and looked at me. "I took care of the pool for Hattie. Thought it was somethin' any good boyfriend would do. Cleaned it and checked the chemicals at least once a week."

"That was certainly considerate of you," I said, building him up to launch into the next question. I gestured toward the one backyard with a sightline to the pool. "Do you know who happens to live there?"

"Her? Oh, yeah. I mean, I know of her. Name's Victoria Blue. She's not one you ever see out much. Not that there's anything wrong with that, just kind of keeps to herself. To be honest, I always figured if there was anyone in this neighborhood I'd get along with, it would be her."

"Why's that?" Heather asked.

Mason shrugged. "Just because you never see her. Not like she's a recluse or anything, but she doesn't seem to put much stock in making appearances like the rest of them here." He paused. "I don't know much about the rest of the neighbors, to be honest. Like I said, I tried to keep some distance between myself and this group. But I'm pretty sure Victoria works from home. She's got quite the little set-up in her yard as well. Liked to work out there when the weather was nice."

I exchanged a look with Heather.

"Probably wouldn't hurt to knock on her door," Mason said, gazing over to Victoria's place. "She's most likely there."

8

CONSIDERING THE FACT THE TWO HOMES SHARED A property line, it took a ridiculous amount of time to follow the winding roads back through the neighborhood until we could pull up the long drive to Victoria Blue's home. It had a strikingly different look than most of the other houses in the area. The yard was in good shape, though slightly more unkempt. Vines grew up the outside of the stone house, almost giving it a castle-like appearance in a place where everyone was striving for modernity.

"Kinda creepy," Heather said as we came to a stop in the turnabout in front of the house. "But I kinda like it."

I laughed. "So maybe you do want to move here after all?"

She rolled her eyes. "Only if I did things like this lady. Keep your head down and out of people's business."

"Maybe," I said. "But maybe not entirely out of other people's business."

I got out of the car and we walked up to the intercom outside the front door. I pressed the button and immediately the sound of chimes rang out from inside the house. Seconds later, the barking of a dog could be heard from inside as well.

"There's that dog you've been looking for," I said. "Maybe this is the home for you after all."

"That dog probably eats nicer dinners than I do." She laughed.

We waited a minute or so, and then, on a whim, I pressed the button once more. If there wasn't any staff to answer, then there likely wasn't anyone in the home at all. But, to my surprise, a second later the small screen above the doorbell came to life. It showed what appeared to be an empty room. Whoever was on the other side was apparently standing off out of the camera's range. A smart move.

"Can I help you?" a decidedly feminine voice asked.

Maybe Miss Blue just didn't like having people around, period, whether they were there to help or not. It seemed to fit with the way Mason had described her.

"Possibly," I said. "My name is Harry Starke. This is my associate, Heather Stillwell. We're with a private detective firm and just wanted to ask you a few questions about the neighborhood."

There was a long pause, long enough for me to think whatever I'd said had been enough to scare off the person on the other end of the video feed. Then, finally, a short reply.

"I'll be down in a moment."

I'm not sure what I was expecting when the door opened, but Victoria Blue was not it. Perhaps it was the mismatch of her name. The one color that stood out when she was finally in front of us was her hair, a fiery red. Along with her pale skin, I had to wonder how much time she actually got to spend working out back. Someone with her complexion would likely go from pale to burned in about two minutes. She had large, round glasses perched on an elfin nose and, in a bookish way, was actually quite pretty.

"Please come in." She gestured hurriedly to the foyer, her eyes darting around behind us.

"Is everything okay?" Heather asked, picking up on the anxiety the woman was showing.

"Yeah, yes," she said, closing the door quickly behind us. "Just this neighborhood." She shook her head. "Phones are probably ringing all over already about the mysterious pair who showed up at the Blue residence."

"That bad?" I asked. "We've barely seen a soul since we've been here."

"That's the way it is," she responded. "They see you and then decide if they want you to see them."

"I don't mean to be rude," I said, "but that sounds a lot like the kind of person who would have a video doorbell but stay out of the camera frame."

The slightest hint of a smile played at the corner of her mouth. "When in Rome..."

I looked down the long hall that led back into the manor, which was really the only word for the place. It was filled with cardboard boxes of various sizes in different stages of packing. "Looks like you're not planning on staying in Rome too much longer."

She glanced at the disarray behind her. "No. Turns out Rome's not the place for me."

"How so?"

"Just not really all it's cracked up to be. Or at least not the way it's advertised," she said.

"Where are you headed?" Heather asked.

"Nashville," Victoria responded. "I know a few people over that way. When I came here, I thought it would be more... neighborly. Y'know, out of the bigger cities but still within driving distance. I guess I was imagining some kind of TV show where everyone got along, kids rode bikes. Pick your trite image. But it seemed safe and I thought it would be pleasant."

"It's certainly peaceful," Heather said.

"Yeah." Victoria smiled slightly again. "Peaceful in that kind of way that drives you stir-crazy after a while. Don't get me wrong; it's not like everyone just holes up and peers through the curtains at one another all day. They certainly have their moments. It's just that a social gathering here is more work than fun."

"I heard you like to keep to yourself," I said. "From the way you describe things, I imagine I'd do the same."

She gave me an inquisitive look. "I suppose I shouldn't be surprised a detective has already talked about you when one shows up at your door. Just out of curiosity, is this something to do with me specifically, or are you out gathering up the neighborhood gossip?"

I was a bit surprised it had taken her so long to get to the topic at hand. Most people find it incredibly intimidating to have an investigator show up on their doorstep. Then again, Victoria seemed like one of those quietly confident people who knew they hadn't done anything wrong and weren't worried who knew.

"Well," I said, "since we're on the topic, is there any neighborhood gossip you'd like to tell me?"

Her eyebrows drew together. "Could you be more specific? I'm not really sure what you're asking me."

"We just came from Hattie's house," Heather said, gesturing toward the back. "Her boyfriend, Mason, is the one who hired us."

The look on Victoria's face told me everything I really wanted to know, but to her credit, she owned up to it immediately.

"You want to know what I saw."

"It would be helpful," I said. "You are the person who made the anonymous call."

She looked down, then up, her expression confident but not defiant. "I don't think there's really anything more to say than what I told the dispatcher initially." A little brown and black Yorkie sauntered into the room, stretching before walking over to give Heather a sniff. "Dipper and I," she said and gestured toward the dog, "went out into the back as usual. I had some work I wanted to get ahead on and he likes to lay in the sun. Instead, he went straight to the fence and wouldn't leave his post for anything. I went to see what had him all wound up, and that's when I saw Hattie's body."

"You could see her from your property?" I asked. "Even with the fence?"

"I drug a chair over." She shrugged. "Like I said, folks like to see without being seen. I'd just about bet everyone who doesn't have planters along the fence line has a chair or a stool or something. Of course, they'll tell you it's just curiosity, but there's something a little beyond curiosity here. Voyeurism, almost." She sighed and shook her head. "One of the many reasons I'm ready to pull up my stakes. Though I guess I'm guilty of doing the same thing."

"When you saw Hattie, she was already in the water?" I asked.

"Floating face down. I'm not a medical professional, but even I knew the emergency call was probably going to be pointless. That's one reason I decided to do it anonymously. Getting myself involved in things wasn't going to help anyone, and it would more than likely make things a little chaotic for me."

"Did you notice anything the night before?" Heather asked. "A party? People outside?"

Victoria shrugged and shook her head. "I wasn't out too late the night before. Hattie would have her parties, but they usually

57

weren't subtle. Most people around here tend to try and avoid subtlety at all costs. You've probably noticed. The Heights is one or the other. Either 'hey everybody look at me' or 'mind your own business.' To be honest, the strangest thing in my mind was that Hattie was even up. I don't know when she fell in the pool, I guess, but she was never much of an early riser."

"Could she have been up all night?"

Victoria shrugged again. "Could've been. My bedroom isn't on this side of the house, so even if she had been, I never would've heard anything. One thing I will miss about this stone house," she said and patted the wall behind her. "It's quiet."

There was a slight lull in the conversation and Victoria picked up the string again. "Well, if there isn't anything else, I've got a lot of packing yet to do. I'll let you know if I think of anything; but other than what I told you now and before, all I did was see the body and make the phone call. I don't know what else to tell you."

"Well, if you think of anything," I said, handing her a business card from my jacket pocket, "even if it doesn't seem like much, don't hesitate to give us a call."

"Of course." She set the card on a box and walked us to the door. "I don't know if you're allowed to say, and maybe it's none of my business, but it was just an accident, wasn't it?"

I turned back to her. "That's the thing we're trying to figure out as well. Have a good day."

Heather and I headed down to the car, hearing the large front door to the home close before we'd even covered a few steps.

"She's a quiet one, all right," Heather said, opening her door.

"And a busy one," I said.

She raised an eyebrow.

"Someone that reserved, in a home like that, how long do you think it's going to take her to pack up all those boxes?"

"Maybe she'll convince herself to hire movers."

"For her sake, I hope so. For now, though, I'm starving. Lunch?"

"As long as it's somewhere cheap. I've had enough of the high class for one day."

I laughed and began the winding path back toward the entry to the subdivision.

9

I took us to a sandwich shop not far from the office, contemplating grabbing our food to go, but the long silence of the car ride let me know Heather's mind was working overtime. Figuring we weren't in any real rush, and that our cell phones would keep us as available as anything else, I decided to dine in with Heather and give her some time to think out loud. Sometimes, the biggest part of the job is just letting our thoughts tumble out with someone who is informed enough to listen and clever enough to help. Heather had both of those traits in spades.

We got our food and found space at one of the high wooden bars by one of the front windows. Perched on her stool beside me, Heather looked out at the traffic, and I waited for her to break the silence. It didn't take long.

"So here's where I'm struggling," she said, unwrapping her food. "Most cases, there is a clear problem to solve. Someone has gone missing. Something is stolen. Someone has died. Which, I suppose, is what we've got here. But I feel like right now, the biggest problem is deciding if this is even murder. If so, then there are certain steps we'd obviously take. But we'll be spinning our wheels if it turns out this was an accidental death. We interview people until kingdom come, but if no one else was in the yard with her, what's the point?"

"True," I said, letting her continue.

"When we work on a murder case, we think of motive, opportunity and means. The fact that she is so wealthy would usually make me think of a motive like robbery, life insurance payout, a business competitor who wants her biz, or maybe even blackmail. Maybe she had a gambling addiction and owed a loan shark. But we were both in the house and it didn't exactly look ransacked to me. Honestly, it looked like she might come walking back in at any moment. I suppose Mason would've known what to take without making things look suspicious, but then again, he's the one who brought us the case. She doesn't seem old enough to have a lot of insurance or have a business that's worth killing over."

She took a bite of her sandwich and chewed slowly.

"So here's a question on having the means," she said after a moment. "How would one even go about murdering someone with alcohol and a knock to the head? If she really didn't drink, then I suppose it wouldn't have taken much alcohol to have a pretty big impact on her. And I didn't see any alcohol in the house, making me think she wasn't a drinker."

She paused, and I was just about to reply when she started again.

"But, like you said, alcoholics usually have more bottles tucked away than squirrels do nuts. And I suppose drinks would likely flow at any of the classy soirees up that way, so she'd have to have some tolerance. Unless she really didn't drink."

She paused again.

"Thoughts? I'm open, Harry."

I wiped my mouth with my napkin, smiling a bit. "You're

good at what you do," I said. "Don't ever let anyone tell you otherwise."

She smiled. "Asking questions I don't have the answers to? It's a real skill, let me tell ya."

"It's the only way to find answers," I said.

"But you don't have any yet, either, huh?"

"I've been thinking along the same lines you have. Getting her drunk enough to pass out and then dragging her into the pool, it's not entirely impossible. I'm sure there was at least one story in your high school about a kid dying from alcohol poisoning, choking on their own vomit, that kind of thing."

"But there wasn't any vomit in the pool, was there?"

"I'll have to look into that, but the autopsy seems to imply there was alcohol in the system, a bump to the head, and water in the lungs, but nothing else out of the ordinary. Now, getting an alcoholic drunk enough to pass out is a different animal. It's much trickier."

"And costs a lot more."

"Sometimes," I said. "The thing with late-stage alcoholics, the ones who've really put the time in, is that their tolerance doesn't just continue to go up. It comes in waves. Sometimes, yes, you could have a guy knock back whiskeys all day long and the only sign of intoxication would be that he was tired. Then again, a month later, that same guy might be on the low end of things. His tolerance is shot because his body can't continue to process the alcohol forever. Those are the guys who get picked up for DUIs not because they were driving erratically, but because they passed out or had a seizure."

"Seems like it would be tricky either way," she said. "Unless someone was willing to put in the time to wait around for that day." She glanced at me. "Someone who'd put in a lot of time already, maybe."

"Maybe," I said, gathering up my trash. "But for now, maybe

is all we have. Let's give Tim the electronics to play around with and we can see what turns up. I know it's frustrating to not even have the real question pinned down, but you're going about this the right way. In my opinion, at least," I added with a smile.

"Well, the boss's opinion is usually the one that counts," she said. "Usually."

We chatted for a few more minutes while she finished up her meal, mostly smaller, easier topics. She asked about Jade and Amanda, talked about her family, and before too long we found ourselves back at the office.

Jacque met us as we came into the lobby, handing me a list of names. I raised an eyebrow.

"Just people we might want to talk to," she said. "Neighbors mostly, and the security guards. Some of the boyfriend's contacts, old clients he'd worked with, and some of Hattie's employees and business associates. There's some structure to the neighborhood. Not exactly a neighborhood watch or anything, but certainly what I guess you might call levels."

"Tiers," Heather said with a grin. "The ultra-wealthy wouldn't have something as mundane as levels."

"That fun, was it?" Jacque raised an eyebrow.

"Eh." Heather shrugged. "The thing with rich folks is they seem to make everything complicated just because they can. For my money, I'd take a good old mugging or drug bust any day of the week. These people are just... vindictive."

While the two women discussed Heather's and my trip to the Heights, I walked down to Tim's bunker-like cave at the end of the hall. As usual, he was perched on a desk chair, back ramrod straight, and his eyes flitting back and forth between the monitors on his desk.

"Word on the street is we caught a whale," he said without looking over. It was almost eerie sometimes, not that he was aware of who was there—on a team the size of ours, you get used to one another and could name who was walking down a dark hall just by the rhythm of their steps—but the way he always knew everything I was getting ready to tell him. As if to confirm my thoughts, he typed a few things quickly and then turned to look at me. "I assume those are the electronics you're going to want me to jailbreak."

I unhooked the two bags from my shoulder and handed them over to him. "Couple laptops. A pair of tablets, I believe. And not to rain on your parade or anything, but there's also this." I handed him the file. "The boyfriend says all her passwords and information should be on these pages. Less hacking, more reading."

Tim's jaw dropped open just a little bit. "I guess I've heard of people doing this, but if you're going to have a password, why store it on a sheet called..." He flipped open the folder and looked at the heading on the first page. "Passwords."

"Bad memory?" I said. "Or maybe just nothing to hide?"

"Everyone's got something to hide." Then glancing at me, he added, "And yes, present company included."

"See what you can find," I said. "Maybe there's more to it than we think."

The excited look came back to his face. "That's true. This could all be a smokescreen. Make everyone think you're an open book while actually hiding your secrets somewhere else. It's clever."

"Have fun with it then." I started to walk back down the hall when he called after me.

"This phone is hers, too?"

I leaned on the doorframe. "The boyfriend said if it was in the bag, it was hers, so I guess there's only one way to find out. I'm curious to know if she posted anything on social media the day she died. Oh, and look into any other deaths in Hilden Heights over, say, the last five years. Especially drownings."

"On it, boss."

What had convinced the entire staff to keep referring to me as "boss" was beyond me, unless they just happened to realize it was the one thing that I didn't care for. A little good-natured ribbing, I suppose. But we worked as a unit, and just because I was the one who signed the checks didn't make me any more valuable than anyone else. Besides, the fact that I could surround myself with some of the most brilliant people in the area and not expect them to find my buttons probably meant I deserved the jokes.

10

I HAD SPENT THE REST OF THE DAY TRYING TO CATCH UP ON the more mundane side of running a business. Whether it was vending machines or missing persons, there was always more than enough paperwork to go around. Usually I can just keep myself occupied and do what needs to be done, but something about Hattie kept lingering in the back of my mind. Maybe it was what Heather had pointed out, that we were having a hard enough time deciding if there was even a crime to investigate. Maybe it was the neighborhood itself that just seemed unusual, even for someone who's used to money. Whatever it was, I kept catching myself staring out the window, thinking about the pool, the homes, the people.

By the time I gathered my things and headed out, I was more than ready to be home. An evening with Jade and Amanda sounded like just what the doctor ordered. A toddler is not unlike trying to herd cats, and I welcomed the distraction.

After we'd eaten, gotten the little one cleaned up, and put the house back into some kind of reasonable order, I walked up to the master bedroom where Amanda was starting her evening routine. Most nights this could last anywhere from a quick brush of the teeth and splash of water on the face to a more involved, hour-long routine. I'd always assumed it had depended on how much Jade had been running around during the day, but I'd also noticed it depended a lot on what kind of true crime podcast Amanda had turned on.

Tonight, though, the bathroom was silent except for the usual sounds of getting ready for sleep. I wasn't entirely disappointed. After living true crime all day, it was tough to turn off when it was playing in the background at home as well. It wasn't that I had any problem with it. In a lot of ways, it gave us things to talk about and helped her understand what my job was actually like. But in other ways, it made it almost impossible for me to tune out. Maybe it's just force of habit, or maybe it's something intrinsic to people like me, but if I heard the beginning of the story, it was almost guaranteed I'd be listening to the end, either to confirm what I'd already figured out, or to try and learn something new from a fresh take.

"No horror stories tonight?" I asked as I walked over to the sink on my side of the room. The layout of the master bath technically had us standing back to back when we were both at our respective vanities, but the mirrors made it possible to still keep eye contact and carry on a conversation with relative ease.

"Well, that's what I've been wanting to talk about," she said, looking at me in her mirror.

"Meaning?" I started to brush my teeth.

"Meaning, what's the news on Hattie Baker?"

I laughed under my breath and held up a finger, letting her know I needed to at least finish brushing before we jumped back in. To her credit, she went back to removing her makeup and waited till I'd spit and washed my face.

"You're intrigued by this one," I said, turning around and leaning on the counter so I could see her. "Moreso than usual, it seems."

She grinned at me in the mirror. "It's not because they're wealthy," she said, "if that's what you're thinking."

"There's nothing wrong with it if that's exactly why. It's a group of people who live close to us but have an entirely different lifestyle. Nobody would ever fault you for being curious."

"It's really not, though," she said. "I remember the other woman up there. Or at least reading about her."

I thought for a moment. "You mean Beatrice Loftis?"

She pointed at my reflection. "That's the one. I know this sounds silly, but you've said yourself that a news reporter gets hunches just as often as a detective. And you also know how hard it is to turn that part of your brain off."

"You didn't buy the accidental death story there, then?"

"I'm not sure." She leaned down to look into a circular mirror with higher magnification. A light around the edges turned on at her movement. "Diving into the shallow end of your own pool? I don't know how drunk and disoriented you'd have to be to do that. And I know it's not exactly the easiest thing to explain if you take the more menacing, murder-y aspect. But..." She sighed and turned around to face me. "It just seems strange, doesn't it? And now another pool death that doesn't quite add up."

"It doesn't quite add up," I admitted. "But it doesn't *not* add up either."

She let out a breath. "Maybe it's the fact that Hattie Baker was so young. Not even thirty yet. Can you imagine what her parents must be going through?"

I paused for a moment. "Honestly, I've never even considered it."

"Harry!" She turned around, eyes wide. "How could you not consider it? How could none of you have considered it?"

"Jacque just finished up the list of names to talk to this afternoon. I'm sure the Bakers are on there."

"But isn't that the first place you should've gone?"

"Mason was the first place mine, and everyone else's, thoughts have gone."

"All the more reason to talk to the Bakers. You said he wanted to marry her. They must've met him a time or two, if for no other reason than to deny him their blessing. If you can't come to a conclusion on Mason, I think it's only logical to talk to his girlfriend's parents."

"You've got a point," I started and then stopped. She didn't just have a point; she had a great point. I'd been telling Heather over and over that the very fact Mason was so willing to help led me to believe he wasn't involved. But I had been blind to my own flaw. I was only seeing the Mason that he wanted me to see, the very same idea Heather and I had been discussing about what electronics he chose to bring to us.

I looked back over at Amanda. "You're saying that, even if the Bakers are biased against him, it would at least balance out the impression we've gotten so far."

"Bingo."

"I knew I kept you around for a reason," I said, walking over and bending down to kiss the side of her neck. "I'll track them down first thing in the morning."

"And keep me posted as you do," she said.

I smiled and went off to the bed. It probably wasn't entirely legal to be sharing as much with her as I did, especially since she was at least somewhat associated with the media. But she was also my wife, my sounding board. In a lot of ways Amanda was as much a part of the agency as anyone else who walked through the doors to the office.

I stripped down to my jockeys and got under the covers. At least now I had a more direct plan. Just running down the list of names Jacque had provided seemed not only tiring, but tedious. I could practically imagine the conversations just based on how the person was involved. It's like the old joke: if you want a real reference for someone, don't use the list of people they put down. Find their enemies. Find the bosses they didn't get along with. Of course your friends will stick up for you.

I put my hands behind my head, looking up at the dim ceiling, the only light coming from the bathroom now. The plan seemed like a good one. But it didn't really solve all of my problems. I replayed the conversations Heather and I had had earlier in the day. Maybe the Bakers wouldn't do anything but muddy the waters more. The fact of the matter was, when someone dies, the people left behind have a lot to deal with. There's a gap in their life. They want to understand why it happened. Maybe for folks with religion it's a simpler process; everything is part of a grand plan. But even then, I'd seen enough grieving parents, widows, and friends to know even invoking the good Lord didn't necessarily bring peace.

And people who are looking for answers, nine times out of ten, will find them. The problem is when the answers aren't the same as the truth.

11

My sleep was restless that night, something that I'm unfortunately used to. Amanda likes to tease me that she can tell how thorny a case is by how much I toss and turn. "The funny thing," she always pointed out, "is that it's not how gruesome the case is, just how tricky."

And she was right. I'd tracked down some twisted individuals over the years, but if I knew who they were and what I was up against, it's like my brain was able to file the problem away more simply. It was the times there were too many questions, like with Hattie, or the times that the path of action wasn't clear, also like with Hattie, that I couldn't let things rest.

I woke up early and went for a run around the neighborhood, partly just to get up and moving, partly to give Amanda a chance to rest without some oaf rolling back and forth on the mattress beside her. The exercise didn't entirely clear my head, but it at least got my blood moving. More importantly, it gave me a tangible goal. Five miles is five miles, no matter how you look at it. Sure, some areas in Tennessee are hillier than others, some routes are more congested or more peaceful, but you still have to cover every yard before the job is done.

By the time I got home, I was feeling at least slightly more focused. I took a quick shower and got ready, telling Amanda to take advantage of one of the few mornings Jade hadn't woken up with the sun. I slipped out the door and grabbed a quick coffee and breakfast on the way, thinking I might have a bit of time to myself.

Of course, one of the problems with hiring a team as driven as mine is that you're rarely the only person coming into the office early. When I pulled into the lot, I saw Heather's car was already there. Tim's was as well, but that wasn't entirely unusual. I know the kid had an apartment somewhere, maybe even a house, considering what I paid him. But he had a laser focus and no problem with sleeping on the floor of his office, or in his chair, or just not sleeping at all, for days at a time when he was on a tear. I figured Hattie Baker and the Lifestyles of the Rich and Famous might've been one of those tears, and it would appear I hadn't been wrong.

I walked into the office, tossed my laptop bag on my desk, and walked back down to the small kitchenette where Heather was standing, her eyes up at the ceiling.

"Think we should get a painting up there?" I asked. "A nice mural of God and everybody?"

She looked over at me. "I didn't even see one of those in the Heights."

"We didn't see all that much of the Heights either," I said. "It wouldn't surprise me."

"Yeah," she said. "Me neither, now that you mention it. How crazy is that? To be so rich you spend money on things other people couldn't even think of?"

"Like I said, the more you spend, the more you have to worry about."

"Unless your bank account gets hacked. Then spending

would've been the right choice. They can't carry away everything."

"You'd be surprised. Anyway, what brings you in early?"

She patted a few printed sheets that were sitting on the counter beside her steaming cup of fresh coffee. "Figured if we were going to get on these names, then there wasn't any sense wasting the morning choosing which way to go first."

I nodded. "Fair enough. What did you decide?"

She laughed a little. "That I might be wasting the morning anyway. These people are all over the place." She picked up the sheets and leafed through them aimlessly. "Both literally and figuratively. Between Mason's family and Hattie's, not to mention the people who don't even live in the Heights, we could book a month-long tour and still be pressed for time if we want face-to-faces."

"True." I folded my arms. "But that's also why you're here. You've got one of the most organized minds I've ever seen, and I think we'd both agree that the disorganization is the one thing that's really driving you crazy here."

"Maybe," she said. And then, sounding almost exactly like Amanda. "There's just something that seems off about this case."

"Well, do you think it could be that there isn't any case at all? You can search for patterns and hidden agendas and secret schemes all you want, but at the end of the day, alcoholics fall in pools, and sometimes they don't climb back out."

She looked at me, one eyebrow raised and clearly irked.

"I'm not saying that is the situation here." I patted the air with open palms in what I'd been told was a calming gesture. "And if it makes you feel any better, Amanda's on your side."

"It does make me feel better, actually. What's her take?"

I shrugged. "Honestly, it's not much different than yours. Something seems wrong, but she can't figure out what. We did come up with a plan that might help you out at least a tiny bit, though."

"What's that?"

"I'm going to the parents' place."

"Like, today?"

"Like, as soon as I can figure out who and where they are."

"Great," she muttered. "So that's two down, two hundred to go."

I gave her a look.

"I know, I know," she said. "I'm overcomplicating things. I need to go through the list and prioritize. Half these people probably haven't even been to the Heights in years. That place just gets weirder and weirder."

"What do you mean?"

"I mean, it's like...you know how we were joking about the Stepford Wives thing? It really is like that." She flipped back the upper sheet on the list and started pointing out names. "This woman runs the local book club. This one has a baking club. No joke, Harry, this lady has a sewing circle. It's like 1950 in that place."

"Wealthy folks have a lot of time on their hands."

"Maybe the feminist in me is a little irked by it all. I mean, do these women really just sit around and live off their husbands?"

I started to reply and then let her balance out the thought.

"Because the husbands like to flash how successful they are by their bank accounts, and the wives like to flash how successful they are by their leisure. Okay, okay. But still, there couldn't be like one woman there who had her own job?"

"There was," I reminded her. "We went to her castle."

She looked down. "Okay, fair enough. But," she said and held up a finger, "that's also the one woman who couldn't stand being there."

"Hey." I held my hands out. "I'm not defending the Heights. Just making observations and drawing conclusions."

"As we do," she said. "One conclusion that I've drawn is that these women don't leave their neighborhood much, so that might be the easiest place to start."

"I think you've drawn another as well."

She laughed, almost reading my mind. "Yeah, but it sounds mean."

"You're making observations and drawing conclusions. Not judging."

"So you think it's gonna be a gossipy little hub as well?"

"Victoria Blue basically told us as much. Go ruffle some feathers. Kick over some rocks and see what crawls out. It might be nothing but cattiness and a long day for you, but you never know."

"And you'll find the parents?"

"That's the plan."

"All right." She exhaled, blowing her hair out of her eyes. "I have the feeling 'long day' is going to be an understatement."

"Think of it this way." I patted the counter. "Outside of Miss Blue, these people have fought tooth and nail to buy the address they have. I'd guess that they aren't going anywhere soon. That zip code is a lot to give up."

She nodded. "Still, sooner rather than later is kind of my style."

"Then do what you think is best." I turned and started walking toward my office when I thought of one more question. "When you got here, was Tim here already?"

"I think he's going to be here for a while. He's really getting a kick out of this one."

"Any news?"

"Not that he told me, but you know how he gets. I'm surprised he even realized I was in the room."

I nodded. "I'll send out an email here in a moment, but since we're talking already, I wanted to let you know we're going to bring the full team together on this one. Meeting at the end of the day today."

She laughed a little. "Kind of an interesting choice for a guy who isn't even sure there's a case to be discussed."

"If there's any group of people who can figure that out, they'll all be in this building by four PM. Find out what you can, but don't break your back over it. Meet us back here and we'll see what we can do."

"You got it."

I almost thought I'd gotten out of a conversation scot-free when she tacked on "boss" at the end of her sentence.

Well, if that was how they wanted to refer to me, maybe I'd claim it. After all, I had an email to write, and I'd never signed one quite like that before. Just as long as Bruce Springsteen didn't mind, I supposed.

12

NOT SURPRISINGLY, IT DIDN'T TAKE A LOT OF DIGGING TO track down the late Hattie Baker's parents. I knew I'd been frustrated just being in the Heights, let alone around the people that live up there, but I had to give them credit for one thing. Folks with money usually like everyone else to know. Having said that, my father's a billionaire, but aside from his Gulfstream, you'd never know it. August likes to live the quiet life. When he's not in court, he likes to play golf and can usually be found on the course. So a few quick Google searches had given me just about all I needed to find Mr. and Mrs. Baker.

What did surprise me was to find out Hattie Baker wasn't exactly what I'd expected. Victoria Blue had given us the impression that everyone in the Heights was new money, and it wasn't something most people would disagree with. Old money didn't tend to flock into a subdivision, no matter how grandiose it might be. Perhaps that was what made Victoria's presence there so uncomfortable. She wasn't around her own kind, or at least not in the ways she'd hoped to be.

The Bakers, a Thomas and Patsy, had done mighty well for themselves, though, opening a law office and apparently only taking cases that either guaranteed a big pay-off or a lot of attention, which eventually amounts to the same thing. People talk about CDs and day-trading without ever quite considering a bit of both can go a long way. Fame clients are like that. The right person saying your name can earn you as much money as an open and shut case or a client willing to put you on a serious retainer.

The thing that really struck me, though, was that Hattie did have a lot of the new money about her. Mr. and Mrs. Baker had done more than well for themselves, but from what I could piece together online, it had been a very different kind of familial situation. I'd heard stories of people trying to do this, though mostly they were grand plans from some pair of young parents who hadn't had the time to realize their idealized versions of themselves would likely fail when compared to the general desire to take care of one's children.

Amanda and I had talked about it. I'd talked with my own father about it. But the newly wealthy often truly believe that, when their children grow up, the kids should have as normal a life as possible. What that usually looks like is a college degree and then the son or daughter setting off on their own, wholly responsible for making his or her way in the world. But, like I said, no matter how moral this plan might seem, the vast majority of the times I'd seen it play out, the child made its way in the world with a new car every few years, a home of their own or rent payments being made, and at the very least a healthy allowance that appeared in a bank account every month without anyone ever quite admitting to what they were doing.

No, I couldn't fault people for that. I knew what life could hold. I'd seen more sides of it than almost anyone would ever want to. Did that make me want to cut the apron strings with Jade as soon as she turned eighteen? In some ways, yes, but a dad never stops being a dad.

Unless you're Thomas Baker.

It seemed the man had stuck to his guns, something that I kept in the back of my mind as I read through the articles on the family. If he was willing to be that hard with his own child, there wasn't much of a chance that I could buffalo any information out of him. And his being a lawyer to boot, there was a great chance that I'd show up and be told his representatives would answer any questions I might have.

But, this was what I'd come in for and sitting around pondering it wasn't going to get me any closer to the answers. So I pulled up directions on the computer and wasn't surprised to see his office was fairly close to my own. Somewhere over between Ridgeside and Highland Park, a fair enough address and likely the most convenient for what he needed to do.

I grabbed my jacket off the back of my chair and, after sticking my head in Jacque's office to let her know where I'd be, headed out to the car. I noticed as I crossed the lot that Heather's car was already gone, so clearly she'd followed my advice as well. Walking into an office building before nine might be a little different than making the rounds at the Heights, but the girl was tenacious; I couldn't do anything but be proud of her for that.

The receptionist at the law firm actually laughed at my request, something I'd hardly expected. "I haven't seen either one of them in... oh gosh," she said and looked up at the ceiling. "Well, there was the Christmas party last year. They usually try to make an appearance at that. But as for coming into the office, well, let's just say if you see Thomas or Patsy Baker come through those doors and it wasn't planned, something must've gone horribly south."

"But they do come in occasionally?" I asked, feeling my plan for the day slipping through my fingers. I'd been so sure Thomas Baker would be sitting in a top-floor office, the king of his castle, that I hadn't even considered the fact that he might have turned things over to his underlings. It made sense, in a way, I supposed. But I couldn't help myself from thinking a man who would cut his own daughter off must have a difficult time letting go of control of anything.

"I mean," the woman said and shrugged. "I guess it depends on your definition of 'occasionally.'"

I gave her a polite smile. "You're certainly working in the right place with answers like that."

She giggled again. "Lawyer jokes. What can I say? They rub off on you." She leaned over and glanced at a schedule on her computer screen. "I can tell you that, considering there's nothing on the agenda for today and, like I said, we all know when either of those two makes an appearance, your best bet would be the country club. If you don't find them there, someone might be able to point you in the right direction. If that doesn't work, then..." She held out her hands. "You'll have to come up with a new approach. The Bakers are known for being a bit... hm... spontaneous."

"And what is your definition of 'spontaneous'?"

She laughed. "Quite a bit different from theirs. Mine means splurging on a dessert at Applebee's. Theirs is more like, splurging on a dessert by flying to New York."

"Well, at least they're in the States," I said.

"Maybe." She shook her head, though the tone of her voice was clearly one of awe. "They'd be just as likely to splurge on a dessert in Italy."

I rubbed my chin. "At least there will be dessert involved." I thanked her for her time and headed back toward the front doors of the building.

"Do you need the address of the country club, if that's where you're going?" she called after me.

"No, thank you," I said as I turned back. "I think I know the place."

"All right. Well best of luck, Mr. Starke. If I see Mr. or Mrs. Baker, I'll be sure to let them know you stopped by."

I waved over my shoulder and headed out to the lot, climbed into my car, sat for a moment and heaved an exasperated sigh. Of course, they'd be at the country club. It was likely more than a little silly I'd come to the office in the first place. But at least I knew what I was getting myself into. Though it didn't make me any the more excited about it. I'd spent a lot of time there in the past as a bachelor, making connections and eating delicious food that I didn't have to cook. Now that I was a family man with a wife and daughter, I didn't have any kind of affinity for the place these days.

On the way over, on a whim, I took out my phone and found Kate's number. It was probably something I should've done earlier, but the fact was, I didn't realize things were going to get so muddy. And maybe, I still thought, or maybe hoped, they weren't. But there were too many people convinced that something had gone wrong here for me to not track down every possible lead I could.

As usual, Kate answered on the second ring. She always checks the number first, and if it takes longer than two rings, she's usually tied up with something important.

"Harry, what's the good word?"

"You sound chipper."

"Another day in paradise." She laughed. "And usually, a call from you means something interesting is happening. What's up?"

"Interesting might be a stretch as of yet," I said. "The jury's still out. But I have a question for you."

"Shoot."

"Do you happen to remember a woman who was fished out of her pool in the Heights about a month back? Hattie Baker?"

She was quiet for a moment. I could almost see her chewing the inside of her lip. "Yes..." She drew the word out, still thinking. "Wait. Okay. There were two, right?"

"Exactly. The first appeared to have dove into the shallow end—"

"And the second was just found facedown," she interrupted me. "Bad neighborhood in which to own a pool."

"Seems to be that way," I said. "But I had a question for you about the responding officer."

"Tobin?"

With anyone else, I would've been surprised, or more honestly, suspicious that the recall was so precise. But with Kate, once something was filed away in her mind, it was always there, just waiting. I had no doubt I could ask her nearly any detail about either of the deaths and she'd be able to fill me in as accurately as if she had the case folders in front of her.

"He's a good officer," she continued. "I don't cross paths with him too often, but when we've worked together, he's always been very professional and by the books. You'd like him."

I flicked my signal and made a turn toward the country club. "I thought that might be the case," I replied thoughtfully.

"You're always welcome to come by," she said. "I don't think I have to reiterate that."

"Not at all." I started up the long, winding drive toward the clubhouse. "And I may do just that."

"You sound like you're grasping at straws again," she said. "This one has you puzzled." It wasn't a question so much as an observation.

"I'm not sure what to think. I'm figuring out what I can and looking to see what seems out of place."

"Fair enough," she said. "Well, like I said, come on in whenever you like. Tobin actually was responding officer on both of those cases. Hattie and... Beatrice. I knew I'd think of it."

"Same officer on both, huh?" I asked.

"I know what you're thinking, and don't get too excited. It's part coincidence and part keeping things moving smoothly. Tobin gets along with the people in the Heights, for whatever reason. So, when things happen up there, if he's available, he's the one we send."

"Meaning the rest of you don't get along with those folks?"

"Meaning, when you find something that isn't broken, you don't try and fix it. He works well in that district, so we keep him there."

"Got it." I pulled into a space and looked up at the clubhouse, partly wanting to stay on the phone to avoid having to go inside. "I appreciate your help, Kate. I may take you up on that offer to talk with Tobin, but let me think on it for a while."

"Whatever you need, Harry. Like I said, I'm always interested in what gets your gears turning."

"And like I said, I don't know if it's anything just yet. But I'll be in touch."

"Sounds good."

She clicked off and I stuck the phone back in my pocket and let out a slow breath. I wasn't exactly keen on going into the building in front of me, an expensive copy of an English country house, which I knew was ironic considering who my own family was. And it was probably just as bad of me to judge the ultra-rich the way some people judge the ultra-poor. But nobody's perfect. And the ultra-rich have a way of forgetting that fact, and my father is no exception at times. Whatever the case may be, I didn't exactly have any reason to keep sitting there, and the chore wasn't going to do itself. So, I shook my head, unbuckled my seat belt and stepped out of the car.

13

Patsy and Thomas hadn't exactly made themselves hard to find, especially after having seen photos on my Google search. In fact, they seemed to be the type to only attire themselves in clothes that said, "Look at me." Patsy's hair was thick and teased to the size that, on anyone else, I would've thought it was a wig. Heavy eye makeup, reminiscent of Tammy Faye and a ring on every finger.

Though to be fair, Thomas wasn't falling behind in the jewelry race either. His dress shirt was unbuttoned halfway, showing off his gold necklace and suspiciously deep tan. The pair were on the back patio of the country club, sitting in one of a group of love seats gathered around a low table. The other two couples with them weren't anyone I recognized, but given the way things worked with this class of people, I wouldn't be surprised if I had to know them soon.

It was almost funny, in a way. The more these people tried to show off their affluence and prestige, the more they looked like gangsters and molls from a bad mafia movie.

The young lady at the front desk had been helpful enough

in letting me in and pointing me their way, though the look in her eyes was more difficult to parse out. At first, I thought she didn't want me to cause trouble. But there wasn't much she could do but let me in; not without causing a ruckus. I hadn't driven all the way out there to be turned away. Be that as it may, I figured that she could tell I meant business and if she pointed the way, it would just make things... quicker and a whole lot less bother. That, and I'm sure she recognized the family name Starke, as both my father and I were still members.

The Bakers sat under the awning, sipping their mimosas, looking like if the doctor told them they needed to start jogging, they would, with a straight face, say, "Fine, we'll pay someone for that."

I approached from the side, a man in one of the other couples noticing me first. But as soon as his eyes flicked up, puzzled and perhaps trying to remember if he should know me or not, Thomas Baker turned around quick enough.

"Thomas Baker," I said, holding out a hand as I walked up. "Harry Starke. I'm a detective, and I'd like to ask you a few questions."

It wasn't the most graceful approach, but it made the impression I hoped for. Thomas and Patsy were both on their feet in a split-second, ushering me inside to a private area. Maybe they were just concerned about keeping the details of their daughter's ongoing investigation low-key. More likely, they had no idea why I was there, but brushing up with law enforcement, unless it's an officer you've bought, never looks good to these people.

Thomas waved off a waiter who came over as we crossed the main dining hall, saying, "I'm taking the private room."

Just like that. Not a question in his voice. He was a man used to saying what he wanted and just taking it.

The waiter, obviously used to such behavior, simply nodded and went back to whatever task he'd been doing.

Thomas opened a small door off the main hall and again, with almost too much graciousness, held out a hand, allowing his wife and me to enter before he pushed the door closed and took a seat at the small, round table with us. I adjusted my chair, pulling back from the table slightly so I could see both of them at once. It wasn't that I suspected anything so much as I wanted to be able to watch their interactions, how they reacted to one another. Probably a useless move. These two had been together long enough their conversations would be as smooth as the doubles tennis players outside.

"So, Mr... Starke, was it?" Thomas began. "What can we do for you?"

It was a smooth beginning, pretending to forget my name to remind me I was, in their eyes, below them. But you don't usually forget the name of the detective who just pulled you away from your champagne. Unless, I suppose, you'd had more champagne than you wanted anyone to know.

"I'd like to talk with you about your daughter," I said.

The reaction was less smooth, but they did a fine job of masking it for the most part. Still, it didn't take an expert to see the way their shoulders relaxed, the way Thomas leaned back in his chair. Whatever else they had going on in their lives, I was apparently not going to bother them about the bigger secrets. And I'd have no problem with that if they didn't seem to act like the death of their child was less important than some shady deal they had going on.

"Hattie, yes," Patsy said, her tone immediately switching to Grieving Mother. It was quite the contrast to her laugh when I'd first walked up on their conversation outside. But, I tried to remind myself, it had been a few months and everyone grieves differently. Still, this felt just a little too perfect.

I waited for her to continue, but she seemed to be under the impression that was her line, so I turned back to Thomas.

"I've been hired to look into her death," I said.

"Whatever for?"

"Just to make sure it was an accident and not something a bit more complex."

"Meaning?"

I sighed. "Meaning, your daughter was rather well-off and..."

A chuckle came from Patsy and I looked over to her, eyebrows up.

"I'm sorry," she said, trying to regain her composure. "Hattie did okay for herself, that's true. I shouldn't speak ill, after all. But saying she was well-off is like saying Orin Swift is a good wine."

I raised an eyebrow.

And then Thomas said, dryly, "It depends on your perspective, my dear. I'm sure Orin Swift is perfectly fine for some people, maybe even, as you said, 'good,' but I think there are certain levels of success we should keep track of."

"And Hattie was not at the level you hoped?" I said.

"Hattie was..." Thomas leaned back in his chair, looking up at the ceiling. Clearly, he hadn't loved Patsy's answer, but something about his body language told me he didn't necessarily disagree with his wife's assessment. "Well, considering you're here, I'm sure you know who we are. But I'm curious, detective, have you looked into us far enough to know about Hattie's brothers?"

I admitted I hadn't.

"James and Archibald," Patsy said. "You might know the

names, actually. If you..." She looked at my clothes, without even realizing she was trying to note the labels. "Well, if you happen to invest someday, they're quite well-known around Wall Street."

I put a hand over my mouth to hide a smile. Patsy was one of those debutantes who you almost couldn't be mad at. She sincerely didn't understand what it was like to not have money. There was more than likely a yacht somewhere named after her, maybe more than one. And I understood the irony, considering my own family's sizable net worth. But when she talked about levels of success, I wondered if she'd ever considered becoming more grounded as an achievement.

"I'll keep that in mind," I said. "But Hattie had her own businesses as well. More than one."

"Oh, those little shops," Patsy said, earning herself a glance from Thomas.

"A long way from Wall Street, I suppose," I said.

"Well, darling, they're *local*."

I nodded. "Very true." Part of me wanted to point out that Hattie was providing jobs for people who really needed them, that starting any business, let alone several retail shops, and having them succeed was more than impressive. I wanted to ask which part she found the most off-putting, that the shops were local, or that her daughter was actually working a real job instead of marrying some rich playboy. Mostly, I wanted to point out that, considering where her sons lived, Wall Street was just another local business as well.

Instead, I shifted gears. "Hattie was seeing someone, is that correct?" I don't know why, but for some reason, I had no interest in telling them who coughed up the money for this investigation just yet. If things were to go south, I didn't want Mason taking any more heat and disrespect. And if something came up, well, maybe it's vindictive, but I wouldn't have minded saving this bit of news till the end.

Thomas showed the first bit of real emotion I think I'd seen out of him. He leaned forward and folded his hands on the table, not quite angry with me, but almost more exasperated. "You're talking about this Mason fellow?"

I nodded.

He shook his head. "He was just a hanger-on. Saw *Lady and the Tramp* too many times, perhaps. I told Hattie a thousand times she needed to distance herself." His voice trailed off and I knew what he was about to say.

"To the best of my knowledge," I put in quickly, "Mason has nothing to do with what happened to Hattie. I'm just trying to make sure I have my facts straight. I believe he was at work when her body was discovered."

"Doing that... oh... HPV or QVC or whatever it is," Patsy said.

I considered correcting her but decided to let it go. "Yes."

"The boy needed to work," Thomas put in. "Just finding some rich person and shacking up with them is no plan for life. You've got to figure out what you want and how to get it. Don't get me wrong, we met the boy a time or two and I told him the same thing. Working with your hands is fine, but it's never going to get you anywhere. You have to find other hands to do the work, find people to invest. That's how you make money."

I suppose, to a certain extent, it was the bare bones of a business plan, but I had a hard time understanding how Thomas Baker didn't see that the advice was empty as a deflated balloon.

"You remember the ring, honey?" Patsy turned to him, putting a hand to her chest and then looking again at me. "It was... shameful." She pointed to her finger. "Even this one here was fifty thousand dollars. And we told Hattie that. 'If he can't even scrape together the price of a good ring, he's not going to do anything else for you.'"

I had to laugh inwardly. The true sign of wealthy people is that not only do they forget talking about money is considered impolite, but they say it with the utmost sincerity, as if anything below fifty-K came from a quarter machine at the grocery store.

I looked at my watch, not entirely displeased when I saw Patsy apparently approve of the brand. If I needed to show some bling to get better answers, so be it. "I won't take up any more of your time," I said. "I'm sure it's valuable. But I do have one more question."

"Fire away." Thomas laughed and made a point to look at his own watch, the diamonds in the face sparkling. "We won't charge you for this meeting."

I wondered what his hourly fee was. Amanda and I had talked more than once about taking on clients like this and jacking my rates up by about four hundred percent, but only ever as a joke. There was no way I'd have the patience for it, let alone be able to live with myself for leaving people like Mason out in the cold.

"When Hattie's autopsy was done, there was a large amount of alcohol in her system," I said. "Some people I've talked with seemed to think this was unusual for her. I understand that you weren't around her every day, but did you have any impression that she might've been an alcoholic, or had at least begun drinking more lately, just before she passed?"

Amazingly, the pair looked at one another and laughed. I assumed they were about to tell me just how absurd it would be; that's what Mason had been convinced of after all.

Instead, Patsy spoke up, and after I heard what she said, I knew I needed to end the meeting, not because of the price, but because I was going to get myself into trouble if I didn't get away from them. I thanked them for their time through gritted teeth and walked back out to my car, her words still ringing in my ears.

"Well, of course, she must've been drinking more," Patsy had said. "Franny Cullins told us more than once that it was going to happen. I mean, who wouldn't drink if that's what your life was? It's depressing. If you can't even get a fifty-thousand-dollar ring, what's the point of any of this?"

14

By the time I'd gotten back to the office, I'd at least settled down somewhat. But the idea of people, especially someone's own parents, being so flippant about a death was hard to stomach. Money does a lot of things to people, the main one perhaps being the blinders that get put on. Suddenly, when your bank account reaches a certain number, you forget that other people are real. The size of the stack of your bits of paper is bigger, so you matter more. It's a twisted kind of logic. Especially since they are just bits of paper. Shoot, these days, they're even more imaginary than that.

I tried to keep my mind occupied with some emails and paperwork and then, thankfully, it was time for the team meeting. I was curious to find out what Heather had heard when she made the rounds, and by now, Tim was bound to have made some progress on the tech as well. I grabbed a water bottle from the mini-fridge in my office, thinking briefly that maybe I was fooling myself as well. After all, it's a little extravagant to have your own fridge just for water, isn't it?

When I got to the conference room, the others were already there. I took a seat at the end of the table and leaned back in my chair, opening the bottle with a crack. The others looked over at me and I held my hands out, palms up. "I can go first, or someone else can. Anyone have any big news?"

Our meetings, in fact most of our interactions, had become smooth enough over the years that, after the email I'd sent, everyone knew what the meeting was about, so no one needed the preliminary nonsense and ego-stroking of most business meetings.

"I'll go," Tim said. He was sitting cross-legged in his chair, his glasses, for the moment, not about to slip off the tip of his nose. He had nothing with or in front of him, but I knew there was no doubt he would recall everything he needed to say, and everything that was about to be said, for use later.

I nodded at him.

"So first off, the boyfriend was actually right, if you can believe that. She actually had a file with passwords. She actually didn't have anything shady going on. She just was like, actually that trusting."

"Actually?" Jacque asked, a grin on her face.

"Actually," Tim said and leaned into the word, "yes. But listen. Here's the thing. And maybe this won't be all that surprising to anyone, but she was doing quite well financially. I mean, it's not numbers that'll make your head spin, but she didn't need to work anymore if she made good choices and like, didn't pick up a crack addiction or something."

"She was a Baker," Jacque said. "I can't imagine they'd let one of their own get a reputation for being less than ultra-rich."

"But she wasn't ultra-rich," Tim countered. "At least, not what I'd consider ultra-rich. Which I suppose is kind of a tricky thing to specify. But the point is, Hattie's money came from Hattie's businesses. Her investments were all her own. This isn't mommy and daddy money. From what I can see, she built this all herself."

"Pulled up by the bootstraps," Jacque said. "With a stack of money to help her get going."

"Your jealousy is unbecoming," Tim said. Then, when she raised an eyebrow at him, corrected himself. "Who'm I kidding? You're always quite becoming."

I had to laugh. Tim's lack of social skills was something we'd all just accepted and embraced. This back and forth between him and Jacque was, I knew, her way of trying to help him acclimate to life outside the computer screen. As far as the two of them went, he had about as much a chance with her as he did winning a Super Bowl ring. As the saying goes, he wasn't playing for the right team.

"The point is," he went on, "financially speaking, she had nothing to worry about. It would've been actually difficult for her to spend all her money, really. The rate it was coming in was steady and impressive. So, if we're trying to scratch things off the list, money troubles is one I think we can let go."

"That's exactly what we're trying to do," I said, jumping in. "I don't know if we have the exact same perspective on money as people in her circle, but if more money was coming in than was going out, I'd say you're right. Who gets her assets when the estate is settled?"

"Since she died single, her parents get everything. Actually, not everything."

"Explain." I crossed my arms.

"The beneficiary of her life insurance gets one million dollars," Tim said with a quick raise of the eyebrows.

"And the beneficiary is?" I prodded Tim, giving him a stern parental look to stop with the theatrics.

"All right, all right. Mason Willis. Her grieving boyfriend and our client, gets one million dollars when the life insurance company pays out."

The room went silent, except for Jacque, who said, "No way!"

"Way," Tim said and shoved his glasses further up the bridge of his nose.

Everyone looked shocked, including me, I'm sure, but I continued. "That might be motive for Mason, but he mentioned to us that he was doing well financially for himself. Tim, check into his financials as soon as we're done here."

Tim nodded, and I continued, "What else did you find?"

"She did have a therapist," Tim said. "Lots of emails over the last few years, some text messages, a few calls. From what I can tell, it was just a standard, bi-weekly schedule that she'd had for the better part of the last decade."

"Anything particular you could find out?" Jacque asked. "I mean, besides the fact that her life was so good and her family so rich that she just couldn't stand it?"

"That's the thing." He looked over at her, finally having to push his glasses back up. "And people do this a lot. Yes, she was rich. Yes, her family is rich. But the main thing they talked about, at least from what I can piece together, was her parents."

"Poor little rich girl."

"Actually." I held up a finger. "I'll vouch for her on this one. Don't forget I just spent some time with Mr. and Mrs. Baker."

Jacque nodded. "And they weren't your cup of tea?"

"I'm not sure if they'd even drink tea. It's probably for peasants," I said with a grin. "But in all seriousness, these people are as close to heartless as we've seen in a lot of our other cases. The only difference is they truly don't seem to realize it. A lot of the people we've brought in, and I think each of you could attest to this, at least had some sliver of conscience. They knew what they were doing was wrong, but they felt like their backs were up against the wall. Or they didn't see any other way out. Or they just got caught up in the moment. The Bakers..." I thought for a moment. "The Bakers seemed to think Hattie was a bad investment, and that was that. The deal's over and they're focusing on their more lucrative children."

"Harsh," Jacque said.

I nodded. "But also blind. I think we could explain to them all day why what they're doing may have played a role in all this, and they'd just keep coming back with spreadsheets. They didn't come out and say she deserved to die; no self-respecting parent would do that. But they did say, in so many words, they weren't surprised she'd killed herself."

"And they did nothing about it?" Jacque asked, her eyes wide.

"According to the mom, and I quote, 'if you can't get a fifty-thousand-dollar ring, what's the point'?"

Jacque shook her head and ran her hands through her thick hair. It was the one true sign of frustration with her; but despite how her temper could be, I also knew it made her mind sharp as a razor. "The thing we have to consider here," she said, "and I know this sounds like a stretch, but you also said we're crossing things off the list. So, did you get the vibe they could've had something to do with it? Black sheep kind of deal?"

I considered it for a moment. "It's not an unfair question. I mean no disrespect to Hattie here, but I would guess that if you asked her parents about it, she was absolutely the child they were least proud of. But would they have her killed for that?" I scratched the back of my head. "Honestly, and I know this sounds harsh, but I got the impression that would've been too much work. They were more of a 'let's pretend this doesn't exist' couple when it came to Hattie, at least as far as I could tell." I thought for a second and turned to Tim. "You said the money Hattie made was all from Hattie's work?"

"As far as I could tell," he said. "Obviously, I didn't pore over every single thing yet."

"But you've pored enough," Jacque said.

"I've pored enough to say with some confidence that Hattie's life would've been pretty much the same whether her last name was Baker or Burroughs."

"So they just didn't care," Jacque said. "One way or the other."

"Or maybe they cared just enough," I countered. "They left her alone. Caring about themselves might not have been the best way to go about it, but maybe Hattie preferred it that way. Was there anything else in the emails you could find?" I asked Tim.

He bobbed his head from side to side. "I mean, I was just reading these as a third party. I didn't know much about anything as far as her family went. I can run back through them and see if anything jumps out. Or if one of you guys wants to, it's not gonna hurt my feelings."

"You got this," Jacque said, giving him one of her most charming smiles. "And besides, we need to bring something else to the table here." She turned slowly in her desk chair to look at Heather. "Do we need to open The Case of the Missing Vocal Cords? What's going on with you, girl? I wouldn't think you'd be this quiet even in your sleep."

I was thankful Jacque had broached the topic, but Heather's calm demeanor, her lack of even a smile throughout the meeting, had been grating on me. But, when it comes to certain questions, Jacque has a way of asking them that I know I'll never acquire. Again, it's why I hire who I do. Know your deficiencies and compensate for them.

"I don't have much to add," Heather said. "I spent most of the day in the Heights and no one seemed to know anything at all." She glanced at me. "When we met Miss Blue, she all but told us she avoided the place like the plague. But with Hattie, I didn't get that feeling. Did you?"

I thought back to what we'd learned so far, most to what Mason had told us, and said, "I guess I hadn't considered that she would actively stay away from people. After all, the boyfriend said he didn't go to dinners with her because of how catty the women were. And then there were the clubs as well. Unless Hattie was going out of her way to stay out of sight, like you mentioned with Victoria, I find it a little hard to swallow that no one would know anything."

"That's the story I'm getting," Heather said. "They're sad that she's gone, but only in that kind of detached way. Like if you heard your neighbor's pet died. Which, I mean, that's almost the saddest part of the whole thing. Her parents didn't care, apparently. Her friends drove her fiancé to the point he wouldn't even come to her house. And now that whatever happened has happened, life just rolls on with a few token alligator tears."

Jacque reached across and put a hand on her shoulder. "It doesn't have to," she said. "You've been here long enough to know that just because people aren't talking doesn't mean they don't know anything. What's your gut telling you?"

Heather looked up at the ceiling, over at Jacque, then down at her hands. "I guess it's telling me that the people in the Heights are about to get real tired of me knocking on their doors, because I'm not buying anything they're saying just yet."

"That's my girl." Jacque grinned.

"Before we get carried away," I said, proud of her grit and enthusiasm but having a bad feeling in my own gut, "what would you say was your success rate today?"

"Meaning?"

"Meaning, how many of the doors you knocked on actually had someone home?"

She scrunched her face, no doubt doing the calculations in her head. "Fifty-fifty?"

I nodded. "All right, that's about what I figured. We will go back to the Heights, the two of us, but let's wait a day or two. We've made some waves there and now we can sit back and let things take care of themselves." I pulled out my phone and checked my calendar. "What would you think about Monday next week? In the evening."

She nodded. "More likely to have people home on a Monday night than any other, I'd think."

"At least more than on a Friday afternoon." I glanced around at the rest of the team. "If there's no other pressing business, I'd say we're all up to date. I appreciate your work on this. Have a good weekend."

The group disassembled and I knew at least half of them were going straight back to their offices instead of home, but that was up to them, not me. All I was concerned about at the moment was getting home to see my own family. And that Heather had unconsciously agreed to wait for me before she went back to the Heights. I couldn't exactly say what it was about the place that felt off to me, but I knew I didn't want her there wandering around alone anymore.

15

HAVING PUT HEATHER OFF UNTIL MONDAY, I TRIED TO DO the same with my own mind. It's far too easy to get caught up in a job like mine. There isn't really a time that you are required to be in the office, but the other side of that is true as well; there isn't really a time that you couldn't be working. I was used to the long nights and days without sleep. And that was something that was just fine when I was on my own. But with Amanda and Jade in the picture now, I had really been trying to become more of a nine-to-five father and husband. I suppose I met this goal with varying degrees of success at best, but I'd been working on it. Pizza Night was one way of doing it. Another was making the weekends be weekends. No work, no files at home. It didn't always pan out that way, but I could tell Amanda at least appreciated the effort.

So, after a lazy Saturday at home, we'd planned a trip to the zoo for Sunday. Jade was still small enough to be in that strange middle-ground of experience. Part of her was baffled by the strange animals, but before too long, she seemed to accept that such a level of oddity was actually quite normal in this new world she was learning about.

The chimp show had her standing in Amanda's lap and clapping, though if this was due to the tricks and training, or the fact that it was the only place in the zoo that had air conditioning and didn't smell like it needed a good wash down, I'm not sure. Anyway, after a while, we left the animals to themselves and fell in with the trickle of a crowd and headed back out to the sunshine.

"Do you want to eat here in town or just wait till we get home?" Amanda asked.

I was just about to answer when I felt my phone buzz in my pocket. I'd turned the ringer off in hopes of keeping myself unaware of work for these two weekend days, but there was also a part of my brain that couldn't turn it off entirely. You can want some time to yourself, but I think my position is closer to a doctor than a taxi driver. There are certain times you're needed and no one else can take your spot.

But I was surprised when I saw an unknown number on the screen. Typically anyone who needs to call me is already in my contacts.

Amanda glanced at my phone and then up at me. "Go ahead." She sighed.

"I'll be quick."

I swiped the screen and answered in the standard way. "Harry Starke speaking."

"Good!" the male voice came back through the speaker, immediately aggressive. "I wasn't about to leave a message for you."

I held the phone out and looked at the screen again. "All right. Now you don't have to. Who am I speaking with?"

"The husband of the woman you've been harassing, that's who. I don't know who you think you are, but you best keep a good distance between yourself and my home. I play poker with the Chief of Police, you know."

"No, I didn't know that," I said. Amanda could only hear bits and pieces. Mostly the tone of voice was what made it to her ears, but I could tell she was intrigued. "I'm sure you're quite proud," I continued. "Now, not to deflate your ego or anything, but would you mind telling me who this is? What woman have I been harassing?"

Amanda raised an eyebrow, not out of concern but almost more in amusement.

"This is Isaac Coffee," the man said. "You were at my house yesterday and..." A voice came faintly from the background on his end of the conversation. "He what?" he asked, and from the muffled tone, I could tell he had a hand over the mic on his end. "Who?"

There was a rustling sound as Isaac Coffee was no doubt having the situation explained to him, the one that I was just piecing together as well.

"Well, he's still in charge," I heard the man snap.

"Mr. Coffee," I tried to break through to him. "I think I know what's happened here."

"You and your staff have been harassing my family, that's what happened here. And it's about time you admitted it."

"I believe you may have spoken with an associate of mine," I said, trying to keep my voice calm. "A young woman, probably yesterday afternoon. Heather—"

"That's the one," Coffee came back, his voice still angry but now more offended than anything. "She had no right to come here and upset my wife."

"I'm sure that wasn't her intention," I started.

"Whether you intended to or not is irrelevant. The damage has been done."

"I see." I glanced around and spotted a bench under a shade tree. I gestured toward it, letting Amanda know where I'd be, and went to get things straightened out. Isaac Coffee was in the middle of a good long rant by the time I sat down, but I was only giving him half an ear at that point. Whatever had happened, the last thing I would believe was that Heather had gone out and offended some complete strangers. But I also knew guys like this needed to have their big fit, let the wife see how brave and indignant they can be, and once the steam blows off, then you have at least some chance of a regular conversation.

I held the phone slightly away from my ear, and when it sounded like he was finally winding down, I tried again. "I can appreciate how Heather's presence might have been emotional for your wife," I said, doing my best to keep my voice calm and balanced. "However, I also have the utmost faith in my employees. As I believe we have discerned, I was not present for this conversation, and from what I'm understanding, you were also elsewhere. Is that correct?"

"Of course, it's correct," he snapped. "Some of us have to work, you know."

I couldn't help but smile. Work was exactly what Heather had been doing. But, potato-potahto. "I understand that as well," I said, keeping my tone even. "Perhaps you and I can discuss a few matters and we will be able to avoid any unpleasantness in the future." I had to roll my eyes at myself on that one.

"Oh, we have a few matters to discuss, all right."

"Excellent," I said, and, as I'd hoped, my chipper tone threw him off-balance. "Let's get this all smoothed out. I'm a private detective, and my associate was canvasing the Hilden Heights area in regard to a death that happened a few months back. Are you familiar with the drowning?"

"Of course, I'm familiar with it. I live here, don't I?"

"That you do, sir." Pandering to these people was bad, but I at least had the reassurance that the more polite I was, the more information I was likely to get. More importantly, the quicker this would be over. "We've been hired to look a little deeper into the matter. Certain parties are concerned that misinformation may have gotten into the reports and that, unfortunate as it is, Hattie Baker may have been the victim of foul play." It was all hot air. Don't get me wrong, the gist of it was true, but some people really like it when you sound like a cop. He was probably already imagining telling his buddies at the club. *Yes, victim of foul play, that's really what he said.*

"And that's precisely what has upset my wife so much. Do you not look into these things before you begin banging on doors? It's been a terrible few months for Marilyn. Those two were more like sisters than neighbors."

"And Marilyn is your wife?"

I could hear him let out a sigh that was almost a groan. I smiled again. Pandering was one way to get information. Playing dumb was another. Over the phone they were two of my favorite approaches because the person on the other end couldn't see your grin.

"Marilyn Coffee, you mean?" the man said. "Why yes, in fact, Marilyn Coffee does just happen to be my wife. Now I understand that you have a job to do, and I certainly wish you the best in whatever you pursue. But I'm requesting you keep your distance from our home. My wife doesn't need someone coming in here and upsetting her all over again."

"I completely understand. I have a wife myself, Mr. Coffee. In fact, maybe you can help me out, help both of us out."

I could almost see him chewing over my words. He had a solution right in front of him. If he would just talk to me, he could avoid upsetting his precious Marilyn. But then again, the drama would be over and he would have to find something new to talk about.

"What do you want to know?" he said finally.

"Well, for starters, was Hattie known to be a big drinker?"

"Oh for goodness..." He sighed again. "How am I to answer

that? Did I ever see her stumble down the front steps, martini in hand? Of course not. But if these are the kinds of things you want to know, I can tell you right now this is a waste of your time. I didn't know the woman other than to wave at, and my Marilyn is in no state to have her constantly brought up. If you want answers, just contact the women's group. They're nothing but a bunch of gossips, anyway. I'm sure they'll be happy to tell you some tales."

"Is that a fact?" I thought back to Heather's comment that no one seemed to know anything at all. Things were getting curiouser and curiouser, as they say. "You wouldn't happen to know who's in this group, would you?"

As the third exasperated sigh came across the line, I knew I had just about pushed things to their limit. "Look on the website," Isaac Coffee said. "And harass them instead. They'll probably love it. They've got nothing better to do, after all."

I started to thank him for his time when I realized the connection had been lost, or more likely, ended. I shook my head and put the phone back in my pocket. Amanda and Jade were across the way, waiting in line for an iced lemonade.

"Everything okay?" Amanda said, her voice a mix of concern and amusement.

"Just one of my many fans."

"He didn't sound too excited."

"Oh, he was excited." I laughed. "Just not in the way that helps me."

Amanda raised her eyebrows at me, undoubtedly questioning what the hell I was talking about.

I laughed again. "It's Sunday and I'm with my family. He can be as excited as he wants. We've got better things to do."

She gave me a lingering look and then shrugged. "You're the boss."

16

As much as I wanted to put Isaac Coffee out of my mind—all of them, really—I couldn't help but find my thoughts wandering back to the case through the rest of Sunday evening. I knew it was going to be another restless night, but I was at least thankful Amanda and Jade had worn themselves out in the sun at the zoo. I certainly didn't have any qualms about lying down myself when the time finally rolled around, but it was all I could do to keep my eyes closed. And by sunrise on Monday morning, I was lacing up my sneakers and slipping out the door for a run.

As I jogged out of the neighborhood, my stride quiet on the concrete sidewalk, I knew I needed to let my mind run as well. It wasn't that there was anything particularly off about Isaac Coffee. Just a rich guy throwing around his clout.

I corrected myself, or at least tried to. Maybe he was just a regular guy protecting his wife. After all, I'd played around with him. Maybe he felt like I wasn't taking him seriously. And that would be enough to make anyone upset.

It was strange though, I thought as I rounded a corner. Heather had acted as if no one had a word to say when it came to Hattie Baker, and now this man was livid that we had dared to upset his wife in her time of grief. I supposed it could've been the fact that there were people poking around the Heights at all. Reactions there tended to be, at best, unpredictable and, at worst, litigious. Or maybe, as I'd thought before, he was just finding a way to keep himself in the know, one step ahead of the gossip chain.

But, I amended, if that were the case, wouldn't he have wanted to know more about what I knew? He'd all but foisted me off on whatever the women's group was the first chance he had.

I googled them the night before. It wasn't anything more or less than what I'd expected. "The Ladies of the Heights" looked to be part social organization, part charitable group, but mostly a clique. Their social media pages looked as if, even though they'd all left high school long ago, mentally they'd never really left those adolescent needs behind them. Whoever was in charge of updating their information, almost assuredly someone who was neither a Lady nor from the Heights, hadn't been doing his job too well. The latest photo, a group shot, was from some kind of gala event, all the Ladies in their finest evening gowns. And, of course, smiling right along with them, was Hattie Baker.

This didn't surprise me so much as what was missing from all their pages and accounts. Not a single article mentioned Hattie's death. When I'd checked the dates, there were obviously a few posts made since Hattie had died, but of the incident itself, not word one. I figured maybe it was unladylike to get drunk and drown in your own pool, but that didn't mean it could just be swept under the rug. The wealthy were always finding ways of acknowledging things without admitting them. Look at that Rockefeller guy in the jungle.

I figured there was always a chance this was all coincidence and happenstance, that maybe it was just an accident with Hattie. Maybe it was just an odd turn of events that she wasn't the first to drown as well. There was always a chance that the reason the people in the Heights were being so close-lipped was that they didn't want to be bothered. Or I was getting fed false information. Or any one of a thousand other things.

As I rounded the corner to head home, I at least knew what my next few steps would be. Shower, eat, and find Heather. I glanced down at my watch. If I knew her, she was probably heading to the office already anyway.

It came as no surprise, then, that my car was yet again not the first in the lot when I pulled in at the office. I was pleased to note that Tim had apparently gone home, or wherever he went, at some point. But, as I suspected, Heather's car was in her usual, unofficially claimed spot. I grabbed my bag off the passenger seat and headed inside, dropping off my things before walking over to her office.

I rapped my knuckles on the door jam. "Got a phone call from a friend of yours yesterday."

She looked up at me, her expression questioning.

"Isaac Coffee."

She leaned back in her chair, tapping her pen on her lower lip. "The Heights?"

"Indeed, and something tells me he'd be very disappointed to find out you don't remember him. Though, in your defense, you may never have met him. He was calling in regard to a conversation you had with his wife. Marilyn Coffee?"

"Yeah..." I watched as she pulled a notebook out of her purse and flicked through the pages. If the meeting between Heather and Marilyn had been as traumatic as Isaac seemed to believe it was, I didn't think Heather would have any trouble remembering who I was referring to. "She was one of the ones who was home," she said after a moment, running her finger down the list. "I'm surprised he would've gotten ahold of you though. Or any of us, really. Did he have news?"

"In fact, he did." I walked into her office and sat down in the chair across the desk from her. "But now I'm starting to think I want to get your version of events before I go much further."

"My version?" She laughed. "I'm not sure how many different versions of this there could be. Like I said, she was one of the women who actually happened to be at home, but she was also probably the woman who had the least to say."

I looked at her, my head to the side.

"I introduced myself," Heather said, "explained why I was there, who you were, what we're trying to do. She pretty much said 'no comment' and closed the door."

I leaned forward, resting my chin on my hand. "She didn't say anything at all?"

"Well, it wasn't quite as blunt as that," Heather said. "And you know how those people are. Gotta throw in some big words to show off that fancy education. So it was probably something like, 'as much as I regret to inform you, I am inclined to express that I have no information on the topic you wish to discuss.'" She put a hand to her chest in a shockingly accurate impression of Hattie's mother.

"Hm, that's interesting."

"Why? What did the husband have to say?"

"Pretty much the exact opposite. He said Hattie and Marylyn were basically best friends."

She sat back, her eyebrows coming together in disbelief. "If that was Hattie's best friend, it might explain why nobody has much to say. You'd hope your best friend would be willing to answer a question or two if it could help solve your murder." She shook her head. "That place gets stranger every time we come in contact. Honestly, Harry, I was more than prepared to scratch the Coffees off the list and move on to the next ones. So much for my detective skills, huh?"

I smiled. "Technically, your detective skills are exactly what brought this to our attention. If you hadn't upset poor Marilyn, Isaac wouldn't have needed to play knight in shining armor. I'm prepared to pretend that you did it all on purpose."

"Ooooh, that's right. You caught me. I have many layers to my detecting."

"Just to be on the safe side," I said, "let's hold back on the Heights for the time being."

"No door-to-door this evening?"

"Oh, we'll do that all right," I said. "But let's keep out of it for a few hours. See what happens. It might be nothing, but you've seen more than once how giving people time is often enough to wear them down."

"Enough rope to hang themselves?"

"Something like that. We'll lay low till this evening, then we'll come up with a new plan."

She nodded and looked at the clock in the corner of her computer screen. "That's going to make for a long day."

"I'm not the one who told you to show up at six thirty in the morning." I patted the top of the desk and walked toward the door.

"Six forty-five," I heard her call after me. "And that's basically seven..."

17

As much as I'd hoped Heather would be off the mark with her "long day" comment, I knew better than to believe myself. I'd already been chewing on Hattie Baker's case for the better part of the previous evening and for nearly all of my morning run, and the first thing I'd done was go find the one person who could get my gears spinning even faster.

The thing with Hattie's case was—nothing was changing. Tim had made the comment that we were scratching things off a list. I'd said as much myself early on. Slowly remove the impossible, as Occam had told us. But the list of impossible things wasn't usually so long. Maybe I'd just gotten used to simpler cases. Find the spouse, find the boyfriend, find the estranged wife or jilted lover, and you were typically on your way to a simple solution.

Here, the lover was the only person who truly believed anything had happened at all. Granted, the fact that everyone else in the Heights was so desperately trying to believe nothing had happened set off more than a few warning bells in my mind, but that wasn't an entirely suspicious behavior. Humans, as thinking animals, are extraordinarily difficult to understand. I'd learned my fair share of psychology, both in the classroom and on the streets, but in the end, what the science had to teach us was generalities. In a lot of ways, trying to figure out what a person will do in a given situation is less reliable than a weather forecast. You can look at past events and make a guess, but a guess is all it really is.

I thought about Mason some more. He could either be the only person acting honorably, or he could be the man who proved the unpredictability theory. Maybe it didn't really make sense for him to kill Hattie. They weren't married, but he was the beneficiary on her life insurance. In the grand scheme of things, though, one million wasn't a lot of money when we're talking the Heights. He'd have to have something more complicated lined up behind the scenes. And if he was smart enough to do that, wouldn't he be the last person to bring in an investigator? Sure, it might be the best way to clear his name once and for all, but it was a serious roll of the dice. And, arrogance aside, if that was his play, there were plenty of other agencies he could've brought in who would've been happy to make a cursory glance, cash his check, and get on to the next case.

The parents were cold, but that very coldness is what made me think less and less about them. Being a parent who ignored a child, as terrible as it is to say, tends to be a convincing argument that you wouldn't go to all the trouble of killing the child. And that's without considering how horrific the crime itself would be. Besides, if anyone had a lot to lose, it would be the Bakers.

Then again, there was another famous family, Bakker with two Ks, who didn't know when to stop either. But by their own admission, Thomas and Patsy didn't look at Hattie as anything other than their wayward child, not unlike other families I'd known who almost blushed when they admitted their trust-fund brat had decided to do something unspeakable, like join the

Peace Corps or "waste" their medical training by signing on with Doctors Without Borders.

There was no law against being a jerk, though, and based on my brief interaction with the Bakers, as well as what I'd seen online, that seemed to be the only thing they were really guilty of.

Which left...

I looked out the window, much like I'd been doing most of the day. I'd run by Tim's office early on, not really expecting much. The fact that he hadn't been there when I arrived as much as told me that he'd gotten to what he felt was a stopping point. Even if he'd exhausted himself, he would've just slept in his chair. So it was no great surprise, even if it was a small disappointment, when he said he'd keep looking, but there was only so much to read.

I'd taken lunch on my own, thinking that if I could just put myself in Hattie Baker's place, maybe that would be the quickest route to understanding what someone could be after. But, try as I might, Hattie Baker seemed like everyone else in the Heights. She was a little aloof, maybe a little outside what most folks would call reality. But she was also a ground-up, at least partially self-made woman. I'd made a note to look into her initial financial situation, but I could almost guess what it would be. Money from mom and dad got her started, then, when the businesses were up and running, she'd either been cut off for staying *local*, or she'd paid back what she would've considered a loan from her parents and cut out on her own.

So who could she have burned along the way? She could've made people jealous, sure. But she could've done that a thousand other ways. Just her address was enough to make most people do jealous, half-disguised eye rolls. But in my mind, at least, she seemed like one of the good ones.

That afternoon, as I leaned in my chair, watching the traffic go by, I came to an odd realization. It's not that I ever want there to be crimes committed. Obviously, it's how I make my living, but in a perfect world, I have no doubt I'd find something else to do. This just happened to be in line with my skill set. But if I got to the end of this and it turned out Hattie just got drunk on a whim, slipped, and that was that, well... I almost felt like I was going to be disappointed.

I also felt terrible for thinking that way.

Thankfully, around four, Heather poked her head in the office. "It's driving you crazy too, isn't it?" she asked.

"What gave it away?"

"The silence. It always gets quiet as the grave in here when you've got a tough one."

I smiled. "I've told you all a thousand times, and I hold myself to it as well, in this line of work—"

"Just because it doesn't look like work, doesn't mean you aren't working," she finished for me. "I know. And I appreciate it. But I've been doing a lot of invisible work too and..." She looked down, then back up at me. "It feels *weird*, right? I mean, I know that's hardly the professional term, but do you get that vibe?"

I crossed one leg over the other and leaned back in my chair. "I think that's exactly the term, and it's what I've been trying to figure out all afternoon as well."

"Okay." She flashed a relieved grin. "As long as I'm not the only one. Because I had a question. I know it's going to sound a little odd, but, when we go back to the Heights tonight, what would you think about taking TJ?"

I laughed. We were hardly an outfit that needed to make an impression, at least most of the time. But in Hilden Heights, TJ was going to stick out like a pig amongst their purebred dogs. He was great at what he did, but his years in the military and then sadly later on the streets, were something that weren't exactly easy to hide. "Is that the statement you want to make?"

She thought for a moment. "I don't really know, I guess. If a statement needs to be made, I figured he's about the best we have."

"So you think someone killed Hattie, and that someone lives in the neighborhood."

"I think..." She chewed her lip for a second. "I think that if someone killed Hattie, someone in the neighborhood has information about it. And I think that, at least last time I went, I didn't make much of an impression on my own. Maybe he can stay in the car, or maybe we can play it by ear. But I don't see any reason to *not* have him there."

"Fair enough," I said. "But you have to ask him for the extra hours."

She laughed. "You think he can say no to me?"

"If anyone could, it would be TJ, but I'm not sure even he's got the guts for that."

I watched as she turned and headed across the breezeway toward TJ's office. Maybe making it a group outing wasn't such a bad idea after all. It might ruffle some feathers, but playing dumb and pandering to egos hadn't gotten us much so far. I took my cell phone out of my pocket to call Amanda. With another set of eyes on the neighborhood, TJ might make quick work of tonight's outing. Then again, he might see a lot of things Heather and I didn't. Either way, I needed to let Amanda know I'd be home late that night, something we were both disappointed about.

18

We—TJ, Heather, and I—left the office around five and went to grab an early dinner. We needed to give the Heights people enough time to get back from whatever important jobs or meetings or dinners they were having and, to be fair, I didn't want to do this any more times than we had to. Not only because it was the Heights, but because it was keeping me away from home, and I was more and more interested in spending time with my own family than I was in getting the runaround from anyone else.

We went to Captain D's, more because it would take longer than because we were interested in the fish and fries.

Heather was showing her usual forms of nervous excitement —chattiness, wringing her napkin, straightening her silverware on the table—while TJ was being typical TJ. He sat in his chair, looking out across the restaurant, eyes subtly moving as if, at any moment, someone might toss a hand grenade inside. I would've been concerned if he hadn't always been that way, and also if his attentiveness hadn't saved us more than once.

"So what's the plan?" Heather asked after the waitress set

our plates down. "Work toward the middle? And what do you want to do about the... well, the gender thing."

I smiled. It was the same question every time, not just from her but from the rest of the team and myself as well. It was about a fifty-fifty shot when doing cold interviews like this. If I walked up to the door and a woman answered, she'd either be standoffish or overly eager to talk. Same for Heather, just in reverse. We'd gotten a lot of good information out of cocky husbands who saw her as someone they could manipulate into bed, despite how virtually impossible that would be from her side. But then again, sometimes the women felt more comfortable talking with another woman and not having some random man showing up at their door asking about things they maybe didn't want to talk about.

"I thought we might split up," I said. "You two take one end, and I'll take the other."

Her eyebrows immediately pulled together. "You think I can't handle a bunch of overly confident white guys?"

TJ cleared his throat. "He thinks if I show up on my own in the Heights, the cops are likely to get called on us." He glanced down at himself. "And I'm not exactly what one would call eloquent."

Heather laughed a little, calming herself down. "Okay, fair enough."

TJ looked at her with an eyebrow raised.

"You said it," she grinned.

"The point is," I said as I dipped my fries in a puddle of ketchup, "we'll start at either end and meet in the middle. If you guys get any good leads, don't hesitate to stick around as long as it takes. I don't necessarily want or envision this becoming a multi-night thing. Truth be told, I wouldn't be surprised if we're out of there an hour after we start. But if someone starts talking, let them keep going on as long as they please. Nobody outside of

Miss Blue has had much to say, and even she didn't really give us anything of substance. But at this point, this seems to be our best bet, so do your best to be charming." I looked over at TJ. "Or at least not intimidating."

He shrugged. "I'm just me. Not my fault if folks get intimidated by it."

I looked at Heather. "Be doubly charming."

Around seven, after we'd killed as much time as we could at the restaurant without belaboring the wait staff, we got out of there and drove up to Hilden Heights. The security guard didn't seem any more pleased to see us than he did the first time —markedly less so—in fact, when he saw the grizzled man sitting in the back seat, but, having let us in once, he couldn't very well go back on his statement that we had a right to be there. I decided now was not the time to ask him about any visitors Hattie might have had the night she died. I'd have Heather do that when I wasn't there, sure she'd have better luck using her charm and good looks without us. He waved us through, and we drove ahead to the end of the subdivision.

I dropped TJ and Heather off, making sure they had their phones and knew where I'd leave the car in the middle of the place. I didn't anticipate any trouble, but it was more force of habit than anything. And besides, affluence often makes people slippery in more ways than one. After that, I drove back to where the Heights splits in roughly a T formation, parked the car, left the doors unlocked and started up the street.

It was funny, in a way. I never leave my car unlocked if I can help it, and you would think that doing so in a neighborhood like this would be the safest place to leave the car. But by the very fact it was such a wealthy enclave, the chances of an open car was known as well to every juvenile on the street as it was to me. If you could find a way in, there were purses worth more than the cash inside them just sitting in unlocked cars in driveways and on street sides. But, I also made it a point to never have anything lying about that I couldn't do without. So, with my CZ safely holstered under my left arm, I stood for a moment, looked around and...

As I walked up the street toward the house at the end, I felt my cell phone buzz in my pocket. It hadn't been nearly long enough for TJ and Heather to have run into any trouble, but if it was one of them, I was at least still close enough to turn around and jog back. More than likely, though, it was Amanda, which made my heart rate pick up a bit. She knew I'd be out this evening; we'd talked about it a mere few hours ago. But, unless Tim had had a breakthrough or Kate had something pressing she needed to tell me, I wasn't expecting anyone to reach out.

I was even more surprised when the screen showed just a number, no contact information at all. I swiped and answered.

"Harry Starke speaking."

"Mr. Starke," the voice was pleasant, if a little overeager. There was a tinge of nerves as well, something that you wouldn't usually notice in three small syllables, though it became clear why with the next sentence out of his mouth. "This is Officer Tobin Henry. I heard you've been lookin' into the Hattie Baker case and thought I might be of assistance."

"Officer Henry," I said, walking up the pristine sidewalk past immaculately trimmed hedges. "It's good to hear from you. Kate had nothing but praise for your work ethic, so don't worry about that."

"Kate? Oh. Captain Gazzara? That's good to hear."

It was an interesting comment. To most ears it was just a toss-off, a way of deflecting a compliment in the proper Tennessee fashion, but I'd been around enough to make a mental note of it. Then again, as I'd initially assumed, it may have just been nerves causing the waver in his voice and the uncertainty. What I did know was that when a guy calls you up and sounds like this when he starts talking, he's going to be more than happy to talk until he loses his voice. Maybe tonight wouldn't be a total waste after all.

"I assume you've got some information for me," I prompted.

"Well, to be honest, uh... detective?"

"Harry's fine."

"Well, sir, I don't know what all you know and what you don't. But word got back to me you were looking into Hattie again and I wanted to make sure you knew I was here to help, hunnert percent."

He had an interesting locution, as if his backwoods accent and style had been all but stomped out of him. But there were still hangers-on.

"I appreciate that, Mr. Henry. If you want to run me through what you know, or anything that might have come up that I don't know, I'd be quite obliged."

"So, here's the thing, Mr. Harry, sir..."

I sighed as he began to recount every detail of the case that I already knew, as well as laying himself wide open in areas where there were things he didn't know, but I did. He hadn't talked to Victoria Blue; she hadn't answered the door when he'd rung the bell. He had gone over the ME's report, but to him, it seemed "pretty much open and shut."

"Gal gets her drink on like that, especially if she ain't used to it, well... things happen, right?"

I wondered if Officer Tobin Henry was getting a bit of his drink on as well, considering how his tone and timbre became more and more relaxed as the chat went on.

"These things do happen," I agreed, more to let him know I was still listening than to add anything to the conversation. I'd covered a few hundred yards by this point, and if Officer Henry didn't start giving me something worth hearing, I was working my way toward ending the call.

Just about that time, I thought of poor Hattie floating in the pool, and a thought occurred to me.

"Did you speak with an Isaac Coffee?" I asked.

I heard the shuffling of papers in the background. Maybe he was a bit in the cups, but he was at least prepared and apparently sincerely trying to be as helpful as he could, with notes, reports, and all.

"Lemme see..." The phone clunked to the table as it undoubtedly slipped from between his shoulder and ear. "Sorry about that, sir. You said Coffee?"

"Yes. Isaac."

"Okay. Yeah. Yeah, let me find him here in the file. If you want to know the truth, just between me and you, there wasn't anything particularly interesting about any of the chats. That neighborhood is closed up like Fort Knox. Even if someone did know something, I don't know if they'd say it. But I kinda find it hard to believe a person could live up there like Miss Baker did and never have any contact with anyone. But..." He sighed. "According to the statements, that's the case. Nobody knew anything."

"Did you get the impression it was because you were a cop?"

Another sigh. "I s'pose that could've been it. But it wasn't like they saw a cop and slammed the door. The husbands, the boyfriends, the boy-toys," he said and laughed a little to himself, "they were happy enough to talk about anything you could think of, so long as it wasn't the case. Half the time I couldn't get out of there without an offer of scotch or whatnot. So I guess maybe it didn't matter to them at all I was a cop."

"But they wouldn't talk about the case," I repeated. "From what you're telling me, I'm assuming the wives and girlfriends had even less to say."

"Couldn't get a word out of 'em," he said. "Most times, if the female answered the door, they'd take a look at me and just go get the man. I know we're Southern and all, but geez. It's not like a gal can't answer a question or two."

"I've been seeing similar things," I said. "If it helps."

He laughed. "Ain't no sweat off my back."

"So, Isaac Coffee." I tried to coax him back to the topic. "He also had nothing to say?"

"Oh *Isaac* Coffee! Now I remember. The husband of one Marilyn Coffee. We had a conversation. But not about Hattie. He knew nothin' about her."

"And?" I said. "What was your conversation about?"

"Oh, yeah. Well, I had talked to his wife, Marilyn, about Hattie. You know. Just the usual questions. She told me in no uncertain terms that she had nothing to say. Then Mr. Coffee calls me up and chews me out for upsetting his wife, who he said, was best friends with Hattie. It defies logic, it does." Officer Henry finally took a breath.

"I appreciate your call," I said, coming up on the end of the street. "I'm in the Heights now, about to start some interviews. If I need anything else, I'll be sure to get in touch with you."

"You feel free, Mr. Starke. This here's my personal phone. I don't have it on me at work, of course, but I'll keep an eye out for your call. I've never worked with a private eye before. This is really something."

"Indeed it is," I said, and, unable to resist, tacked on, "Get some rest tonight and some water in you."

He laughed. "You sound like my old man."

I ended the call before we could get into any more long and wandering conversation, looking at the homes around me. If these people had clammed up around Officer Henry, who they were familiar with, how were we going to get these people to talk about Hattie?

19

I took a folded sheet of paper out of my back pocket. It was a makeshift map Tim had given the three of us that listed the last-known occupants of every house. Real estate deals in this area weren't something to be taken lightly, so I had to assume it was about as accurate as I was going to get. I looked up at the three-story brick home, lights glowing in the dimming night. It was what kids thought adults would buy. The windows were spaced evenly and had a small candle-shaped light in each one. The chimney was just off to one side, no doubt puffing jolly plumes of smoke at Christmas. But, as I'd seen far too often, that's all these places were. Smoke and mirrors. More than likely, the couple inside was up to their ears in debt and didn't have a dollar to their name. But the home, I couldn't fault them there. It was an investment that guaranteed at least some kind of return.

The sheet read "Andrew and Franny Cullins." It wasn't a name that meant much to me, but sometimes that was how these folks wanted things to be. I walked up the long concrete path to the door and knocked. A dog barked inside, and then, after a few moments, Andrew answered the door.

"Mr. Cullins?"

"You found me. What can I do ya for?"

I looked him up and down quickly, a habit from usually doing blind knocks on places that the person answering might have a weapon. Andrew Cullins was in a pair of gray jogger pants and a Harvard University shirt. Whether he actually went there or not, I didn't know, but there was nothing about him that said anything other than he'd just been watching TV with his wife. His hair was still gelled almost to perfection from the workday, just a few strands having come loose across his forehead, and his smile seemed genuine. Together with the calm demeanor and greeting, it seemed like all good signs.

"I'm Harry Starke," I said. "I'm a private investigator and I've been asked to look into the untimely death of your neighbor, Hattie Baker. I was hoping I could ask you a few questions."

"Oh, yes, sure." He hung his head slightly. "That was too bad, wasn't it? I didn't know her terribly well. Kind of one of those wave-at-the-neighbor type of situations. Seemed like a nice enough young lady. Wait." He paused, looking up. "I thought that was an accident. Is that not the case now?"

"Officially, yes, that's still very much the case."

"Okay." He laughed, a bit uncomfortably, but in a way that seemed like a natural response. "I don't mean to say I'm glad to hear it, but if the other option is, well, murder, I guess I'm glad to hear it wasn't that."

I bobbed my head from side to side. "The thing is, if it wasn't an accident, there isn't really another option, is there?"

I wanted to see how he would react, but his shrug and raised eyebrows were completely in line with what I would expect from someone nonchalantly telling me the truth. He didn't have a care in the world, as far as I could tell. Maybe they did have a few dollar bills tucked away after all.

"I'm not sure how I can help you," he said, "but ask away.

The reason I moved here was because it seemed like a safe place to live. Now that I'm married," he said and leaned in conspiratorially, "and hopefully with one on the way soon, I'd hate to find out this place wasn't what I expected."

I considered reminding him there seemed to be an oddly high number of pool deaths of late, but it seemed like an unnecessary jab.

"Congratulations," I said. "And no, to the best of my knowledge, you're still safe. But we had an individual come into our office with some concerns and we're checking them out."

He snapped his fingers. "Hah! The boyfriend?"

"I'm really not at liberty to discuss that."

"Ah." He grinned. "NDA? I get ya."

I nodded despite the fact he wasn't quite correct. It was close enough to keep Mason's name out of it. But he also knew that "the boyfriend" existed, which was interesting. On a whim, I changed my line of questioning. "I understand you didn't know Hattie all that well, and this may seem like a random inquiry, but did she strike you as someone who... well, who enjoyed more than a nightcap every now and again?"

I wasn't surprised when he laughed, but I was surprised at why.

"That's a quaint way of putting it." His perfect, straight, white teeth almost reflected the porch lights.

"Meaning?"

"Meaning, and I don't mean any disrespect, but Hattie enjoyed a nightcap, a morning cap, a brunch cap. If the sky was blue, she was more than happy to celebrate it with a drink."

"So she knew her way around the bottle."

"Mr. Starke, if Jack Daniels, Jim Beam, and Johnny Walker were the three Musketeers, Hattie would've been their D'Artagnan." He paused. "Again, I don't mean to speak ill of the woman. She was kind as could be when you'd see her, but," he said and shrugged, "people talk around here."

I was intrigued by the comment. In my experience, the exact opposite of talking had been happening. Before I could ask my next question, there was a rustling in the background and Franny Cullins, attired in an almost matching outfit of sweatpants and a college tee, looking slightly abashed that someone would see her that way, came into the foyer from a room somewhere off to the side.

"Who's this?" She looked to her husband. "Can we help you?"

I went back through my spiel, explaining who I was, trying to downplay the idea that anything out of the ordinary had happened, more than anything trying to convince this woman they themselves hadn't done anything wrong and I was just out trying to chat with the neighbors.

"It's awfully late, isn't it?" She looked from me to her husband, as if he should be thinking the same thing. Andrew, for his sake, seemed oblivious to the signal.

"It is indeed," I said, "but I didn't want to bother anyone during their workdays. Evening seemed like the polite time to stop in. Most couples are at home together by then, aren't they?" It wasn't a question that required an answer, but her eyebrow raised the slightest tick at this, as if the very fact that I had considered approaching a woman on her own was a sign of more devious things. "I don't know what there is to say about Hattie Baker that I didn't tell your little friend who called the other day," Franny finally huffed out. "I'm sure my husband told you everything any of us would know. The woman wasn't exactly the friendliest in the world and, I'm not saying I'm happy she died, but perhaps we'll get someone more suited to our neighborhood in that place. If it ever sells. It's an eyesore."

It was my turn to feel my eyebrows go up. It wasn't animosity, at least not quite entirely, that this woman was expressing. Moreso, she seemed to be seeking a quick end to a conversation she didn't want to be a part of. It was more of a hunch than anything, but something was off, and even that feeling was at least something pointing me toward further involvement.

"She wasn't suited to the neighborhood?" I asked.

"She wasn't... oh, you know," Franny said, looking to her husband who was merely listening, a calm smile on his face. "It's just one of those things that happens. And those things seemed to follow her. Even after the grave, apparently, considering here you are."

"I was asked to inquire," I said.

"Well, be speedy about it." She put her hand on the open door. "That's not something anyone would want lingering around their neighborhood. Good evening, Mr. Starke."

Before I could ask if she meant Hattie herself or the potential murderer, Franny Cullins was closing the door.

I stood on the porch for a moment, my brain rapidly shuffling and filing this new information. Except it wasn't information; it was feelings, thoughts, impressions. Whatever was going on was apparently beyond a simple swimming accident. There was obviously the chance that Franny was just ruffled and didn't feel comfortable talking to an investigator. But when that was the case, most folks responded like her husband, eager to share anything they could. It was like Tobin Henry. I couldn't get the man to quiet down. Pulling back isn't a sign of guilt necessarily, just like opening up isn't a sign of innocence, but it's certainly a sign of something.

I turned and walked back down the driveway, hanging a left on the sidewalk and heading up the concrete sidewalk to the next house. What I experienced there was going to apparently be the pattern for the night.

The lights were on outside, and several rooms were lit up

inside as well. A flash on one set of curtains told me a TV was on in one room, but after ringing the bell three times, not a soul appeared. Initially I thought it might be a family on vacation, their lights and appliances set to timers in order to give the appearance of someone being home. I shook my head and moved on.

But by the third house, where I even saw a shadow pass by a curtain in an upstairs room, I knew word had gotten out that there was some random man walking about the neighborhood knocking on doors. I had a good feeling Franny Cullins was the one making the calls.

As I walked back to the sidewalk, my cell phone buzzed in my pocket. I took it out and checked the screen: Heather.

I swiped the screen. "Striking out?"

"We started out all right." I was surprised to hear TJ's voice, then realized he didn't typically carry a phone unless he was on his own, and even then it was hit or miss. But, if they were struggling, Heather had most likely asked him to hang back so as to not give them any more problems than they were already dealing with. "After a couple more houses, though, nobody'll answer. As far as I can see, they're home. Or at least it looks that way. Seems odd everybody'd go on vacation at the same time."

"Well," I said. "That might be my fault. I talked with one family and since then, nada."

"Ah. You spoiled it for the rest of us."

"Seems that way. Or maybe you did. Whatever the case, I'm not holding high hopes for tonight."

There was a pause as TJ made a comment over his shoulder to Heather. A moment later he was back on the line. "Yeah, she says nobody's answering, even if she sees them looking at her through the curtains. I'm not gonna tell you how to run this show, but it's looking more and more like this is gonna be all for naught."

I sighed. I'd spoken to the Cullins, and it sounded like Heather had maybe gotten one door to open as well. TJ was right; it was a lost cause. "All right," I said. "Meet me back at the car. There's no sense in banging our heads against these high-end walls."

"Will do."

He clicked off and I started back down the sidewalk. Part of being a detective is training yourself to see what's there, the things that other people might miss. But the finesse of being a detective, the more nuanced side, is being able to see what's not there that should be. And that was all I could think about. These people should be talking to us, even if they didn't have anything to say. They shouldn't be hiding behind closed doors and making discreet calls to one another about the people asking questions. The feeling of something being off that I'd had with Franny Cullins grew with every step I took back toward the car. Someone, any of them, should've had something to say. And outside of Andrew Cullins's jovial, off-the-cuff demeanor, outside of Victoria Blue's straightforward, if curt, cooperation, we were finding little to nothing. Maybe having Heather make calls and do rounds on her own was a bad idea, but I couldn't imagine it would've caused the kind of response we were getting, even if she'd been ham-handed about it. No, something here was very wrong.

I strode down the sidewalk, lost in thought, the shadows of the trees passing over my head and the shadows of the perfect hedges passing under foot. It was quiet, and as Heather had pointed out when we'd first come by, almost eerily so. When this neighborhood rolled up its mats, it may as well have been a ghost town. I reached in my pocket for my keys, figuring I could just turn the car around and pick up TJ and Heather on their walk back when something stopped me.

Something was certainly off; something with the whole

place was off. But in the moment, it wasn't the neighborhood or their lack of common courtesy that was bothering me. I looked off to the side, then ahead of me. Something wasn't... then, as I started to turn back, I felt something hard crack against my skull.

The pain was blinding, bewildering. I crumpled to my knees and then down on my hands. The ability to control my limbs fading fast. That was when the first boot caught me in the ribs. Gasping for breath, I instinctively tried to put a hand to my side, but my arm wouldn't move. That was when the next kick caught me in the jaw. I was flipped onto my side, providing a free target to whoever was about to exact some punishment. I saw vague shapes, blurs, forms. The stars were bright in the sky as anonymous fists crashed down, creating more flashes of light in my slowly tunneling vision. It was the sound of scuffling feet, the thud of fist on flesh, the crunch of boots against my ribs. But not a barking dog, just like Heather said. As if I'd summoned her, or maybe just imagined her as I slowly drifted out of consciousness, I thought I heard her voice in the distance.

20

It was the beeping that woke me, but it was a sound I shouldn't have been hearing. My phone played a chime; Amanda's played a song. A beeping alarm had been one of the first things I'd gotten rid of after college. The sound grated on me. But this wasn't the buzz of an alarm clock either. It was rhythmic, steady, almost too faint to really notice.

I opened my eyes to bright lights. Immediately shutting them again. My head throbbed along with the beeping. I was in a bed, but not my bed. It felt different. Smaller. Elevated in the back. And someone was touching me.

My eyes darted open again and I caught the briefest glimpse of Amanda before the fluorescent lighting caused me to close them again. It was normal to touch Amanda while we slept. But not like this, not to hold hands. She would snuggle under my arm or onto my chest, but this was wrong. I reached up with my free hand to shield my eyes from the light, wincing as my fingers touched the bone above my right eye.

Amanda leaned in. "Harry, honey, thank goodness."

I tried to smile. Even not knowing where we were, even not

knowing what exactly was happening, my instincts to set her at ease kicked in. "You should see the other guy."

"Was the other guy Mike Tyson? Because you look like you went ten rounds."

I could tell she was doing the same as me, trying to put on a positive, confident persona, but the look in her eyes showed more concern than I ever wanted to see there.

"What happened?" I asked, my throat sore and dry.

"I was going to ask you the same thing."

She cupped my hand in both of hers and I rubbed my thumb over her fingers. Even that sent a dull thud of pain up my arm.

"Are we at the hospital?" I knew it was a stupid question, but it was an easy one. The more that she could start feeling like she had a hold on things, the calmer she would be.

"Club Med, actually," she said, the hint of tears in her voice. "I knew you'd never get around to a vacation unless I..." Her voice hitched. "Harry..." She put her head on my chest. "What did you do?"

I petted her hair for a moment and realized, with a start, I had no idea.

"Honestly, Amanda, I don't know."

"What do you mean you don't know? I got a call in the middle of the night that you were here. No one seemed to know why. Heather was telling me some story about you getting mugged or jumped, or I don't know what. I thought you said that neighborhood was safe."

That neighborhood... a flicker of an image came to mind. That's right. The Heights.

"Well..." I intended to tell her how the safest neighborhoods could also be the most dangerous, that it was a thing with averages, but the idea, even the thought of explaining it, made my head hurt. "I thought it was," I said finally. "Did Heather see what happened?"

Amanda leaned back, looking down at me and clearly trying to put on a brave, business-as-usual face. "She saw someone beating on you, but when she yelled out, he ran off. TJ tried to chase after him, but the man lost him among the houses somewhere. What did you do up there?"

What *did* I do? I remembered stopping to talk to the security guard. I remembered dinner with TJ and Heather before. I remembered sending them off together because TJ didn't want to talk to anyone he didn't have to. We had driven to one end of the Heights and I'd dropped them off. I'd parked the car. And... a phone call? Someone, maybe. Or the radio? No. Something about a voice.

I felt my brows pull together. There are a lot of strange situations in my line of work, but there's only one rule. Always know and remember everything.

And I had nothing past parking the car.

"I don't know," I said after a pause. "I can't remember anything."

Amanda looked at me, side-eyed, as if assessing the possibility that I was just trying to protect her and Jade by withholding something from them.

"Honestly, Amanda. I'll tell you everything I do remember, but none of it matters. The last thing I recall is getting out of the car to go..." I racked my brain. "To go talk to people about the case."

She held my gaze a moment longer and then sighed. "Nothing?"

I shook my head slowly, pain keeping a steady beat with my pulse.

Just then, a rattle on my opposite side caused me to look over, despite my aching head. The door opened slowly and, with a look of equal parts concern and anger on her face, Kate walked in.

Before I could say a word, she started. "You really know how to make an impression, don't you?"

I smiled a little. Even my cheeks hurt. I reached up and realized it wasn't without reason. The right side of my face was covered with a dressing. I looked at Amanda and said, "What?"

"Someone slashed... Oh, Harry..."

"Go big or go home, as they say."

"It looks like you got the 'go home' part of the deal here," Kate said as she pulled a chair over next to the bed opposite Amanda and sat down. "But if you wanna go big, the Chattanooga PD is ready to do so as well. So I need some info, Harry. And I'm not saying this as a cop; I'm saying this as the friend of a person who was beaten half to death and only saved by the fact your attacker got spooked. So what do we know?"

I took a breath. I knew she wasn't going to like what I was about to say, but there wasn't any other way to work with Kate than by dealing with the cold, stark truth.

"We don't know much." I sighed. "Very little might be the better way to put it."

Kate pinched the bridge of her nose. "I was afraid that's what you might say."

"It's the Heights," I offered. "There shouldn't be a square inch of that place that isn't covered by someone's security camera. Or even one from the HOA, I'd imagine."

"You're right about that. We've certainly got video of the attack. The problem is that it's from a light-pole camera about twenty feet away. We see you walk into frame. You stop. Someone comes up behind you and commences to beat on you like your grandma's rug. After a few seconds, the attacker looks up, darts out of frame, and then a second later Heather enters."

"And the fact that you're sitting here talking to me means it's worth about as much as the tape it's on."

"Pretty much," Kate replied as she sat back in her chair. "It appears to be a man around six feet tall. But that's just our best guess based on his appearance when he comes up to you. He could've been hunched over. The angle could've made the perspective seem off. It's a great tape if you ever want to see your worst-case scenario played out, but even if we knew who it was, it wouldn't hold water in court. It's just a figure who is a little shorter than you."

"The definition of inconclusive."

"Exactly." She tucked her hair behind her ears. "So what I need to know is, who did you tick off yesterday?"

I shook my head. "Not anyone that I recall."

"Harry." Her tone was stern, one I expected and one I had grown accustomed to.

"I remember pulling into the Heights. I remember taking TJ and Heather to one end. I remember parking the car. After that..." I held out my hands.

"C'mon, Harry," she said. "You've got to give me something. That tape is fine if we need to prove you got cracked in the skull, but this place," she said and gestured around, "the bills oughtta prove that just fine as well. Who did you see? A name? An address seems like a stretch, but you have to give me something to start from."

"You've got the Heights," I said, probably a little more sharply than I intended. But I didn't like any of this, not where I was laying, not the look of concern on Amanda's face, and certainly not the inability to help solve a problem when I was so clearly directly involved. I sighed. "That was harsh. I'm not upset with your questions; but I believe you know that, if I knew anything, you would've been the first person I told. You've got tape that's basically useless and I'm laying here bandaged up without even the comfort of knowing who I need to go give comeuppance to. I just woke up about five minutes before you came in and, believe it or not, this isn't exactly an ideal morning."

She reached over and patted my hand, an out-of-character gesture for Kate. Usually, she wanted to be one of the guys, or at least seen as an exceedingly professional woman. But the gesture was almost motherly, kind.

"I know, Harry," she said, her tone softer, more human than cop. "You took a pretty hard hit to the head. I'm probably just worked up over having seen it on the tape. Be thankful the two of you haven't. I..." She looked up. "Honestly, I'm torn. Part of me is just glad you're alive."

"That bad?"

"If it had been anyone else," she said and looked down, giving a kind of sigh and chuckle at the same time. "Well, let's just say, for once, I'm glad you're so hard-headed."

She glanced over at Amanda and then back to me. I knew she was angry and I knew she wasn't just trying to do her job. This had all suddenly become very personal for Kate. And for me as well.

"I wish I could remember," I said, hating how empty and useless the comment was.

"I know," she said, her voice low. "It's not unusual to have some memory loss with an injury like this. I guess I just got a little fired up. Get some rest. The doctor will know more about it than me anyway, right?" She tried to sound upbeat, but I could tell she was more than a little disappointed she wasn't walking out of the room with a name, description, and address.

"You'll be the first person I call whenever this..." I gestured vaguely. The brief conversations, or perhaps more the realization of what had happened, were weighing on me. My eyes hurt. My ribs hurt. My arm hurt. Talking hurt. My head pounded.

"I expect nothing less," she said.

She turned to Amanda and said something, but I was already falling back into slumber. I tried to listen, tried to be useful, but my body was fighting against it. I needed to rest. I needed to heal. The last thing I heard before drifting off was the soft, comforting murmur of Amanda and Kate, somewhere around me, somewhere close.

21

When I woke up again, nothing seemed to have changed. Kate was gone, but I knew she would have to be. Amanda, still in the same clothes, just looking a little more disheveled, sat beside me, my hand in hers. Her head was down, lying on her arm as she slept. I looked around the room, trying not to move too much, both to avoid the pain that coursed through my body and, maybe more so, to let Amanda rest.

I looked up at the drop-tile ceiling, and I thought.

We had gone to dinner, I remembered that. TJ and Heather had joked, but we were worried because TJ isn't much of a talker and Heather had... Heather had already talked to people. We were looking at the Heights, obviously. We went to the Heights. We had to do something there. Find someone. Talk to someone.

No.

Not someone. We wanted to talk to anyone. Or maybe, everyone. Because...

I clenched my jaw. We were in the Heights and I parked the car.

Wait.

The realization hit me about as hard as my attacker must have. I was being ridiculous. Trying to remember what happened when I was attacked was pointless. But I knew who I was. I knew Amanda. I even had the fresh memory of Kate coming by and trying to help. I knew what she told me. I remembered all of that. I remembered everything except maybe two hours. So, what did I remember from before the attack?

I thought back, trying to reconstruct the days. I was a detective, for crying out loud. If I couldn't reconstruct my own story, then I should probably put in for retirement.

My brain gave me colors. Blue water. Red brick. Black shadows. No.

Red hair.

Blue...

Victoria.

Victoria Blue. The woman whose name didn't match her look.

And...

Hattie.

I sat up, startling Amanda out of her sleep.

"Oh, Harry." She threw her arms around me, her embrace tight and hard.

"I remember," I said, trying to sit up. "Not everything, but I know why I was there." I tried to piece the random images together. "I know I will remember."

"Harry, we thought you weren't coming back," her voice broke.

I pulled back slightly, trying to look her in the eye. "I didn't mean to doze off."

She pushed me lightly, a playful gesture that had more emotion in it than I would've expected.

"What?"

"You've been unconscious for two days, honey."

"What?" I sat up, pain rushing through my back and arms, centering in my head, but I shook it away. Two days? What kind of hell had this woman been sitting through while I just lay there? "What's wrong with me?"

"Baby." She reached over and put a hand on my chest, easing me back into the pillows. The half-smile on her face didn't make up for the tears that ran down her cheek. "So much." She tried to laugh. It was a joke we always made, but never in front of anyone. I was too involved with my work. I was too headstrong. I was too everything to find someone to put up with me. I knew it and, while she joked about it, Amanda knew as well. We were custom-made for one another. There wasn't another soul in the world who would tolerate our behavior.

I reached over and wiped her cheek with my thumb. "So much," I said, giving the pat answer, "or just enough?"

She leaned down and put her head on my chest. "Just enough." I felt her sigh, her warm breath through the hospital gown I was wearing. "But this is pushing it, Starke."

I laughed a little, my ribs aching but my brain knowing she needed to hear me be upbeat, on the mend.

"Hold on," she sat up, and immediately I missed the warmth of her touch. I knew I needed to find out what happened in the Heights, but at the moment, all I wanted was to take care of this one woman and our child. The job could take a hike. Amanda and Jade were my only true responsibilities.

I watched as she reached over and pushed a button on the wall by my head.

"Nurse's orders," she said, wiping her eyes with the back of her hand. "Or doctor's orders, I guess is how the phrase goes. I don't know. I'm a little frazzled."

"You stayed here for two days," I said. It wasn't a question, and not entirely something I intended to speak aloud.

She looked up at the ceiling, smiling and crying at the same time. "What else does a girl have to do?"

I opened my mouth to ask another question, and she waved it away.

"Believe it or not, Rose and your dad. They have Jade."

I laughed, wincing at the pain. "I don't know who got the shorter end of the stick on that deal."

"Jade loves Rose, and August. And they love her. It was Rose's idea, actually, but he insisted. Maria offered to stay with her, but I thought... oh, it doesn't matter." The tears were flowing freely. "I thought I was going to lose you."

"I'm... sorry," was all I could think of to say.

"There's nothing to be sorry about," she whispered. "It's good to have you back, Harry."

I rubbed a hand over my face. "What about Jade?" I said, changing the subject. "After all the work we've done to raise her up like a regular girl, now she's probably spent the last two days eating creme brulee for breakfast and shooting skeet after brunch."

"Hey." She shrugged. "They're there for her. That's all that matters."

I nodded. My father and I got along well enough. We didn't always see eye to eye, but the man had his moments. This was apparently one of them. Not that either of us would ever mention it, other than a quick "thanks for taking Jade" followed by an even quicker "glad to see you're feeling better." He had his faults and he had his strengths, but talking about anything that wasn't a court case or a business investment or his golf handicap wasn't something he'd ever spent too much time on.

The door opened silently off to my right, the hinge slowly shutting behind the doctor.

"I see we're back among the living," he said, pulling over a chair, the chair Kate had used, I remembered. It was likely a pointless exercise, but if I was going to try and remember who had put me there, I needed to pointedly remember everything. Unfortunately, neither the face nor the nametag rang any bells.

"Despite how many people wish that wasn't so," I said.

"You're a lucky man." He had his requisite clipboard in hand. I'd been to hospitals plenty of times, seen too much of them since my teens, to be honest, but usually I was the one in Amanda's position. I held the hand of my mother. I talked people through their crimes. I was the person who reviewed cases with Doc Sheddon to find out exactly what had happened based on the injuries. Now, maybe for the first time, I really felt what it was like to be the victim, the one attacked.

And I didn't frickin' like it.

"Lucky or hard-headed, depends on who you ask," I said. "I don't mean to be rude, but this isn't the first time either of us has had to hear bad news. May as well cut to the chase."

The man was thin, tired-looking. He rubbed a hand over his bald head and glanced down at his clipboard again.

"I suppose that'll make things quick for both of us. I'll have to run some tests, of course, but if you want the laundry list, here goes. Cracked ribs, multiple, periorbital hematoma, both eyes." He glanced at me. "That's—"

"Black eyes," I said. "I assume."

"Ah. Well, multiple lacerations to the face, specifically labial, partially broken nose. Surprisingly," he said, almost smiling, "no tympanic injury. Those can be very disorienting."

I raised an eyebrow.

"I suppose I can skip a few tests then. You seem to be well within your," he said and looked at Amanda, "typical state of mind?"

"Very much so," she said. I felt her hand grip mine a little tighter. Neither of us needed to know what had been done. We were both ready to get on to figuring out what we needed to do.

"Um..." He flipped a page. "Internal bleeding, of course. Nothing drastic. No brain swelling. No organ damage that we can see as of yet..."

"I basically fell down a flight of stairs," I said, trying to hurry up the process.

He laughed. "If you mean you fell down all the stairs from the top to the bottom of... oh... say, the Empire State Building, then yes. I'd say that's accurate."

I took a deep breath. The man was just doing his job, and, in all fairness, he was doing it well. I've never been good at being the patient in any circumstance and, even if the joke was bad, he was at least shooting me straight and trying to put a light spin on it.

"All right," I said. "So what's the story here? I'm out of here today, or—"

He laughed. The man actually laughed. Perhaps the best or worst thing a doctor can do. "Absolutely not," he said. "I'd lose my license if I signed off on you. Maybe Empire State wasn't the best way to express it, but, Mr. Starke..." His eyes flitted toward Amanda and I could practically hear him running through the options. "You... you were a bit of a touch-and-go case for, well, for the better part of a day. Then, of course, after yesterday..."

I could see Amanda's eyes well up, and I knew I needed to have this conversation in private. Perhaps two private conversations, one to find out what happened and another to talk her through her trauma.

"Whatever happened yesterday, you apparently fixed," I said, trying to sound confident, almost stern. "So I owe you a thanks for that. And I'm sure I'll see whatever reports I need to that tell me I got the tar kicked out of me, but that seems pretty self-evident, doesn't it?" I gestured around, taking in the room, the doctor, Amanda, myself. "I need to know what we're looking at as far as the mend time goes."

The doctor looked down at his papers again and, thankfully, after a moment put them off to the side at the foot of the bed. "I see you aren't one for a bedside manner."

I shrugged. "It's easier to deal with facts when they aren't sugar-coated."

"Fair enough." He looked at Amanda again, and I suddenly realized this was exactly the doctor for me. He wasn't going to mess around with pleasantries, but he had enough compassion in him to choose his words carefully, not for me, but for the woman sitting beside me. "In my opinion, the worst is over. This..." He patted the clipboard. "...says that things are going to take a few days. You're not entirely out of the woods, as they say, but you can see a clearing up ahead, so to speak. Actually," he said, flipping a page and reading something. "Are things clearing?"

I looked at him, confused.

"I was under the impression you were having some memory troubles."

"Oh," I said. "That." I thought about it for a moment. I remembered plenty of things. I'd only lost an hour, maybe two, but it was piecing itself back together. And if I couldn't remember it, there were a couple other people who could tell me what I did. "It's fine," I said finally. "It'll be fine."

He looked down at me dubiously, obviously doubting the confidence I had. And to be fair, he had the medical degree, not me. But I needed him to believe me, not so much for me, but for my wife.

After a second, he nodded and patted my leg. "I'm sure it will be. If you need anything," he said, addressing Amanda, now, "just hit the button again. The nurses know to get ahold of me at any time."

"Thank you." She reached over and shook his hand, a strange gesture but one of those Southern things that people can't seem to stop doing. We have to treat everything like it's a polite business deal. "I appreciate you keeping my husband from dying and all; have a good one."

As the doctor slipped back out of the room, she sat back down and looked at me. "So?"

"So now we know in which particular ways I got bested."

"I thought more information was always a good thing?"

I reached over and took her hand, laughing softly. "Not when my pride's involved."

"When isn't it?" She leaned toward the bed and put her head on my shoulder.

I reached over and rested my hand on her head. It had been twenty minutes, maybe, since I'd woken up, but I felt so tired again already. I rubbed my thumb on her hair and waited till her breathing had found its slow, steady, sleeping rhythm. Then I closed my eyes and let myself go as well.

22

"Harry."

For the briefest moment I was granted a reprieve. My head on the pillow, Amanda's voice waking me. If for only a second, it felt like the Saturdays I'd been trying to create for us. Then I moved my leg and the scratchy, almost papery hospital sheet dumped me back to where I really was.

I opened my eyes to Amanda looking down at me. Thankfully, her eyes were showing care and not worry this time. "Morning?" I asked.

"Afternoon. But the doctor's been in and he's says to just let you sleep. So..." She poked my chest, making me wince a little. "You let you sleep."

"So why am I up?" I tried to situate myself on the pillows. There is nothing that makes you feel more vulnerable than laying in bed with dozens of people knowing more about you than you do.

"Visitor." She gestured toward the door.

I looked over and Heather was leaning against the jamb, her face a mix of emotions. Amanda had seen the worst of it. She'd heard the doctor. She'd slept in a chair beside me. Heather, on the other hand, was getting this all brand new.

"Hey, boss," she said, a slight quiver in her voice. "How're things?"

I shifted myself up. There's not really any way to make yourself appear calm and confident in that particular setting, but I had to try.

"Been better, been worse."

"Not since I've known you." She flicked a glance at Amanda.

"Fair statement." Amanda laughed.

Heather walked over and pulled out the familiar chair it seemed everyone except Amanda was using. She scootched into the same exact place, had the same exact look on her face that made me feel like I was the only one who didn't know I was but a heartbeat away from a coffin.

"But..." Heather looked down, her fingers wringing themselves around one another.

"I'm okay," I said. "Or at least okay enough. Just working from a different office at this point."

Amanda shot me a look, and I squeezed her hand. I knew she hated this, but I also knew we were both fully aware that I had one thing on my mind right now, and it wasn't going to stop till I figured it out.

"Since Heather's here, I think I'm going to go to the ladies' room." Amanda stood up, giving me a hard glare that I completely understood, and which we both knew I would completely ignore. To be honest, I think Amanda hoped I would ignore it too. Someone did this to me, and someone needed to have a name real fast.

Heather watched Amanda walk out and then looked back at me as the door closed. "So maybe I've been calling the wrong person 'boss'?"

"The greatest gift is a boss who wants you to be successful."

She scrunched her eyebrows. "Kierkegaard? He doesn't seem like the guy who'd say 'boss' though."

"Jon Taffer."

She cocked her head to the side.

"Amanda likes his show. Don't worry about it. We've got things to discuss and Amanda is giving us time, but she's not going to give us the day. I'm technically stable but also, in her eyes anyway, concerning. Tell me good news."

The way she sat back in her chair immediately told me there wasn't much good news coming my way in the next few minutes.

"Well... it's like," she stumbled over her words. "Okay, hang on." Her hands wrung at an almost alarming pace and I reached over.

"Begin at the beginning."

She laughed, but I saw her shoulders relax. "Okay. Let's reverse it. What do you remember? After the Cullins."

I raised an eyebrow. "Who?"

She looked at me, her eyes wide. "The Cullins," she said as if the repetition would make it mean more. "You talked to them first."

I racked my brain. We had obviously been there to look into Hattie. I remembered Hattie. I remembered Victoria. Cullins though, that wasn't ringing a bell. I ran a hand over my face, hit the gauze dressing and winced.

"We went to canvass," Heather said hesitantly.

"I dropped you and TJ off," I said, running through the memories for the thousandth time, but now, at least, it was to ease her own anxiety that I'd not lost everything. "You were mad because you thought I didn't believe in you. TJ pointed out why I really did it."

She chuckled.

"I dropped you and TJ off, and I went and parked the car. I got a call when I got out..." The name was on the tip of my tongue. It was so close, but it danced around. T something. Or H something. HT? Or was that just close. I slapped my hand on the bed.

"Hey." Heather leaned forward. "We can look on your phone. I doubt the guy who jumped you would've called first. Besides, you talked to TJ after the Cullins. You were A-OK at that point. You're missing maybe an hour. Don't sweat it."

"Did you ever get blackout drunk?" My tone was sharper than I intended, but I also knew Heather wasn't someone I needed to walk on eggshells with.

"No," she said, her shoulders squaring. "But I've certainly spent more time than I'd like telling my friends what they did." She paused. "So it's like that then? Just gone?"

I held up a hand and extended my fingers. "Like it never happened."

"Okay." She sat back and crossed her legs. We were at least in a situation where she felt like she knew what to do. Which was good for both of us. One, because I needed information if I was going to figure anything out, and two, because Heather needed to feel confident if she was going to help me do so. "So what do you know?"

"I know I got blindsided at some point and ended up here."

"That's it?"

"I remember... your voice?" I connected the dots. "You and TJ interrupted whatever was going on. Correct?"

"That's a polite way of putting it, but yes." She folded her hands and leaned forward on her knees. It was always a good sign from Heather, maybe the best. It meant she was all business now.

"I'll remember," I said.

"Oh, I have no doubt about that." She gave me a tired laugh.

"The great Harry Starke doesn't forget anything." She paused. "That was mean. I just meant—"

"I know what you meant." I tried to smile. "And you're right. So don't you forget that."

She grinned. "It's just...this is becoming a real thing now. Not that it wasn't before, but..." She leaned back and exhaled, blowing her hair out of her eyes. "The residents saying that whatever happened to you had nothing to do with the case or the Heights or whatever. Word is that you brought trouble to the neighborhood, not that you found it there."

I sighed. I should've seen that coming. If I hadn't been laid up and in and out of sleep, I probably would've seen it. "So this is basically my fault and the people there are offended by it."

"Pretty much."

"Well." I shrugged. "They were offended when we showed up in the first place, so I'm not crying over it. Are you?"

"We were there to help."

"Exactly. So let's forget about the Collins—"

"Cullins, a U."

"Whatever. Kate said there's a tape of the attack. Let's focus on that."

"Oh, there's tape all right," she said. "When was Kate here?"

I held out my hands. "Two days ago? Things are a little gray."

"There isn't only one tape. There are about a dozen tapes. I guess you probably know, but not much of the Heights isn't under surveillance."

"I would expect no less."

"And we may or may not have had Tim figure out how to get his hands on it."

I wanted to scowl. We did everything above board at the office. It was not just a moral issue; it was a legal issue as well.

"It's not copyrighted," she said hopefully.

"If he didn't break any laws." I thought for a moment. "Shoot, even if he bent one or two, what did he find?"

"Oh gosh." She laughed. "No. I just meant," she said and brushed her hair back, "some girls can flash a smile and convince people to hand over anything."

I laughed. "The guard? He hated us."

"He hated *one* of us. But don't get too wound up. I don't want the doctors coming in and blaming me for something. The point is, we have tape. We have a whole, whole lot of tape. And it tells us two things. So as you convalesce here, think about them."

"And they are?"

"One, the guy wasn't from the Heights. They've got footage of him climbing over the fence on the back side of the division. So, good job. You may have a bona fide hitman on your heels."

"Super."

"Two, he came in on a motorcycle." She leaned back in exactly the way I hoped she wouldn't.

"That's it?"

She shrugged. "It's more than you had a minute ago."

I rubbed my face. "What kind of bike?"

"I don't know."

"Bike people are more cliquey than high schoolers. If it's a Harley, he's got money and wants you to know it. If it's a crotch-rocket, he's probably got a death wish." I paused. "If it's a Gold-wing, he's probably old enough to have broken his hand on my hard head."

"Seriously?"

"Seriously. Everything a person is shows up in what they do. Get Tim to look at the tape again. All Kate told me was he was about six feet tall. Now we know he's six feet tall and has a bike. That isn't much, but, like you said, it's more than we had before."

"So check the bike and boot shops?"

I gestured to myself. "Only one of us can do much right now."

"Yeah." She reached out and put a hand on my shoulder. "Just so you know, I know you're trying to make me feel like this isn't a big deal."

"It can't be a big deal," I said. "I'm not nearly done with this yet."

23

Regardless of what I thought or the confidence I tried to instill in Amanda and Heather with what I said, the next few days were a blur. The doctor had decided to keep me on a morphine drip for the pain, but the pain was something I needed to keep me lucid and valuable in catching my attacker. But, as he argued, the guy who jumped me would probably still be out there somewhere in a week; if I didn't heal up, I wouldn't be able to do anything about it. He had a point.

So the hours went by in a fog. There are still memories, but the type that I can't say for sure are real. It's like dreams of reality, the most mundane things. Did Amanda really bring me that cup of water? Did she really spend so many nights sleeping in the chair by the bed? Or worse, what was that flash of recollection? What was that image I had that seemed like it was the answer to all my questions?

The morphine made me feel like the first time I had one too many in college and vowed never to do that again. My body was tired, and my limbs felt exhausted. And at the same time, my brain would be both hyperactive and lethargic all at once. In the moment, I was elated that I'd remembered something, so confident and excited that I was sure I would remember it. Then, after a day or an hour or fifteen minutes, I'd moved on to something else, only suddenly realizing that I had forgotten something and that whatever it was had been extremely important.

I have images of the ceiling, the bedsheets, always Amanda. The fog would lift at times, at least I think it did. I seem to remember the doctor coming in once or twice, adjusting my morphine and then, vaguely, allowing Amanda to sign me out. I had a vague recollection that she helped me dress, my bulky frame leaning too hard into her but both of us laughing, me because of the drugs, her more likely out of excitement that I was, at least theoretically, out of the hospital and therefore out of the woods. I seem to remember the drive back; everything was strange because she rarely ever drove when the two of us were together.

There was the house, quiet with Jade still at my father's. And that I remembered perfectly fine, a memory that I had developed since the accident, during, or slightly before the morphine regiment.

The stairs seemed daunting to both of us, and not wanting to let my two hundred pounds knock both of us down them, especially after what I'd already been through, Amanda had put blankets on the couch, ice water and warm tea on the table in front of me, as well as a few small snacks.

I'd like to say I remember her doing this. I hope that I thanked her. But the truth is, when I opened my eyes, finally feeling clear-headed, if a little groggy, it took more than a moment to figure out where I was. We'd slept on the couch before, but typically never a full night. Jade would wake up or one of us would get too uncomfortable, and around three or four in the morning, we almost always moved up to the bed. Seeing the sunlight come into the room, realizing I was still fully dressed, albeit in pajama pants and a t-shirt, I knew immediately something was off.

I looked around the room. It was empty except for what Amanda, I assumed, had left on the table. A flicker of a thought came back, just the briefest image of her setting things down, saying she knew I'd be hot and cold at some point and wanted to be ready for either. My stomach growled at the sight of the bowl of pistachios, a few eaten and their shells on a paper towel beside it. So she had been here. We had been on the couch together.

I rolled onto my back, my body sore, and I saw, with more curiosity than surprise, my wrist in a soft Velcro-type cast. I held my hand up, looking at the swollen fingers.

Just then, as I tried to calm my brain by creating a logical chain of events, Amanda walked down the stairs. Her hair was sleep-tousled and she was dressed almost exactly like me. She looked at me and smiled a tired smile.

"You're up. Are you with us today?"

I turned my arm back and forth in front of me, trying to remember what the doctor had said about... well, anything. "Most of me is here," I said finally. "But I've got some questions."

She laughed a little and came to sit beside me. "If that's the first thing out of your mouth, then I'd say you're all here, at last."

"How long has it been?"

"Almost a week. But if you mean since you got home, just last night."

"Broken?" I held my arm out, and then slowly, my brain started to pick up the pace. "No. Fractured."

She nodded, looking slightly away. Obviously me being back amongst the living was a good thing, but the idea of having to talk about whatever happened was never going to be easy for Amanda. She'd told me countless times that my job worried her.

To her credit, she'd never told me to quit, but she was confident enough, transparent enough, to let me know what she thought without any kind of sugar-coating.

"The doctor said you were hit from behind, most likely tried to catch yourself and fractured your... carpal bones?"

I nodded. "Sidewalks can be pretty unforgiving."

"So can blunt force trauma." She looked down again, though not quick enough for me to miss the glint of tears welling in her eyes.

"Hey." I reached over with my good hand, taking hers and rubbing my thumb along her knuckles. "You always said I was hard-headed."

She laughed, the sound a mix of giggle and sob. "Lucky for us, I was right."

"A week," I said, trying to move the conversation back to a point away from the actual attack. "I owe you one, don't I? Your back's got to be killing you."

She shrugged. "I slept in the bed whenever the nurses weren't around. I doubt you remember that, though. You were pretty spotty there for a while."

"I feel spotty still." I sat up, groaning at the pain in my ribs. "Cracked?" I touched my side.

"It wouldn't be a proper beating without that, would it?" She smiled a little, her old feistiness coming back to the surface.

"I suppose you have a point." I reached up to touch my face, wincing as my fingers touched the still-tender scrapes and bruises. "I feel like the doc set me back with his drugs instead of letting us get this over with."

"Oh, you let him know." She laughed this time, full-throated.

I smiled. "No uncertain terms, huh?"

"I'd say that's putting it mildly."

I shrugged. "I guess everybody's got a job to do. I just wish his didn't interfere with mine. Morphine's not something to mess around with."

"He said it needed to be done."

I glanced around the room, trying to reconstruct what most likely had been happening. "He's got the medical degree," I said finally. "But wiping somebody out for seven days is a heck of a way to solve a problem."

"But it's solved." She took my hand in both of hers. "At least, as much as it can be. You've got some mending to do, but he seemed pleased with where you are. He said the fogginess would wear off, and it seems to be doing just that. Now we just have to give it some time."

I looked over at her, and before I said a word, I could see her guessing what I was about to say. She got up and walked over to the end table at the foot of the couch. When she turned around, she had my cell phone in her hand.

"I know giving it time isn't the Harry Starke way," she said mildly. "I knew that when we first started dating, and I've seen it ever since. Now, to be fair," she continued and jiggled the phone in her hand, "it's not an entirely unattractive trait. But I swear to you, Harry, if you go out and exacerbate this situation by doing something stupid, you will never, ever hear the end of it."

I smiled. "I'll take that deal."

She looked at me a moment longer. "Heather's been calling." She held the phone out. "Just for updates on you, not because of the case. Think about that before you make the choice we both know you're going to make."

"What did you tell her?"

"That I was considering going out and finding a drug dealer just so we could keep you on the drip and out of trouble."

I laughed as she handed me the phone. "That's my girl."

"And I'd like it to stay that way. I'm too young to be a widow."

Her tone was playful, but the underlying seriousness was difficult to miss.

"I'm going to take a shower real quick." She walked back toward the stairs. "Whatever scheme you come up with, at least consider doing the same thing. You're a little... ripe."

I shook my head. "No sponge baths?"

"Not on my husband."

I grinned as she walked up the stairs, swiping my phone open and finding Heather's number. The list of recent contacts wasn't entirely out of the ordinary. I usually spoke with most of my team at least a few times a day via voice or text. But knowing that I had been basically AWOL for all of these calls, even if I had been in the room, was a jarring thought. Worse yet, I wondered if I had been a part of any of them.

I tapped on each call individually, checking the times. None of them had been overly long, likely just long enough for Heather to touch base and Amanda to give her whatever news there had been, but seeing tangible evidence of the time I'd missed was hard. Not just hard—frustrating, irritating. I knew the doctor had done what he thought was best and I knew there wasn't any use crying over spilled milk, as they say, but I was ready to start getting things back in order and making them right. And a week of my team on a case like this meant there had to be some breaks in the case. I pressed the call button.

She answered before the first ring had completed. Whatever else she was doing, she must've been anticipating this call. "Amanda?"

"Sorry," I said. "You're stuck with me again."

"Oh, Harry, thank goodness." I heard her breathe out a deep sigh of relief, then the sound of a closing door. "Are you... good?"

I rubbed my temples with my thumb and forefinger. "I take it we've talked."

"You had a few things to say, but... well, let's chalk it up to the drugs."

"Bad?"

She laughed. "No, more like... incoherent? You were all kinds of chatty the first day or so, but once the morphine built up all I could hear was snoring in the background when I talked with Amanda."

"Bygones be bygones?"

She chuckled again. "I can't promise I won't bring this up again at some point, but right now, I'm just glad to hear you lucid."

"Then let's go from there. I missed a lot of days, Heather. Tell me something good has happened while I've been out."

"Not just good, what I think you might call 'great.' How much do you remember?"

I shook my head and looked down at the soft cast on my wrist. "Not enough to be of any help."

"Do you remember where you were?"

I paused. I did, vaguely. Or at least I knew we had been working a case... somewhere we didn't usually go. Somewhere... in a flash I saw it. "The Heights?"

"A-plus. Now, here's the real test for your deductive skills. Do you remember what the Heights has more than anywhere else?"

I started to say "money" and then another vague, half-memory came back. "Surveillance cameras."

"You're on a roll. Three gets a prize. Do you recall who happens to work in your office and is the most obsessive technology nerd we've ever seen and couldn't live without?"

I felt my heart rate pick up. "Tim found something."

"We think so," she said. "He was being his usual self, but

times ten, if you can believe that. He really took this one person-ally. It's like he made a deal that if you were out of commission, he was out of life. That kid hasn't left since we got him the secu-rity footage."

I nodded to myself. We were more of a family than a group of work associates. I never wanted to rely on that, never wanted to make anyone feel like they had to be more committed than they wanted, regardless of how I felt toward them. But more than once, a situation like this would occur where someone gave everything they had for one of us. I was proud of every one of them.

"Positive ID?" I asked, figuring Heather must've heard enough of my rambling in the last few days that an even slightly emotional comment would be questioned and devalued.

"He's pretty sure and it looks good to me. Definitely worth checking out."

"Who is it?"

There was a pause on her end of the line. "Maybe you should just let us check this out. No sense in getting too excited until we know for sure."

"I've been the definition of not too excited for a week now. I want to ride along."

The pause was longer this time. "I don't know if that's a good idea."

"Heather, good or bad, it's the only idea right now."

She laughed nervously. "There's always the idea of the man who was beaten half to death waiting a few days before he goes out and confronts his attacker. That one might need some consideration."

"It might," I said, standing up and trying to muffle the grunt of pain I felt. "But, sadly, things don't always work out the way we plan. I'm coming along."

"I don't mean to delve into your personal business," she said, obviously using her last gambit, "but—"

"Amanda knows," I said. "Or she will know shortly. But listen." I limped toward the staircase, trying to work the stiffness out of my unused legs. "I don't think I'm quite ready for driving, so I'll need you to come pick me up."

"At least you're saying one reasonable thing." She sighed. The phone was silent for a moment and I was more focused on reaching for the banister without succumbing to my woozy head than anything. "Harry," she said after a moment, bringing me back to the present.

"Yes?"

"If we get going on this and it gets shaky, I'm walking away and taking you straight back home. Agreed?"

For the second time in ten minutes, I took the deal. I knew these women had my best interests at heart. I knew they had more than valid reasons, medical reasons, to back up their position. But I also knew this was something I had to do. Heather promised to be there in twenty minutes and I ended the call.

Limping up the stairs, I called out to Amanda. "Leave the water on. I'm going to work."

24

I was pulling on my leather jacket when the knock came at the door. Amanda hadn't been pleased with the news, but she hadn't been surprised either. I got what I know she hoped was a playful eye roll and then a very stern set of questions about exactly where I was going and who I was going with. At the mention of Heather's name, she seemed to relax, if only a tiny percent. The two women had always gotten along, and Amanda knew as well as I did that Heather wasn't a person who needed looking after. She could take care of herself and, in a pinch, also help take care of me.

Which is what made it so surprising that, when I snuggled my CZ75 in its holster and opened the door, Heather wasn't the one standing on the porch.

"Kate," I said. "This is unexpected."

"Heather called." She folded her arms across her chest, surveying me up and down. "Your team's still on it, but she thought it might be wise to bring in some extra help. If this is what the potential outcome is..." She gestured vaguely toward me. "I'd say she might have a point."

I shrugged, not wanting to get into yet another discussion

about whether I should be heading out on a call or not, but Kate and I had known each other for a long time. I was fairly confident she wasn't going to bring it up, at least not directly. She'd rather make a few jabs here and there, knowing full well that once I made up my mind, it was done.

I stepped back into the foyer as Amanda came down the stairs. The two women exchanged greetings and I kissed my wife goodbye.

"You bring him back in..." Amanda started, then grinned mischievously. "I was going to say one piece, but how about just the same number of pieces?"

Kate laughed. "If it was up to me, he wouldn't be going at all. But I've got my partner in the car, just in case."

I could already see Samson, her ever-loyal and fearless dog, standing in the back seat, looking over at us, tail wagging.

"Best in the business," Amanda said.

I gave her another peck on the cheek and promised to be back soon. With that, Kate and I were out the door and climbing into her car. When you've known someone as long as Kate and I have known each other, there are a lot of times when words aren't necessary. There's just that kind of ESP where both people know what the other is thinking all based on a look, or often, even less. So as we pulled out of the drive and onto the road, I was already waiting for her comment.

And she, apparently, was waiting for mine. "Well, are you gonna say it?" she asked. "This is pretty much the golden opportunity."

"What's that?" I feigned ignorance.

"Oh, c'mon. 'You oughtta see the other guy.' I know you're not much for humor, but this is just a wasted chance."

"I wish I had seen the other guy," I said, looking out the window. "Then we wouldn't be messing around like this."

My head ached as the trees blurred by, the sun bright, and

what would be on any other day a very pleasant view. I flexed my fingers. Thankfully, when I'd gone down, I'd had the foresight to fall to the left. I'd heard there was some kind of subconscious instinct to protect whatever side was dominant, and given that I was already only half-conscious after the first blow, I was starting to believe that must be the case.

"So you remember nothing?" she asked, flicking her turn signal and coming to a stop sign.

"Bits and pieces. It's coming back, just not fast and not nearly as fast as I'd like."

She nodded and made the turn. "Have you seen the security footage?"

"No," I shook my head, feeling my pulse pound.

"Mm-hm."

It was one of Kate's tells. Something I'd said didn't please her too much. Most likely it was the fact that we were off to track down a violent offender that I had never actually laid eyes on. "I assume Tim must've gotten a decent image of the guy," I said. "Heather sounded confident."

Kate laughed and glanced over at me. "Of the guy? Absolutely not. Of the bike, yeah."

I rubbed my eyes. "Let me guess. Hood? Bandana?"

"And sunglasses. He took a page from the Unabomber on that outfit. I'm almost surprised he could see well enough to ride, let alone get the better of you."

"Must be one unique motorcycle," I said.

She bobbed her head back and forth. "Yes and no. It's not a custom job, or at least not customized enough to really make it stand out. You know how these guys are. Everything's gotta be about them and their individuality. But, it's not a common bike. About fifty in the state, five in the county."

"But one in the city?" I asked, hopeful.

"You got it."

I looked back out the window. It should've been good news, but a good lawyer would pick it to pieces in no time, and a jury would be hard-pressed to believe "beyond a shadow of a doubt," that the bike and the guy were interchangeable. The bike could've been stolen. It could've been any of the other five in the county. Shoot, with fifty in the state, the pool of potential suspects had grown exponentially, and that's without someone making the point that Tennessee had some real close borders around it.

"So what makes you think it's him?" I asked.

"Honestly?" She made another turn, and without her even finishing the sentence, I was starting to get an inkling of her plan of action. We weren't headed back toward the Heights, which really wasn't all that surprising in itself. If those people wanted something done, especially something illegal, or at least violently illegal, they weren't going to dirty their hands with it. Backroom deals, fraud, white-collar crimes, sure, they probably did it on a regular basis. But cracking a guy over the back of the head? That was "unsophisticated" crime. They would just throw money at someone and hope the problem went away. Same as always.

"I don't know if it is him," Kate continued, bringing me out of my reverie. "But I do know how people react. It's never iron-clad; you know that as well as I do. But..."

"Guilty people run. Innocent people talk too much."

She looked over at me. "You got it."

We rode in silence for the next ten minutes or so, Samson trying eagerly to climb between the two front seats and give me a proper greeting, which to him apparently meant licking my wounds. I scratched his muzzle, trying to keep his head still on my shoulder.

"I'm hoping this is more than me, you, and Heather," I said

as Kate made yet another turn further into one of the shadier parts of town.

She patted the radio that sat in the console between us. "We've got people coming in from all points of the compass. Just didn't want to get too wild with it. Like I said, I don't really know what we're walking into. Can't waste valuable resources and all that."

I rubbed my chin for a moment, thinking. "You keep saying you aren't sure, and I get that. But which way are you leaning? Surely you wouldn't be out here if you were still on the fence."

She looked at me briefly. "You need to take a long look in the mirror, Harry. Literally and figuratively. Someone did this to you. And I think their only regret is that you got back up. This wasn't a warning; this was to take you out entirely. If there's even a chance we've found the guy, or a guy who knows the guy, or a guy who just heard a rumor from his dealer, I'm going after it."

I nodded, not surprised by the declaration of loyalty but not entirely comfortable getting into this kind of emotional talk with anyone outside of Amanda. "You got a name?"

"Jacobi Milton."

"Sounds fancy."

"I think we'll find he's not living up to his name." She pulled the car into a lot and turned off the engine. The asphalt beneath us was cracked, weeds growing up freely between the faded yellow lines. A few concrete parking posts remained, most leaning haphazardly from long-ago drunken impacts. An empty fast food bag blew by, the tumbleweed of present times. And across the street was an auto-body shop, though it wasn't one most folks would feel comfortable walking inside. Beneath the neon signs in each window, one with the shop's name and the other just reading "Open," were proudly displayed patches from the local motorcycle club.

"That seems to reinforce your hunch," I said, gesturing toward the storefront.

"Oh, Harry," she said in a singsong, mocking voice. "Don't you know these are clubs, not gangs? Totally different."

"Nine times out of ten, you'd be right," I replied. "Or maybe I should say ninety-nine times out of a hundred."

"You're not afraid of a few One-Percenters, are you?" She grabbed her radio and checked in with the rest of the teams closing in on the building. It was good to hear the tone of their voices. They weren't overly confident, but they weren't scared either. The problem with clubs like this was you never really knew what to expect. Some days, you'd walk in and they'd be the most helpful people in town. Other days, you'd walk in and not walk back out, at least not without assistance or carried out in a body bag.

"Well," Kate said. "We can hang out or get this over with. You heard the reports. We've got every side covered, so we may as well go say hello before someone else tips him off."

I nodded, almost unconsciously reaching inside my jacket to feel the grip of my pistol.

"You can wait," Kate said, one leg already out the door, though her voice sounded like she knew that wasn't an option for me.

"And miss all the fun?"

We strode across the street, Samson on a short leash at her side, looking like nothing more than cops. I tried to keep my back straight to put off an air of overt confidence, but the hitch in my step, the soreness and lack of use in my legs, was slowing us down. Just as we stepped up onto the broken concrete of the sidewalk in front of the shop, the front door opened. A scrawny kid in jeans and a leather vest with nothing on underneath stepped out.

He pulled a cigarette out from behind his ear and a Zippo out of his pocket.

"How's it going?" I pulled the door open for Kate and looked at the kid.

He scoffed and rolled his eyes, clearly not interested in a chat. The funny thing was, there were only a few reasons you'd expect to see a biker leave his club to smoke outside, and none of them were usually legal. Unless, of course, this one had the good sense to see what was coming when we walked across the street and this was his attempt to get out before things got worse.

Inside, the shop was part clubhouse, part legitimate motorcycle parts store. Or at least it looked that way. One side was gear, parts, and the random mechanical pieces that only bikers would be able to identify or utilize. The other side had a makeshift bar in one corner, a few overstuffed leather chairs and stools scattered randomly around the room from wherever they'd happened to be left last. In the far back, I could just make out a pool table in the gloom.

I nodded toward it, speaking under my breath to Kate. "Keep an eye out for the sticks."

She tapped the back of her head. "You do the same this time."

I started to walk over to a man sitting on one of the stools in front of the bar. He had his elbows perched behind him and was doing nothing to hide his disdain for our presence. Like the kid outside, his leather vest was the only thing he had on his torso, but unlike the kid, this man was carrying another seventy-five pounds, easy. His Harley bandana did little to hide his greasy, graying hair.

"Think y'all may've made a wrong turn," he said, reaching behind him to grab his beer. The thing that people never seem to understand is that guns and knives aren't the only weapons to be wary of. Pool cues, broken glass bottles, those set off alarm bells just as much as any "conventional" weapon will, or at least they do once you've been around awhile.

"Are you Jacobi Milton?" Kate asked. Her voice was already aggressive. She didn't take well to being talked down to, and this man clearly had us pegged as law enforcement of some kind, giving us our three strikes: we might be cops, we weren't in the club, and Kate was a woman.

"Could be," the man said, taking a slow drink. His eyes flicked behind us. "Might not be. Depends. Y'all Publishers Clearing House?"

Disregarding the comment, my battered body and my irritation both heightening my senses, I turned to see just what the man had found so interesting. A split-second later and I would've missed it. The door leading out the back opened and a figure darted through, obviously wanting to get as far from us as possible.

"Out the back." I had a hand on Kate's shoulder, almost dragging her along with me.

"You know y'all come onto our ground here," the man called behind us. "We didn't ask for trouble."

"Not today, you didn't," I yelled back, my pulse pounding in my aching head. "But sometimes you get it anyway."

I threw the door open to a long, narrow garage space. Apparently the place truly was a shop, or at least had aspirations for it at one point. A dozen or so motorcycles lined both sides of the narrow space, each in various stages of repair. Ahead of us, another garage-type door stood open. In the light pouring in from outside, I caught just a glimpse of a young man darting around the corner.

Before I could say anything, before I had time to address the somewhat surprised man kneeling by one of the bikes, an oil pan in one hand, a rag in the other, and a look of sheer surprise on his face, I heard Kate barking orders into her radio.

"Back alley, headed west." She brushed by me. "Wait here."

I glanced back at the mechanic on the floor. He didn't present any threat I could see, but the various wrenches and tools all within arms' length certainly did. And besides, if this was the guy we were after, I wasn't about to hang back and let it go down without me.

I rushed after her into the alley, my head pounding, my legs aching with every step.

And I saw that my pursuit didn't matter at all.

Half a block up, the guy was already bent face-down over the hood of a car, his hands being cuffed as I watched.

"You guys are good." I looked at Kate, trying to catch my breath.

"You oughtta utilize us more often." She grinned, walking briskly toward the car and the man now in custody.

I followed, still feeling my limp as I walked, but finding that it was suddenly much easier to ignore.

25

BACK AT THE STATION, THE ARRESTING OFFICER HAD PUT Jacobi Milton in an interrogation room, handcuffed to the table. When Kate and I walked in a few minutes later, the officer was standing outside the door. It was partly for one added layer of protection, both for Milton and any officers who entered the room. It was also an age-old tactic. Let the guy sit and stew for a bit. We had nothing but time on our hands. Milton, however, had nothing but four pale walls to stare at and an uncomfortable chair beneath him.

"I suppose it's pointless to ask if he's talking," Kate said as we approached the officer on guard.

"Just sat in the back," the man said, his tag reading Witzig, though his demeanor seemed to imply he hadn't the slightest idea his surname meant "funny" in German. "Not even the usual swearing or denying. Acted like it wasn't the first time and probably won't be the last."

Kate nodded and looked over at me. "You're more than welcome to come in. Might help us out to have him staring at the damage he did."

"That or it might make him even more cocky," I replied,

considering the options. Of course I wanted to go in. I wanted to go in and get the guy to talk any way necessary. After all, he'd hardly given me a fair fight. Maybe it would be a way to even the odds and ease my conscience. But I wasn't foolish enough to get carried away like that anymore. Especially not in a police station where basically every word and whisper was recorded one way or the other.

"Cocky talks," she said.

I rubbed the back of my neck. The headache was making its way down into my neck; I could literally feel my heartbeat behind my eyes. If nothing else, going in would keep my mind occupied. Sitting around and waiting would just be a steady throb of pain as the seconds slowly ticked by. And that was the type of thing we reserved for people like Jacobi Milton, not the ones on the right side of the law. I suppose the correct term for me would be "victim," but that was something I never had and never would be comfortable associating with myself. I got jumped, sure. He caught me off guard and that wasn't necessarily my own fault, but it was a mistake, nonetheless. Victim though, that was something I couldn't ever feel right tagging myself with.

"You know he's going to expect good cop/bad cop if we both go in," I said.

"Let him," she replied. "Maybe we'll even give him a show. Bad cop/bad cop is a fun one too, though. Keeps 'em guessing."

I grinned. Kate's approach to policing was one of the things I admired most about her. She knew the rule book, but she also knew it wasn't anything secret. The best way to be a solid officer was always case-by-case, and she was more than ready to adapt to whatever situation presented itself.

"You want to let him stew a little more, or are you ready to go for it?" I said.

She shrugged. "I'm technically in charge here, but I think you've got more scratch in the game. What do you think?"

I glanced at my watch. "If he didn't have anything to say on the ride over, I imagine he's used to sitting in these rooms. Waiting is just going to be a waste of our time and that might be the only thing he's hoping to do right now. I say we go in."

Kate nodded and looked at Officer Witzig. "Cameras are on, I assume?"

"Yes, ma'am. Since we brought him in."

"They show anything?"

"Fiddled with the cuffs a bit," the man said, his back ramrod straight and hands behind him. "Not in an escape attempt from what I understand, more like they were uncomfortable. Which I suppose they are."

"Tight?" I asked.

He shrugged. It was an interesting thing. In all the time I'd spent in law enforcement, I'd rarely come across an officer, lawyer, or judge who'd actually seen the inside of a cell. They would walk in for a consultation maybe, or they'd do arraignments over Skype or Zoom; but to actually sit in one, to have the door close and not know when it would open again, that was a different situation. I didn't have any doubt that the men behind bars deserved to be there, but I wondered at times if the judge really had any understanding of what the punishment was he was handing down. Years, decades of a person's life, just gone. It's easy to jack up numbers and get your rating up, but it's something else entirely to sit in a room, hour after hour, knowing exactly how many more days, months, seasons it would be until you were out.

"Do yourself a favor," I said to Witzig. "Get one of your buddies to cuff you, not as a friend, but like you were a real perp. If you really want to make it in this job, you need to know who you're dealing with on an intimate basis. If you're really feeling bold, ask to spend a night in county."

He looked at me, eyebrows up. It had been years since I'd done that, and I knew things had changed. But back when I was still on the force, it had been something I knew I had to do. Not just to understand the experience, but to understand the mindset it creates. I'd done it twice, once my second year when I stayed a night, once my third year when I'd spent a weekend in gen-pop. Obviously, the circumstances could never be entirely accurate; I knew I could get out whenever I needed to, but I'd wanted to understand who these people were. Because it turns out, what happens on the inside is often more formative than what has happened on the outside. Just not in the way we usually want it to be.

Kate put a hand on my elbow. "Come on."

I realized my jaw was clenched. The constant pain, even more so the throbbing in my head, was making me short-tempered, and if I was going to snap at anyone, this young police officer certainly wasn't the one who deserved my anger. No, that man was sitting just a few feet away.

When Kate and I walked into the room, Jacobi gave us the barest of glances and then leaned back in his chair as far as the cuffs would allow him. It wasn't much of a success, but he gave off the disinterested vibe he was going for, even without the proper posture.

"I'm Captain Gazzara," Kate began, and then, nodding to me. "This is my associate Harry Starke."

He glanced back and forth between us, a small smirk playing at the corner of his mouth.

"Long time, no see," I said.

His smirk turned to a wry grin.

"It looks like you understand why you're here," Kate said,

pulling out a chair and sitting down, flipping her notepad open on the table in front of her.

Jacobi shrugged. "I was just out for a jog."

"Yeah," Kate said. "Jeans and a cut, a vest, are usually what I wear to the gym too."

I leaned against the wall, arms folded. It was the typical "bad cop" pose, but I wasn't posturing for the kid. I was mad and needed to be able to pace, to keep my hands close so they wouldn't do anything to jeopardize this.

Milton turned his hands up as if to say he didn't know how to respond.

"This is going to end the same way, regardless of how long you make it last," Kate said. "You can cooperate or sit there and pretend you don't know anything, but I'm not going to be the one missing dinner at home tonight."

"I wasn't doing nothing," Jacobi said.

"You ran off like your hair was on fire," she said. "Kind of a strange coincidence for that to happen the moment a police officer shows up at your club."

"It *is* a strange coincidence," he said, leaning forward. "Because that's what I was running for. I thought I left the oven on. Had to get home."

I bit my lip, knowing I needed to let Kate run the show here. My presence was almost entirely to try and rattle Jacobi with the after-effects of what he'd done. The problem was, it didn't seem to be working.

"Right." Kate shot me a glance, knowing full-well I was doing my best to keep silent and wanting to encourage it in any way. "So you don't know anything at all about what happened to Mr. Starke?"

"Oh, that?" He laughed, and to my disbelief, bounded ahead. "Sure, I know about that. What I think you don't know is, the job's only halfway done." He shot me a glance of pure arrogance, one that only a man fully aware of the police protection he was entitled to could give. "Got interrupted."

"So you're admitting you were hired to kill Mr. Starke?" Kate kept her voice neutral, not wanting to break the delicate tension in the room. Cocky talks, she was right.

"Kill? Not at all." Jacobi tried to lean back in his seat again, but the cuffs linked to the table pulled at his wrists. "That would make me a hired killer. That's a serious accusation, miss." He smirked as if neither of us noticed the purposeful disregard for Kate's rank he was showing. "I was just asked, as a favor, to make sure somebody stopped asking questions. Plenty of ways to do that. One sure way, but as you can see, that didn't happen, since here y'all are, asking questions again."

"Cute," Kate said. "I suppose you don't remember the name of the person you were doing this favor for either then?"

"It does elude me."

If this had been someone a little higher up the socio-economic ladder, we could've pulled his bank records and perhaps lucked out. This guy, however, most likely took his payment by way of bills in a paper lunch sack. If he didn't want to talk, it was going to be slow-going tracking down where the money came from. If we ever did at all.

"So you just, as a favor for a friend who you can't remember, beat a man half to death?"

Jacobi looked me up and down, his expression almost one of an artisan inspecting his work. "Them's your words. All I can tell ya is two things. One..." He looked at me. "You need to think long and hard how much it's worth to you to keep poking your nose in other folks' business. I wouldn't put my hopes on your buddies saving you next time. And two..." He looked back at Kate. "I do believe I'd like to see a lawyer."

I rubbed a hand over my mouth, almost as if I was trying to keep myself from talking. Seeing the gesture, Kate nodded toward the door. Without another word, we stepped back into the hallway.

"Before you say anything," she said, speaking quickly and quietly as soon as the door closed behind us, "remember that we just got a confession. Not to what we want, and not nearly as much information as we want, but he's on tape saying he attacked you. This is a problem that is at least halfway solved."

I ran my hands through my hair.

"How much do you know about this case?" I asked.

"About yours or about Hattie's?"

"Both."

"With regard to you, and especially with regard to Jacobi Milton, I know that this isn't the first time we've pulled somebody out of that autobody shop. It may say motorcycle repair on the front, but those aren't the types of problems those men typically solve. It's the go-to for rich people looking to get something taken care of without a paper trail. Half the time, from what we've heard anyway, they just call in and ask for Otto. It's some kind of code."

"You didn't consider telling me this before we went in?"

"I was hoping, probably foolishly, that *we* wouldn't go in at all. But I should've known better than that."

I sat down in a chair that was outside the interrogation room. My head was pounding.

"With regard to Hattie Baker," Kate said, taking a seat next to me, "I don't know much. But I know if it's got you this frustrated, you must not know much either."

I hitched a thumb over my shoulder. "As of right now, the guy who tried to kill me has given us more information than anyone."

"Nothing from the neighbors?"

"They act like they never even knew she existed."

Kate leaned her head back against the wall and let out a

slow breath. "It's suspicious, but I need more than just curiously silent neighbors and a guy who, let's face it, Harry, has made some enemies and finally got jumped."

"Finally, huh?"

"You prefer 'again'?"

I laughed, but the sound hurt and I winced.

"Let's get you home," Kate said. "Jacobi can spend his time in lock-up tonight with his buddies and that's no concern of mine. But Amanda's not going to be too pleased if I bring you back more broken than you already were."

"I'm on the mend," I said, though I didn't refuse her hand when she reached down to help me up.

26

REGARDLESS OF THE FRONT I WAS TRYING TO PUT ON FOR Kate, one that was likely useless anyway, considering how long we'd known each other, the look in Amanda's eyes when I closed the door behind me was one of those complicated, deep looks that only people in long relationships can give one another. I could tell she was relieved I was back. But she was also angry, worried, scared. She was frustrated, even as she hugged me.

"That wasn't a quick trip," she said, holding me at arm's length and looking at me. "What happened?"

I'd done my best to never hide anything from her, not unless the case absolutely demanded it, or it was a situation where she or Jade could be put in danger by knowing too much, so I knew I'd tell her everything I could. She deserved it. But, in hopes of at least building a foundation of some kind of normalcy, I asked. "Jade still at my dad's?"

"For the time being." She still had her hands on my forearms, her eyes running up and down me as if she were going to find a bullet wound or a knife sticking out of me somewhere. "I talked to him today. He said they're having a wonderful time.

What that means with your father, who knows. She's probably getting flying lessons in the Gulfstream and developing a taste for *foie gras*."

"I don't know if that would upset or relieve me," I said. Jade, like every child, had very particular interests in food, running from color to texture to placement on the plate before ever getting to taste. Half the time, I think just the name of the food made the decision for her. "At least *foie gras* sounds fun. Better than 'goose liver' at least."

Amanda held my gaze for a moment and then took me by the hand, leading me toward the couch. "Okay, that was your fun jokey moment. Let's get this over with. What happened?"

It was strange. I knew Amanda and I would work. I'd known it somewhere in the back of my mind all along. But every relationship has its quirks, the wrinkles that need to be ironed out or the places each partner rubbed the other the wrong way. Sometimes they could be fixed; sometimes they couldn't. What it came down to was each person's willingness to accept the other, to keep working. Together. When it came to Amanda and me, we'd been no different. But I also knew that, when it came to certain things, I was pushing her limits. She would stay strong. She would accept who I was and what my job entailed. But that didn't mean she'd like it.

For a split-second, I considered trying to gloss over a few details, to try and make things easier for her in the moment. But I also knew that making things easier in the moment would just make them harder down the line. And I knew Amanda was strong enough to hear what I had to say. It was one of the reasons I'd married her in the first place.

"Well." I eased myself down onto the couch, wincing a little. The run, the sitting in cars, even the standing had taken it out of me. "I won't try to tell you you're going to love this story."

She pulled her knees up in front of her, turning toward me

on the couch. "I knew that when you walked in. And don't think you fooled Kate either. You have surrounded yourself with people who care about you, Harry, which is a great thing. Something most people never get. But it also means we can all see through your—"

"Stories?"

"I was going to say lies, but that seems mean. We can go with stories. But I want the real one. I'm Mrs. Starke, after all. Don't make me look foolish by my being the only one in the dark."

I nodded. "I would never do that. So I'm sorry this is going to bother you, but it's what I had to do."

I walked her through the events from the moment Kate and I shut the door to the house and got in her car. I felt like, even if I was going to go all in, giving her the fair proportion of time would somehow downplay the events of the chase, the one thing I knew she'd be upset about. Geez, I was upset about it. Or at least, my body wasn't too pleased with me for doing it.

I explained how Tim had matched the bike, how Kate had gotten involved, why there were other officers, stressing, in fact, how many other officers there were, but I'd barely gotten to the bad part before she rubbed her hands over her face and held them briskly out at me.

"You?" she said.

"And Kate."

"That doesn't make it better. You *and Kate* decided the best thing for you to do, after I spent a *week* nursing you back to health—which I think I've done an arguable job at that—which is beside the point. But you and Kate, you figure, oh, hey, he's been off morphine for a few hours, why not go raid a biker bar? Are you kidding me right now?"

"Listen." I held my hand out slowly, reaching over to touch her foot. "I didn't know what it was at the time. Kate didn't intend for me to go in in the first place. So don't hang her out to dry on this one."

"Oh, I'll hang whoever I'd like."

"It's not Kate's fault," I said, lowering my tone. "You and I both know I'll do what I want to do. And when it comes to something like this..." I gestured at myself. "There isn't a question of whether I'll hang back. I want to... solve the problem."

She rubbed her face again. "You sound like the people you bring in sometimes, you know that?"

"I do. And I don't mean to worry you. But I also want you to know that when things cross this line, it becomes something outside of work."

"Vigilante justice only works in e-books, Harry."

"Which is why I was with Kate."

She looked up at the ceiling and shook her head. "You're lucky she's the one who showed up. That's the one flimsy bit of this story that's not making me kick you in your broken ribs."

"Fractured."

She laughed a little despite the fact that she didn't want to. "Okay, macho man. Let's forget that you got the tar beaten out of you, let's forget that you shouldn't have left the couch today but you went to go pester some one-percenters."

"I didn't say that."

"Harry, I swear, it's like you forget what I used to do. You think I don't know where you were?"

I grinned a little and held out my hands. I married her because she was tough, but I also married her because she was smart as a whip. That and about a thousand other reasons. "All right. Fair enough. Yes, according to the sign on the front, one-percenters."

"So?" She held up her hands. "You came back alive. Or at least alive-ish. What happened?"

I looked at her for a second and fell for her all over again. I never intended to feel this way about anyone. After my mother passed, I made a concerted effort to close myself off from anything outside of a professional relationship. Kate had burrowed her way through my walls and we'd become friends. But even that had made me apprehensive. Amanda, in spite of, or perhaps due to, our rocky initial acquaintanceship, was now the most important person in my life, someone I'd do anything for. Well, one of two at least.

I gave her the story of Jacobi. His aborted escape attempt, his attitude. I hesitated for a moment, but decided if I was in for a penny, I was in for a pound, and told her everything he'd said about needing to stay out of things, about the arrogance he'd shown in the interrogation room.

"You know," she said when I'd finished. "There are homes all over this country where, when the husband comes home, he puts down his laptop bag, he kisses his wife, and they spend a delightfully uneventful evening together."

I nodded, letting her collect her words.

"And we're never going to be that type of home, are we?"

I thought for a moment. I'd tried so hard to pull back from work, to become more of a generic, nine-to-five husband and father, but there were always moments like this where my wife looked at me, my face still swollen, my bones still healing, and my latest news being that I'd put myself right back into the thick of it just an hour or two before.

"I'm working on it," I said finally.

Amanda wiped a tear from her eye, something I rarely saw from her. Then, surprisingly, she laughed, shaking her head. "You know what, Harry? You know what the worst thing about you is?"

I raised an eyebrow.

"I don't know if I *want* you to work on it or not. You're the most frustrating person I've ever met. But you're also the most intriguing."

I looked down, grinning. "I could say the same thing about you."

"Oh, I'm frustrating now, am I? Could you elaborate?"

I leaned over and pulled her closer. "Only in the way that I can't find anything to be annoyed by with you."

She laughed, snuggling up to me. "Good save, Harry Starke. Good save."

I felt her breath against my chest and felt her muscles relax under my hands. "I guess there's no point in asking if you're going in tomorrow," she said.

I kissed the top of her head. "The sooner it's done..."

"The sooner the next one will come up." She tensed up again and I rubbed her back.

"Maybe," I said. "But I'd hate for you to stop finding me intriguing."

She swatted my leg and instantly pulled back. "Oh my gosh, I'm sorry. Did that hurt?"

"I've got a few places that still feel all right."

She rolled her eyes and tucked her head back under my chin. "You're on probation, sir. Don't get cute."

I shrugged. "I can't help what God gave me."

I heard a little giggle and felt her pull closer. I knew it took a lot to stay with me, but this woman had more than enough. I ran my hand through her hair and, for the first time in a week, felt like I was finally going to be all right.

27

Despite the pleasant, restful evening with Amanda, something I hadn't realized we'd missed out on ever since Jade had come into the picture, the next morning was more than a bit of a struggle. My muscles screamed at me when I tried to get out of bed and my head felt like a balloon. Amanda rolled over when the alarm went off, the sound almost visible to my sensitive nerves.

"Are you sure, honey?" she said as she reached over and put a hand on my back.

We'd debated my sleeping on the couch again, but now that I was at least cognizant, I didn't want to risk making things worse by spending the night in such a cramped, unnatural position. So, we'd made the slow walk up the stairs, my hopes firmly set on the fact that just a few more hours worth of sleep, a couple of painkillers, and I'd be back to normal. Or at least normal enough. I was apparently incorrect.

"I wouldn't say sure is the way to put it, but I'm determined," I said.

I heard her sigh. "I figured as much. I'll get breakfast started."

"Just coffee," I said. Then, as I limped to the bathroom. "And maybe some painkillers."

"Way ahead of you, boss."

I shook my head and went to turn on the shower.

By the time I got to the office, which, unsurprisingly for us, was the typical opening hour for most businesses, I was the last to show. Inside, the team was still milling around the small coffee maker in the kitchenette, no doubt discussing whether I was going to make an appearance that day or not. When I walked in, I saw their collective eyebrows shoot up. Tim, for the briefest of moments, looked like he was actually going to clap.

I quickly held up my hands. "No need for any extra noise. I'm on strict orders to keep things calm."

"From the doctor or Amanda?" Jacque asked, a smile on her face as she came over to give me a gentle hug.

"If it was up to the doctor, I'd probably be a morphine addict by now," I said.

"Hey." She looked back at me. "They kicked you out, didn't they? What you do next is up to you. I seem to remember someone telling a whole lot of ex-cons that."

I rolled my eyes. "As far as this all goes, here's the story, or at least my side of the story, since I'm sure Heather has given you hers more than enough times for everyone's sake. After the attack in the Heights, during which I saw nothing of use, I was in the hospital until a few days ago. Yesterday, thanks to Tim's hard work..." He looked down, always nervous to be acknowledged. "We tracked the attacker's bike to an autobody shop on the east side. There, we found the subject. We gave chase, he was quickly apprehended, and is currently sitting in county, apparently rather proud of himself."

"We knew all that," Jacque said, a hand on her hip.

"He also made it clear that we need to keep our distance from the Heights unless we want more of this..." I said and gestured to my face before continuing, "to happen. Now, personally, that sounds like a challenge to me. But I figured you all should know."

"We know that too." Heather laughed.

I shrugged. "Then it's your turn to fill me in. What've we come up with so far?"

"Why don't we move this into the conference room," Jacque said, placing her hand gently on my forearm. "Sitting is a little more comfortable."

I nodded slightly, understanding her subtle way of taking care of me. I appreciated it. Everyone, myself more than the rest probably, knew I shouldn't be there. I was running on painkillers and caffeine and likely wasn't going to have much to add to a case I'd been effectively removed from for the time being. But I needed to be there. I needed to be working, thinking, involved.

Tim scurried off to his office to grab his notes, Heather did the same, and TJ, Jacque and I moved to the larger meeting room. I eased down into the chair slowly, aware of Jacque's almost unnoticeable move of putting a foot behind the casters on my chair, steadying it for me.

"That bad?" she said, her voice barely above a whisper.

"It's got to start getting better at some point," I grunted, sitting down heavily. "But thinking about it hasn't done me any good so far."

"I feel you," she said, then walked over and sat down in her chair. It was interesting. Most times, Jacque was the last to use slang or street talk, but apparently when she was touched by something, when a nerve was hit, she dropped her facade. I remembered a time when Jacque was the one in the hospital during one of our cases. As Heather and Tim slipped back in, taking their seats, I could feel Jacque's eyes on me. If Amanda could've seen it, she would've been proud. We take care of each other in my office; it's the only way we can survive.

"So what's the news?" I asked when we were all settled. "Tim? You usually have some good intel."

"Some," he said, pushing his glasses up and clicking some keys on his laptop. Despite his obvious skill at his job, he never seemed to garner any confidence in his abilities. "There really hasn't been much in the way of news," he continued. "Unless no news is news."

I nodded my head. "Sometimes we just have to check off all the things that aren't possible."

"And what remains, however improbable..." he said, letting the end of the quote hang. "Okay. I checked into deaths in the Heights over the past five years: one heart attack, one lost cancer battle, and the two drownings you already know about. The heart attack victim, Gerald Kingston, was sixty-nine years old and in poor health. The cancer victim, Todd Northfield, had a recurrence of pancreatic cancer and didn't beat it the second time around. He was forty-seven years old. I really didn't find anything that they had in common with Hattie Baker and Beatrice Loftis."

"Good work, Tim," I said. "I agree that those unfortunate deaths don't sound suspicious. What else do you have?"

Tim clicked a couple computer keys and continued, "I've been working on hacking into some of the computers from Hattie's neighbors..." He trailed off, perhaps realizing that what he was admitting to wasn't exactly legal.

"And?" I tried to encourage him. I knew we weren't supposed to gather information that way, but I also knew we weren't the police department. If something fell in our laps, we had a little more leeway than a governmental organization. Probably not much. It was still an invasion of privacy, after all. But the ends justified the means more often than not. And sometimes what people don't know won't hurt them. Or at least not in the way we were planning on putting the hurt on someone. If it took a little backdoor monitoring, then so be it.

Tim looked over at me, eyebrows up. "Well... I mean, on the one hand, strictly speaking as a professional, these guys do not try very hard to protect themselves. Like, I'm getting into these things faster than I could prison-break a cell phone or some kid's Facebook account. Their passwords are like their high school mascot and the year they graduated. Not exactly taking a lot of wizardry to get into these accounts."

"That's good for us, then," I said. "What are you finding, though?"

He sniffed and shook his head. "About what you'd expect. They're all bed-jumping and all convinced that no one else knows about it. A few of them have some pretty serious porn addictions. A pair of questionable purchases from overseas. Probably some fraud. But..." He shrugged. "When it comes to Hattie and Jacobi, nobody's saying anything. At least not that I've seen so far."

I nodded. "Keep working on it. The more we know, the better off we are. Even if it's not related to the case in particular, you might find a pressure point that will make things easier on us when we get back out there."

"Sure thing," he said, nodding.

I glanced over to Heather. "You're all having the same luck as always, I assume? Nobody saw, heard, or was aware of anything?"

"TJ, Jacque and I have been out canvassing while you've been away," Heather said. "The residents of Hilden Heights say they know nothing more about Hattie, and don't know anything about Jacobi. No one's ever seen him before, never heard the name."

"We're basically looking at a neighborhood where no one knows anything, even though we know they know something?"

"Right. The security guard told me he doesn't keep a log book of visitors entering and exiting the property. I asked him about the night Hattie died, if he remembered anyone visiting her, and he said he didn't recall anyone special stopping by, including Mason," she said.

I nodded, another dead end.

She took a sheet of paper out of her file and slid it down the table toward me. "If we're grasping at straws, which we clearly are, I did find this."

I took the sheet Jacque pushed my way. "Hilden Heights Book Club?"

"I know," Heather said, flipping her hair over her shoulder. "It seemed like a long shot to me at first as well. But this is the only connection I can find between Hattie and Beatrice."

"So you're assuming the two deaths are related?" I chewed on it. This whole case had seemed questionable from the start. Now that it was starting to look like multiple murders, I had to keep my skepticism at the forefront.

"I really didn't want to, if I'm being honest," she said. "But since we were striking out everywhere else, I did a little digging into Beatrice's story. Call it a hunch if you want, even though I know you hate that word. But the fact is, these two women had more in common than just the book club. It's... a little freaky."

"Meaning?" I asked.

"I'll get you the details later," she replied, "but for the time being, suffice it to say they're basically twins. Same interests. Same neighborhood, obviously. Similar deaths. But even small things, their ages, the people they dated, the standard day in

Beatrice's life could, for all intents and purposes, be the standard day in Hattie's.'"

"They dated the same people?"

"Not the exact same people. But the same type. You know how Mason was all up in arms because of the flack they gave him for being blue collar? Beatrice had a few beaus of her own that weren't 'their kind.'" She used her fingers to make air quotes. "I know coincidences happen, and sometimes that's all they are, but there are an awful lot of them happening here."

I nodded. "Wrong side of the tracks sounds a lot like our friend Jacobi."

"I haven't been able to make a connection there," she said. "Not yet anyway. But..." She looked at me, her eyes sparkling. "You thinking what I'm thinking?"

I looked down at the sheet. "It might be enough to get a reaction out of him. If he sees all the names, if he feels like we're connecting the dots."

"But you said yourself he's proud of what he did," Jacque cut in, the fire in her eyes juxtaposing Heather's excitement. "You're not thinking about letting him off the hook?"

I tapped the paper. "If this gets him to talk, if this gets us a murder instead of an assault charge, I'd be willing to do quite a bit of negotiating."

She sighed and folded her arms. "He deserves to be where he is. Maybe you haven't looked at your face in a while, but I've been staring at it this whole time and it's not a pretty mug right now."

I laughed a little, wincing at the pain in my ribs. "Pretty was never my goal anyway. Get ahold of Kate. See if she can work something out with the lawyer. If this guy can help us, I'm all for it. And, besides, you really think we aren't going to come across him again someday? Or that Kate might? He'll be back in a cell within six months, guaranteed."

Jacque ran her hands through her hair, frustrated but agreeable. "Okay, that's a fair point. I'll go call Kate and see what we can do."

She walked out of the room, her cell phone in hand. I looked around the table. "If there's nothing else, I'd appreciate it if you all just keep doing what you're doing. This one's going to take a lot of grunt work, but we're making progress. Despite what it might look like."

"What about you?" Heather asked as we all stood up. "Taking a half day?"

"No." I leaned on the table, my head throbbing. "But I'll be in my office if anyone needs me. A lot of things to catch up on."

She gave me a lingering look and then nodded. "I'll be in mine too."

I understood what she meant. It was another one of the subtle ways the team was trying to take care of me without making it obvious. And I did appreciate it. But at that moment, what I needed more than anything was rest.

I walked stiffly across the main corridor to my office. I closed the door, pulled the shades, and then sat gingerly in my chair. I could feel my pulse in my temples. It felt like my very bones were aching. Maybe just a few minutes, I thought, closing my eyes. A few minutes rest and I'd be able to focus again. I leaned back in the chair, letting the murmur of the office swirl around me, and slept.

28

I WOKE UP TO A TAPPING ON MY SHOULDER AND HEATHER'S concerned face only inches from my own.

"Harry?"

"Yes?" I leaned forward, hurriedly taking in my surroundings and realizing what I'd done. "I'm all right."

"It's two o'clock, Harry. You've been asleep for five hours." She perched on the corner of my desk, not something she'd typically do, but something that showed me how concerned she truly was. "Do you need to go to the doctor? I know you're going to say no, but tell me the truth."

I sat forward, leaning my elbows on my knees and rubbing my eyes. "Honestly, that may've been just what I needed. The pain meds aren't messing around." I sat up straighter, realizing I wasn't feeding her a line, or at least not entirely. "But my head feels one hundred percent better. Maybe I should sleep in here more often."

She eyed me, not interested in the light-hearted tone. "You never sleep here. What's going on? Are you sure they cleared you for all the concussion protocol?"

"I think it's been way long enough for that concern," I said, pulling out my phone. It was more to appear natural, to have something to do, than anything. Though the idea of falling asleep in the middle of the day did concern me somewhat. Maybe I'd mention it to Amanda later. Maybe I'd just play the whole thing by ear. But as I swiped my phone open and pretended to check for new texts or emails, I knew that Heather's almost motherly gaze was more than enough to keep Amanda satisfied.

"I'm really fine," I said. "Probably shouldn't have come in early, I'll give you that. But you know as well as I do that this is where I need to be. I haven't taken medicine in..." I checked my watch. "Seven hours, so I may be singing a different tune by four o'clock, but for now, I feel good. I actually feel better than I have since Jacobi jumped me."

Heather folded her arms and leaned back a little, assessing my words and my appearance. "What are we supposed to do today?"

I grinned. "A test, huh? I suppose I can't be mad that I hired the best. We're supposed to go see that very same Jacobi."

"Because?"

"Because one of my crack staff members found a connection between Hattie and Beatrice, and we want to see if that will rattle his cage a bit. I'm with you, Heather. I really am. If anything changes, you'll be the first to know."

Her expression didn't appear entirely convinced, but she lifted herself off the desk and walked around to the chairs, the side where she usually was. "You realize that if we go in there, and you conk out on the floor, he's going to just love it."

"I do realize that," I said. "That's why we should get going before the pain comes back. Don't forget who trained you." I couldn't resist and added, "Boss."

The corner of her mouth pulled up just slightly. It wasn't much, but it was enough.

"All right." She sighed. "Give me five minutes to gather up the paperwork and then we head out."

"Yes, ma'am."

"Okay." She waved a hand as she walked out the door. "Enough funny stuff. It's not your forte."

I leaned on the desk after she left. I did feel better. At least nominally. The throbbing in my head was gone, though I wondered how long it would be until it came back. The pain meds, Neurontin and Toradol, were a far cry from the Oxycodone I'd also been given a prescription for. "Basically Tylenol's big brothers" is how the pharmacist had described them. But if I was going to be back at work, the last thing I needed was a narcotic in my system. Thankfully, Tylenol's big brothers were doing their job. And as childish as I knew it was, I didn't want Jacobi to see me flinch. He'd already gotten an eyeful when we'd brought him in; this time he needed to see Harry Starke at his finest. It might not take him down a peg, but I knew my size and my ability to be intimidating was always there when I needed it.

Heather poked her head back in the office, her eyes still carrying a slight hint of concern. "Ready?"

"Never been better." I grabbed my jacket from the back of my chair and slipped it on, doing my best to hide the wince of pain in my ribs as I lifted my arm. Heather, for her part, did her best to act like she didn't notice it.

We walked out to her car, neither of us discussing who was going to drive. "You know he's gonna be lawyered up," she said as she climbed behind the wheel.

"I assumed so, but that's not my biggest concern."

"What is?"

"What kind of lawyer he has. Jacobi Milton is a public defender guy all the way. We see anything outside of that, then we have some more questions to find answers to."

"Not a high view of bikers, I see."

I glanced over at her as she backed out of the parking spot. "Not a high view of people who jump people from behind. Not a high view of people who advertise One Percent. Not a high view of people who can beat someone half to death and then only be disappointed they didn't finish the job."

"Fair enough." She flicked on her turn signal and turned toward the police station downtown. "You don't think he's got a lot of dirty money lying around? Enough to get a decent lawyer? Or the club might? Those guys are supposed to be like a family, aren't they?"

I shrugged. "I've never been in one. Done a few cases where I pretended to be, and yes, they look out for each other. But you were there when we brought him in, and Kate can vouch for it. They gave him running room, but nobody was sticking their neck out for the guy. He's probably a probie, on probation."

She drove quietly for a few moments. "Are you gonna be okay with this?"

It was a loaded question. She knew full well I could handle myself, but this was a different set of circumstances than we usually walked into.

"Are you asking if I'm going to jump across the table?" I tried to be light-hearted. "Because no. If you're asking if I'm going to be firm, you already know the answer to that."

"Fair enough."

Ten minutes later we were pulling into the county jail parking lot. The building was a maze of hallways and rooms, all of which looked the same. The only place I'd ever seen that put so much effort into making a layout confusing was Vegas, and their motivations were exactly the same. Keep people in. We wandered through the initial check-in, the separate rooms where they patted us down, a male officer for me, a female for Heather, and then were finally brought to a small room that had nothing more than a desk with a clear, Plexiglas divider in the middle and chairs on either side.

Heather and I waited for a moment before Jacobi walked in, with a young, dark-haired man in a sharp suit and a smug expression at his side.

I glanced at Heather. This was going to go nowhere.

"Mr. Starke," the lawyer said. "How nice of you to come see us. You should be glad I was already here or you would've had to wait a while."

I raised an eyebrow. The lawyer wasn't my concern. I wanted to see what Jacobi did, how he acted, how he responded. He was in prison khaki, his hair greasy from the poor washing his indigent kit shampoo would've given him. He had a five o'clock shadow now, but the nicks on his neck let me know he'd been trying to keep up appearances. My guess was he'd been put in a gen-pop kind of situation, waiting to find out what his case was going to be. So the man across from us was new. Otherwise, any decent lawyer would've had Jacobi out hours ago.

"I assume you understand how incredibly complex our current situation is," the lawyer began, not even bothering with an introduction. "You were a police officer. Now you're a private detective. And you happen to be accusing my client of assaulting you while you were in a secure neighborhood." He leaned back, a smug smile on his face. "The conflict of interest here isn't even worth pointing out. Whatever you think you might have is, I assume, garnered from what we might call questionable means. You used your connections in the police department to harass a man who was doing nothing other than working. Things aren't going to go well, Mr. Starke."

I looked at Heather. We'd heard this same kind of rigmarole a dozen times before. "So," I said, "despite the fact that he all but admitted he did it, on camera, when Captain Gazzara brought him in, we're changing things up?"

"My client had been through a very emotionally and mentally hectic situation," the man said.

Jacobi put his hands on his head, leaning back in the chair. For a moment, I thought he was going to put his feet on the table just to prove how relaxed he was.

"So you want to do it this way?" I asked, looking Jacobi solidly in the eyes.

"I officially request that you not address my client," the lawyer said. "I'm here as his legal representative, and he has nothing to say."

I looked over at Heather. Her hands were grasped together firmly in her lap and I could see her jaw muscles clench. "Then I think we're done here," I said.

I stood up and took Heather by the elbow, feeling her anger trembling in her tricep. "Back to the office. We can deal with it there."

29

As we worked our way back out through the labyrinthine layout of the jail, Heather patted the folder of papers on her leg. It was a gesture I'd seen more than once. The same way a dog will get its hackles up, Heather had her tells.

We walked through the first checkpoint and I let her simmer. By the second locked door, I could tell she was on the verge of speaking. At the third, she finally swatted her leg with the folder and darted a glance at me. "He thinks we're just going to do nothing? Because he got some suit to come sit there and glare at us?"

It was part question, part infuriation. My meds were still going strong, but I could feel the stiffness in my body and I wasn't about to let this escalate.

"We came for information; we got information."

"That he's lawyered up?"

"That he's lawyered up with a man well above his pay grade."

She paused for a moment, looking down, thinking. "You think someone footed the bill."

"I can't see how else it could've worked."

She tapped the folder on her leg, a movement that was now more about thinking than venting frustration. A thumbnail went to her teeth. "So if he didn't pay for the guy, there's really only one neighborhood that could have."

"That's what I'm thinking."

"Wait." She put a hand on my arm. "We should go back. We didn't even ask about the book club."

The corrections officer at the third and final door handed us back our IDs and glanced up momentarily at her comment.

"I don't think it would make much difference," I said. "You saw his face. Everything we said got the same smug grin. He's completely confident this is going to be a walk in the park."

"But he's on video with Kate."

"They'll say it was coerced. Or that he was a victim of police brutality and talking out of his head. You know how this always goes. Reasonable doubt isn't quite so reasonable anymore."

She sighed, tucking her wallet back in her purse and stepping up to the metal detector.

"I just feel like we should've asked. Even if he did nothing."

I watched her pass through; the lights on the monitor showing green. "We can always come back," I said. "The more you bother someone, the more likely they are to get irritated and say what they shouldn't."

"It just seems like it would work," she said as I lifted my arms, letting the CO run his detector over me. "If we can get him to react, even the slightest bit, then we'll know he knows about the Heights Book Club. And he'll know we know." She looked down for a moment. "That was complicated."

I was about to respond when the man running his detector over me spoke up. "Hey, uh... I'm not really supposed to get involved here, but are y'all talking about Hilden Heights? The book club there?"

I looked over at him. "In fact we are. You know it?" It

seemed odd. COs weren't known for their high pay grade. In fact, almost anyone could get the job, provided you had a clean record and a high patience level. He was about as far from Hilden Heights as I was from being Santa Claus.

"A bit," the man said, tucking the detector back into its oversized holster on his hip. "I'm not much of a reader." He looked around and shrugged. "Obviously. But my wife, she's one of the English teachers over at Sig Mount." He caught himself. "Signal Mountain. Sorry, she's been there long enough we don't go through the trouble of saying it."

Heather whistled. "Impressive. That place doesn't mess around."

He smiled, his pride in his wife clearly visible. "She does it all. I know I'm just a CO, and she probably oughtta be doing better'n me. Shoot, the stuff that woman is teaching her kids, I mean, eight, ninth-grade kids, pups really, well it's beyond me. But she likes to read and I got my little woodshop out in the garage, so it gives us time to do our own things..."

He trailed off and I wondered exactly where he was planning on going with this, other than complimenting his wife in her absence, a thing I couldn't exactly be upset about.

"Your wife is in the Hilden Heights Book Club?" I asked, trying to bring us back to the topic.

"Oh." He looked down, a slight flush coming to his cheeks. "No, no. She asked to be. It's the closest one to us, really. She's always trying to get more folks' opinion on what she's teaching her kiddos, trying to see if there's something she oughtta be having them read that they ain't. Aren't, I mean."

I nodded. "Sounds like she really cares about her job."

"Oh, she loves it," he said, running a hand through his hair. "I wish I knew a little more about it, but..." He glanced at the barren corridor where he spent most of his days. "We work a lot of tens and twelves around here. Not much of a job, I know. But by the time I get home," he said and shrugged, "I can crack a book if you want me to fall asleep. And she doesn't take it easy on those kids. No pot-boilers." He seemed proud to know the term. "It's all real literature. But that ain't, isn't, exactly what keeps me up at night."

"So the book club," Heather jumped in, "they wouldn't let your wife join? Or?"

The man looked down again, rubbing his hands back and forth on his belt, clearly a nervous gesture. He looked up and apparently decided to just dive in. "Said we weren't the right type. You believe that?"

I glanced at Heather. "Honestly, Mr...?"

"Wally Schatz." He stuck out a hand. "You are?"

I introduced myself and Heather and got back to the topic at hand. "To be honest with you, I don't know if anyone outside of the Heights counts as the right type. I wouldn't feel too offended by it. Not that it isn't offensive."

"Well, that's the thing," Wally said, clearly happy to have even the slightest break from monotony in his day. "It ain't like, I mean, it's not like she doesn't know what she's talking about. She was telling me about Faulkner..." He looked up at the ceiling. "I mean, I went to school. I read. I read every daggone book they gave me. Failed every test on them too." He laughed a little. "But Ursula, that's my wife, she makes them make sense. If I'da known her in high school, I might've ended up somewhere other'n this hallway."

I folded my arms. One of the things that got under my skin the most was people not appreciating what they were doing. Sure, boredom is a thing, but sometimes boredom only means that you're doing an impeccable job. "This hallway is the last stop before some dangerous people can get back out into the public. Don't forget that. You're a guard, Mr. Schatz. We need people like you."

He looked down again, his face reddening just slightly. "You tell my boss that." He chuckled a little. "Maybe I can get me a raise."

I laughed and patted him on the shoulder, turning back toward the exit. "I'll be sure to put in a good word."

Just before I opened the door, Heather turned back.

"Your wife," she said, addressing Wally. "Ursula?"

"Yep."

"Do you think we could talk to her? We're kind of running into some dead-ends and maybe she could at least give us a fresh perspective on things."

"Well, yeah, a'course." He pulled a notepad from his breast pocket and scribbled a number down on it. "I'm not sure how the book club would help you, and between me and you," he said and handed her the slip, "Ursy isn't likely to be too happy to talk about it. But..." He shrugged. "If she can help, she'll always help. Just..." He scratched the back of his head, almost sheepish. "I'd just ease your way into it. That's a woman who knows how smart she is and ain't, isn't, too keen on getting snubbed."

"As all women should be," Heather said. "Thank you."

We walked back out through the main entrance of the jail. "Got a feeling, do you?" I asked.

"We don't have much else going on," Heather said. "Keep kicking over rocks and see what crawls out."

I smiled. "Always the way to go."

30

Outside, Heather paused by the car door, her phone in her hand. I raised an eyebrow.

"No time like the present, right?" she asked.

I nodded, though currently the present was feeling like something I needed to get out of. It wasn't the physical stress, but the intellectual work and the emotional strain that was starting to wear on me. Maybe that nap had only been a taste of what I really needed, just rest.

I was surprised to hear Heather's voice pick up, a genuine friendly tone in it. "Hey, Kate. I've got a thing you might be interested in. Wanted to see if you had any interest in tagging along."

I listened, leaning on the roof of the car as she filled Kate in on how things had gone with Jacobi. Unsurprisingly, it sounded like Kate was already well-informed.

"That's right," Heather said. "S-c-h-a-t-z. Ursula."

Kate said something back and Heather made a writing motion at me. I grabbed the notebook out of my inner jacket pocket and copied down the address Heather repeated to me.

"See you there," she said, clicking off the line. "Looks like we aren't done making friends yet today."

I nodded and opened the car door, easing myself into the seat.

"You sure you're okay for this?" she asked, sitting down and buckling her belt. "Kate and I can handle it."

"I'll be fine," I said, not entirely believing the statement myself. "I need to be out and about. I can be tired later."

"You look like you passed tired before we left the office." She put the car in gear and backed out of the parking space.

When we got to the Schatz residence, Kate's SUV was already parked along the curb. Heather pulled in behind her.

"So this is where we are?" Kate said as I gingerly climbed out of the car.

"Up and moving. That's the doctor's orders." I tried to keep my face neutral as I pulled on my jacket.

"There are limits to those orders," she said. "But I assume you have fully committed to disregarding them."

"These things happen."

She scoffed a little laugh and walked around to give Heather a brief, friendly hug. "So this is our new lead, huh? If we want to find people who got snubbed by the Heights crew, we probably don't need to look far."

Heather shrugged. "At this point, we've got one connection between two deaths. If Ursula tells us nothing, then we're no worse off than we are right now."

"Fair enough." Kate glanced at me, lowering her voice, though not nearly enough. "How's this one?"

"Stubborn as usual."

Kate laughed. "No fighting that then."

Heather nodded and the three of us, me feigning ignorance of their chat, walked up the small concrete path to the front door of the Schatz residence. Kate pushed the doorbell and stood back. A small dog yipped from inside and a moment later, Ursula Schatz was standing on the other side of the screen door.

"Can I help you?"

She'd clearly just gotten home from work. I glanced at my watch. Quarter past four. Seemed reasonable for a teacher who knew what they were doing and had a short commute.

"Hi," Heather started. "I know this is going to take a second to unpack, but I promise we won't take up too much of your time."

Her tone, the glimmer in her eyes, it was one of the things that had convinced me I needed her on the team. Heather had an ability to instantly become friends with strangers, to make every situation seem comfortable and normal. My own husky, sometimes short-tempered demeanor needed a balance like that.

"Oh," Ursula Schatz hesitated for a moment but then, looking between the three of us and back to Heather, smiled. "What can I do for you?"

Heather introduced us and, just like that, Ursula pushed the screen door open. "Come on in," she said. "I'm not sure how I can be much use to you, but I can give it a try."

I looked around the small living room she led us to. A few photos sat on a shelf on one wall, a small TV taking residence on another. There was a couch and two small sitting chairs. Between Ursula and Wally, they clearly weren't bringing in a king's ransom in salary.

Once we sat down, Kate dove in, explaining the barest details of the case but bringing the weight of the CPD with her. She explained who we were, why we were there, and why any of it had anything to do with Ursula Schatz. When Heather handed her the list of book club members, Ursula merely flicked at it before she handed it back.

"Of course I know who they are. I'm a teacher."

I looked at her. "You have their kids in class?"

She laughed. "Oh, they wouldn't deign to sully their reputation by sending their kids to a 'regular' school. But I'm surrounded by teens all day. The one thing teenagers can do is gossip. It would be hard to not recognize these names."

I smiled. It was refreshing. I got so used to chasing down people who didn't want to talk, people who lawyered up, people who thought they were playing a game, that a real, genuine conversation with someone almost felt strange.

"So," I started, "since you're familiar with these people beyond the book club, could you maybe just tell us your general impressions?"

She laughed again. "General impressions? I think you've probably gotten the same general impressions I did." She paused. "Well, that's not entirely fair. It takes all kinds of people to make the world go round, as they say."

I raised an eyebrow, getting a soft chuckle from Ursula.

"All right, that's how the saying goes, and I try to believe it. You spend as much time with fourteen-year-olds as I do and it kind of becomes your mantra. Fragile egos there. But when you meet women who are twice as old but still act the same..." She flipped a hand, as if brushing away the Heights in its entirety. "I just went there because it was close to home and I thought it might be a legitimate book club. Wally and I... well," she said and looked down. "Obviously we don't have any children and that doesn't look like it's going to be in the cards. So I let him work in his shop, and I take care of the kids at school. At least as best I can."

I nodded. "He said you both have your own hobbies."

She laughed. "Hobbies is one way to put it. He really does do some wonderful work out there. I've been trying to get him to sell things online, but... it's Wally. He just gives everything away."

"You as well."

She looked at me, her head cocked to the side.

"Wally gives away the projects he makes; you give away your time. I don't mean to be overly presumptuous, but I assume at least a small part of your interest in the book club was related to your students."

"I just want to do the best I can," she said.

"Commendable."

She glanced down, clearly uncomfortable with even the slightest compliment on her work and perspective.

"We don't mean to take up your whole afternoon," Heather jumped in. "But, if you could, do any of the names on this list seem familiar to you beyond what you've heard at school?"

Ursula perked up again, clearly happy to have an easy question to answer. "May I?" She reached over for the list again. As her eyes scanned the names, I could almost anticipate what she was about to say.

"Franny, Marilyn, Caroline, Nel... then of course Hattie and Beatrice, rest their souls."

"You've met all of them?" Heather asked. It was practically the entire list.

"I might just be a high school teacher, but that doesn't mean I lack culture." Ursula laughed. "I've seen them all out and about. Art shows mostly. It's why I thought the book club might be a good fit for me. But, they didn't seem to think I was a good fit for it. Which is probably fine." She shrugged.

"Meaning?" I asked.

"Meaning, I don't know what that club is, exactly, but they don't..." She paused, her eyes on the ceiling.

"You can say it," I said. "Nothing leaves this room."

"Let's just say they don't strike me as readers." She looked down, grinning a little.

I nodded.

A few minutes later, after Kate had wound up the interview

and the three of us were standing back on the sidewalk outside, Heather turned to me.

"I'm assuming you don't want to get into another chitchat with the Stepford Wives."

I shrugged, putting my hands in my pockets. I was about to agree with her when something flashed through my mind.

"The Cullinses," I said.

Her eyes lit up, the excitement genuine. "You remember something?"

"I was talking to them," I said, almost to myself. My brain was chasing a thought that was just barely out of reach. "She talked about..." No, that wasn't right. I knew I couldn't force the memory, but it was infuriating to have it so close. "That's wrong. He talked. *He* talked to me. He talked about everything. It's not the wives we need to be tracking down."

I looked between the two women, both of them beaming smiles at me. I knew I'd been in a rough spot, but I hadn't realized just how concerned my team had been until now.

"He's coming back," Kate said, nudging Heather with an elbow.

"So what's your plan here, boss?" Heather asked.

"For tonight," I said and glanced at my watch, feeling the weight of the day heavy on my shoulders, "nothing. We'll track down the boyfriends and husbands, but let's do it tomorrow. Get them at work. It'll throw them off balance and keep the Sisterhood of the Traveling Pants out of it."

Kate smirked. "Are you in a book club now too?"

I shrugged. "I listen when people talk. That's at least as good."

31

HEATHER TOOK ME BACK TO THE OFFICE AFTER THAT AND, with a bit more than subtle urging, convinced me to call it a day. Amanda had said she was going to get in touch with my father that afternoon, and I knew that, as much as we'd been through, having Jade back in the house would be good for the both of us.

I drove home leisurely, trying to not overwork my already tired body any more than I had to. I saw Amanda's car in the drive and knew the two most important women in my life were more than likely lying belly down on the floor of the living room, loving every second of being together.

I pulled the car into the garage and slowly, carefully climbed out. I loved the high ride and handling of the machine, but after getting kicked around a bit, I was regretting how much work it took to actually get out.

I stepped through the door from the garage and called out to Amanda.

"In here!" her voice came back from the living room, Jade's giggle not far behind.

"I thought you might be," I said, walking over with as much normalcy as I could.

Amanda gave me an up and down. "You're done for the day then?"

I sat down on the couch, Jade immediately running over to me. "Done with detective duties. Dad just clocked in."

Amanda rolled her eyes and got up on her knees. "Well if you can keep up with her, I'll start dinner. I think someone's dad," she said, eyeing me, "forgot that kids need more than just sugar to survive. This one's been bouncing off the walls." She gave one of Jade's pigtails a playful tug.

"He's not a dad," I called as she walked over toward the kitchen. "He's a grandpa now. Total new set of rules."

I heard her laugh under her breath as I scooped up my daughter.

"Fair," Amanda hollered back. "But we gotta figure out how to get back at him."

I held Jade up, her giggle almost hyperactive as she reached toward me. "Oh, things could be worse."

The next morning I woke up early, intending to take advantage of the extra long night's sleep and try to get my body back on its usual routine. Morning runs were almost always my favorite part of the day. It was a time to think, plan, figure out what I needed to do, what I wanted to do. And it was quiet, calm. I loved my wife and daughter endlessly, but every person needs a moment to clear their head. The morning run had been that for me.

However, this morning, less than half a mile into the regular six-mile path I was intending to take, I found myself leaning against a tree, one hand on the bark and one on my knee. The pace had been aggressive; I knew that going into it. But it wasn't so much that I felt like I was really pushing myself. Nevertheless, my body seemed to think otherwise. Every part of me ached as my elevated heart rate pumped through my limbs.

Maybe six miles was too grand an idea, but I certainly

thought I would've been able to do one. As I limped back toward the house, though, hoping no one drove by who knew me, I realized I was a lot farther from being back to rights than I'd anticipated.

Amanda would be sure to ask, of course. She knew exactly how long it ought to take me to get out and back on a given day. Of course, by the time I walked delicately home, the minutes might not be too far off my typical pace. I shook my head. Something needed to happen to redeem this day, and I'd only been up for forty minutes.

————————

My body wasn't much less achy when I pulled into the parking lot at Andrew Cullins's office, but I had a good breakfast in me and some quality, albeit short, time with Jade and Amanda under my belt. I wouldn't say I was feeling aggressive, I wouldn't even say I was feeling back to normal, but I know when I pulled into the spot and saw Andrew Cullins see me, things changed rapidly.

I threw the car in park and stepped out quickly, trying to show enough confidence to cover up the burn I felt on my ribs at the fast motion.

"Mr. Cullins," I called out, raising a hand. "Harry Starke."

He threw me a quick glance and, for the briefest of moments, looked at the building as if there were a chance he could run inside and get out of whatever conversation we were about to have. It was one of the most tell-tale reactions I'd seen in a long time. No one likes to have a cop or a private detective show up at their door, but the instinct to run is one that only a few have. Most people get overly helpful. Andrew Cullins was just trying to get away.

"Mr. Starke," he said, walking over toward me with one last, hopeful glance over his shoulder at the building. "Or I suppose I should say 'Detective' Starke. What brings you here today?" He flicked his wrist, a gesture that I'm sure worked wonders in his business meetings with the way it showed off his gold watch. "I'm a bit pressed for time."

I offered a hand, which he almost begrudgingly shook. It wasn't a gesture I enjoyed, but it covered my bases for all the CCTV cameras I was sure were attached to the building. "I just had a few more questions for you. I take it now's not a good time?"

"I..." He tapped his briefcase on his knee, looking about. It was obvious there were two things in his mind: one was how to get rid of me the quickest. The other was if it would be more worth his time to just get us into the privacy of his office and away from any other person who might come pulling into the lot. "Can you tell me what this is about?" he asked after a moment of contemplation.

"It should be fairly straightforward," I said. "No need to stand out here though. I'm sure you have somewhere a little more comfortable inside."

He sighed. "You read my mind." He turned toward the building and then slowed his pace as he saw me limp after him. "It's nothing against you, detective. I just..."

"Lots of prying eyes and loose lips," I said, falling into step beside him. "I understand completely."

He gave me a look, a small smile. "And that's why you met me here instead of at home, isn't it? Well played."

I shrugged. "I'm sure you've planned a few of your meetings in the same way."

He laughed. "And had them planned against me." He held open the tall, modern glass door. "So what is this about today?"

I stepped into the lobby and followed him over to the elevator. As he pressed the button for the top floor, I tried to remain nonchalant. "Just curious about a book club," I said. "You know of any good ones?"

Andrew eyed me for a long moment, then sighed. "You want coffee? My secretary can whip some up that's out of this world. But if you want to hear about the book club, you may as well settle in."

32

I pulled the plush leather chair out and took a seat across from Andrew at his desk. It reminded me of talking to my father. Everything was designed to show how important the man across from me was. The difference was that my father had earned it. Andrew looked like a spoiled child who knew he didn't belong where he was.

"You're sure you don't want any coffee?" he asked, unbuttoning his suit jacket and settling in.

"I'll be fine," I said. "May as well make this as short and sweet as we can."

Andrew nodded and steepled his fingers in front of him. "So the book club, you say? I'm not sure which way you want to tackle this."

"I'm just curious," I replied. "Hattie Baker and Beatrice were both members. I've talked to another young lady who was not graced with such a privilege. But at this point, I just want to know a little more about it. Seems pretty exclusive."

He laughed. "It's the Heights."

I looked at him, my head cocked to the side, unsure if I'd heard him correctly.

"Look, Mr. Starke, I know where I live and who I live beside." He gestured his hands out, encompassing the office. "I understand that this is all fluff and window-dressing. But I believe that you also understand how important it is. When you're in business, at the numbers we run here, you have to look the part. You have to live in the best neighborhood. You have to drive the flashiest cars. You want to know something?" He leaned forward as if he was going to impart the direst of secrets. "If you go out in my garage at home, there's a rusted-out Ford Bronco sitting in it. The wife won't let me drive it around because she's afraid I'll be seen and somehow tarnish our good name, but that's my baby. I paid fifteen hundred dollars for it and haven't even decided if I want to fix it up or not. It's almost exactly the same car as the first I ever had. Paints a shade off..." He looked off in the distance. "But the point is, I know the game I'm playing. And I know what I need to do to keep myself grounded. The book club, on the other hand..." He sighed. "Let's just say that books aren't a huge part of that club."

"So it's a social group?"

He nodded. "That would probably be the kind way to put it. And in all fairness, I've never been to a meeting myself. But I can tell you how many novels I see sitting on the nightstand, and it's few and far between. It..." he started and then caught himself.

"This is just between me and you, Andrew," I said. "I'll keep whatever you have to say filed away with the secret of the Ford Bronco."

He laughed, and I knew he was about to open up.

"You're a good man," he said. "I don't toss that about lightly, or at least, I don't sincerely say it too often. I know how we appear to other people, and I know Franny and the rest of the ladies don't do anything to make it easier on people. Money is money, and it's a hard thing to argue with. We all want it, some of us get it, and it's a hard truth. If you want to know my take on the so-called book club, it's just a time-filler."

I raised my eyebrows.

"It's the paradox of wealth," he said, tossing his hands up. "I come here, I do very little, and I watch my bank account skyrocket. The wives though? The girlfriends? The mistresses? They're in a gilded cage. They can't leave the Heights lest they sully themselves by being with the common folk. But they can't do much else either. Those gates, that guard who I'm sure gave you a real run-around before he admitted you, all of that is keeping people in as much as it's keeping them out."

I considered letting him know I wasn't exactly a Dickens character myself, but at this point, he was too caught up in his poor little rich boy speech to likely truly listen.

"So it's a popular girls thing?" I asked.

He shrugged. "Basically. It gives them something to do and something to feel haughty about."

I was surprised. "Heck of a way to talk about your wife."

"No." He rubbed his face. "I'm sorry. That was rude. She's just been..." He twisted back and forth in his chair. "I'm sure you heard about Beatrice."

I nodded.

"Hattie was like Beatrice all over again. I try to encourage Franny to go to the book club, to get out and socialize, to do anything, regardless of what I think about it, because otherwise..." He sighed. "Otherwise, she just sits in the living room, staring out the window. You might think we're a bunch of spoiled little rich kids, and in a lot of ways, you might be right. But when your friend dies... when two of your friends die, it doesn't matter how much money you have. In fact, it makes it worse. We can buy almost anything we want, Mr. Starke, but we can't bring Hattie back."

For once, what he said made sense, or at least sounded

reasonable. "I'm sorry for your loss," I said. "And I apologize if I've given you the wrong impression. I don't have any prejudice against people based on their zip code. I'm just trying to find out as much information as I can."

Andrew nodded, his eyes flitting to the clock on his desk and letting me know my time was about up.

"If you want to know about the book club," he said, "I'd talk to Collie Newman. She's the unofficial president, though Franny calls her the 'dictator for life.' So be aware of that."

"Sounds pleasant," I said.

He rolled his shoulders, his head dipping to the side. "I shouldn't really say one way or the other. I know I personally haven't ever felt too friendly, but... I don't know. Some people just rub you the wrong way, you know?"

"I've met a few."

"Well, consider yourself warned," he said, laughing a little. "She runs some business out of her house. Pretty hush-hush about it, but if you're wanting to track her down, she's usually at home. One of those spinsters. Like that other lady." He looked up at the ceiling. "Veronica something?"

"Victoria Blue?" I asked.

He snapped his fingers. "That's the one."

I nodded and stood up, reaching across the desk to shake his hand again. "I appreciate the tips, Mr. Cullins. I won't take up any more of your time."

He leaned back in his chair and gave me a sad smile. "I have so little to do here it's embarrassing... Any time, Mr. Starke. Any time."

I took the elevator back down several flights to the ground floor, my ears popping about midway down the high-rise. He'd been helpful, or at least as helpful as he could be, but it made me reconsider something. We'd been so focused on what the women weren't telling us, and now on the idea that we could talk to the significant others and get a different perspective, that I'd forgotten the one person who created this case to begin with.

The elevator doors chimed and opened, and as I walked across the lobby, I was already googling the address for Mason Willis's business. A number popped up with the information and I hit send.

"Mr. Starke," he answered almost immediately. "News?"

"Just wanting to talk," I said. "Are you going to be in your office for the next..." I glanced at my watch. "Hour or so?"

"I can be here or I can meet you," he answered, sounding eager.

"I'll be there shortly."

I made my way across the parking lot to my car, already beginning to wonder how long I'd be able to keep up the pace of the day. The run should've been a clear red flag, but I had been hoping if I just slowed things down, I might find some balance. My cracked ribs seemed to think otherwise.

I called Heather and let her know where I was headed. It wasn't a real concern, but more force of habit. This isn't a job where you want to go missing for too long, after all.

Mason met me at the door of his little office. The place clearly used to be a small, ranch-style home, but then again, when you spend your time working out in the field like he did, what more did you need? It made me reconsider the extravagance of our own building.

"Mr. Starke." He held the door, clearly unsure if he should shake my hand, pat me on the shoulder, or not touch me at all. His eyes were all concern. "I'm so sorry to hear what happened. If I'd known it would go like this, I would've never got you involved."

I clapped him on the back. "Sure you would've. It's what people like us do. Besides, it's not like it's the first time I've been in a toss. Usually I see them coming though."

"What's the word?" he asked, ushering me to a small sitting area in what would've been the living room in the home's previous life. "You're up and around; I assume that's good."

"The word is probably not what the doctor would want to hear, but I'm not necessarily sharing that with him. Slow-going, but I'm getting there. My brain is fine; it's just my body that's taking its time catching up."

He gestured to a pair of chairs by a small bistro-type table. "Unless you'd prefer the couch. I'm not sure where you're at, pain-wise."

I pulled out the chair, grunting a little but realizing that if I was going to get through this, I couldn't coddle myself. "I'm getting used to it."

He gave me a questioning look for just a moment and then sat down across from me. "So what brings you here?" he asked, his gaze still clearly assessing my state. "I assume if there was news, you would've just told me on the phone. Or..." He looked down. "Is this the part where you give me the bad news in person?"

"No, no." I reached into my inner jacket pocket, pulling out the list of book club members. "I wanted to have you take a look at something and figured it would be easier if we met up. Besides, the more I'm up and moving, the better off I'll be. Or so I'm told."

He nodded and looked down as I unfolded the sheet of paper and slid it across the table to him. "Do any of these names look familiar to you?" I asked.

He ran a finger down the list, a careful, precautious gesture that I knew had to have come from countless hours doing exceptionally detailed work. "If you're asking if I know them, sure. Hattie's mentioned all of these people before. If you're asking if I can tell you about them, I'll be a little less help there."

"Meaning?"

He glanced at my hand, my ring finger in particular. "Your wife. I assume she has some friends that you know all about but have never really seen or spent time with?"

"Ah. Friends of a friend." I folded my hands, realizing this probably was about to quickly go nowhere.

"Basically, yeah." He shifted in his seat, a hand rubbing at the back of his neck. "I know this is going to sound stupid, but Hattie and I..." He looked off, out through the picture window in the room we were in. "Well, I've told you enough already anyway, so why not go all in? You know how I said the rest of the Heights didn't really care for me? Too blue collar?" He glanced around the small room as if some part of him might've started to believe they were right. "Hattie wasn't exactly throwing me parades when we first started dating, either. I know this is going to sound bad, but for the first nine months or so, I was kind of just waiting for the end to come."

"What gave you that impression?"

"Oh." He rubbed his neck again. "Just things. I would hear about people but never meet them. Whenever she had something to go to, it wasn't a question of if I would attend with her. It was just a statement that she'd be busy until such and such a time. It's probably stupid of me, really. I mean, how long can you date a person who wants you to be their secret boyfriend?"

"Do you think she was dating someone else?"

"Nah." He leaned back. "There wouldn't have been enough hours in the day for it. And look, I know I'm making her sound bad right now, but it was just the way Hattie was. I loved that girl like she was my wife, from day one. I was willing to be patient with her and..." He shrugged. "Let's be honest; you've been there. She was dealing with a whole different set of social rules than the rest of us. I was just giving her the chance to work through that on her own."

I nodded. "Well, after five years, I'd say you must've done quite the job."

He grinned a little, looking down. "I..." He shook his head, almost laughing, though the sound was somewhere between mirth and tears. "I guess I hope I made her happy while I could. Lord knows the rest of the folks up there spent enough time tearing her down."

I leaned across the table and patted him on the shoulder. "That's about all we can shoot for. Pick your person and do the best you can by them." I stood up. "I won't keep you any longer. I'm sure you've got plenty on your agenda for the day. Just wanted to see if any of those names rang a bell."

He shrugged. "They all do to some extent, just not much I can tell you other than gossip. If something comes to me, I'll be sure to give you a call." He glanced back down at the paper before sliding it over to me. "The only one I really heard a lot about was Beatrice. She and Hattie were good friends before she passed."

I nodded. "I'll be in touch. Thanks for your time, Mason."

He walked to the door with me, a kind of tired silence between us. I didn't know what the man was going through, not from personal experience at least, but I knew I was quickly coming to the conclusion that, Hattie or no Hattie, Beatrice or no Beatrice, book club or no book club, Mason Willis was a stand-up individual, and he deserved closure if nothing else.

33

I called Heather on the way back to the office, pleased to find out she was not too far from me, grabbing a coffee with Kate. Keeping CPD, or at least Kate, involved had been something we'd tried to do as much as possible since I'd gone out on my own. I was pleased to see Heather was taking the same stance.

"Meet us at the cafe?" Heather asked.

I turned the car around and made the quick, five-minute drive to where the two women were waiting, leaning toward one another over a bistro table not too terribly different from the one I'd just sat at with Mason. My lower back was reprimanding me for my over-confidence, so I merely leaned down, elbows on the high tabletop, as the women filled me in on what they knew so far.

"It's not a lot," Heather said. "Though, at this point, that may as well be the motto for this case. I mean, pick your trite phrase and I probably heard it today. 'We're all sorry to hear about this loss.' 'She was taken too soon.' Even a 'It's a harsh world that would snuff out her candle.' I felt like I was just listening to people recite Elton John lyrics."

I nodded. "So blandly sympathetic. That seems like the safe bet. I can't say I'm surprised."

Heather shrugged. "These are business people. They know how to say all kinds of things without saying anything at all." She took a sip of her coffee. "I will say this. Collie Newman isn't going to win any popularity contests in that neighborhood."

"What do you mean?"

"I don't know if you remember Caroline Sykes."

"Just the name."

"Well, her husband, Justin? He was the one who seemed to have the most to say when her name came up. I'm not saying he hated her, and he of course would never say that. But if there was one thing he reacted to, it was the mention of Collie Newman. 'Not worth the knock-off sandals she thinks are so trendy,' is the direct quote."

"Wow." I looked out the window. "So two cardinal sins. Poor personality and low-quality footwear."

"Tell him the rest," Kate said, flipping through a small notebook she kept for our particular cases. Her cramped, clear handwriting covered page after page.

"So Justin Sykes was the most vocal," Heather continued. "But there wasn't a single eye that didn't roll when I brought up Collie. I don't know what she's done to make everyone dislike her so much, but she's been incredibly efficient about it. You know how Victoria Blue was choosing to leave the neighborhood? I think if the families could vote someone out, it would be Collie."

"Interesting." I folded my hands, looking down and trying to think in the bustle of the shop. My head was starting to hurt again but I didn't want to dull my thoughts with meds if I could help it. At least not just yet. "Let's have Tim take a look into her a little more closely."

"Already did," Heather said, smiling. "I assumed that's the way you'd go."

"And?"

"And he's puzzled."

I rubbed my temples with my fingers. Puzzled with Tim could mean a lot of things. Usually, in fact, it was a placeholder to let us know he vaguely noticed we had asked him a question, but we were a good few hours from getting an answer. The young man was nothing if not meticulous.

"But not entirely baffled," Heather said, her voice clearly trying to cheer me up.

"Not baffled is good."

"He said she's got a lot of money."

I shook my head, perhaps showing more exasperation than I intended.

"I know that's sort of a given," she said quickly. "But he's not sure where it's coming from."

I looked up at her, my interest piqued. "How so?"

"He was still working on it when I left, and it may be nothing at all. But you know how part of the Heights is being a Stepford Wife and part of the Heights is being a quote/unquote business tycoon? Collie is neither."

"So where's it coming from?"

She tucked her hair behind her ear. "As far as he's been able to see so far, it's not from a sugar daddy, not that she'd need one. And he thinks she isn't doing anything illegal, but that was the part he said was puzzling."

"Parents alive?"

"No. Deceased ten years ago."

"Ah." I rubbed my eyes with my hand. Everything about today, from the choice to take a run on forward, had not been in my best interest. "So we're looking at inheritance?"

She bobbed her head back and forth, Heather's typical

237

unsure response. "It could be. I'll let you know when Tim knows more. He seemed to think it seemed strange, but that's really all I know."

I glanced over at Kate. Nine times out of ten, she would've thrown in a simple Occam's Razor-type solution here. Instead, she shrugged. "Till we have more information, she might just be a woman who is good with money. Those do exist, you know."

I grinned despite my fatigue. "I've heard rumors."

"We were talking about going to visit Collie ourselves," Heather said. "Since you're here, you wanna tag along?"

I didn't love the idea of being a third wheel, but I loved the idea of missing out on the conversation with Collie even less. I held my hands out, palms up. "Why not?"

34

I sat in the backseat as Kate drove, thankful she had brought her own car instead of the CPD issue. She and Heather chatted quietly in the front two seats, obviously trying to not disturb me, but even more obviously trying to not seem like they were hoping to not disturb me. I leaned back in the seat, my eyes closed, telling myself again that sooner or later, I'd be over this. I would heal. This would end. And I'd chosen these people, not necessarily because I thought they'd take care of me, but perhaps subconsciously because I knew they would when I truly needed it.

When Kate pulled up to Collie's house, the place looked familiar. Or at least slightly. Having been in and out of the neighborhood a few times, and having seen the same pillars and brick and sculpted hedges, it was a little hard to tell. This may have been one of the doors I knocked on before the attack, but it didn't seem like one I knew much about. Maybe one of the homes who'd not answered, hiding behind their curtains as if we couldn't all see their shadows dancing in the living room light?

Heather came to my rescue, opening the door for me. "You said no one was here last time." For a moment, it looked like she was going to hold out a hand to help me stand, but thought better of it. "Does that ring a bell?"

"It looks familiar," I said. "But they all do at this point."

She gave me a curt nod, glanced at Kate, and the three of us walked to the front door. Maybe I'd slept on the ride after all, but the two women seemed to have had much more conversation about me than I'd first realized. I needed to set them at ease. I cleared my throat, squared my shoulders, and stood up straight. We needed to do this right, and a half-busted private eye wasn't going to help things.

A moment after Kate pressed the bell, Collie Newman opened the door. Her dog-like expression went rapidly from confusion to a dawning understanding.

"The... investigators? I'm not sure what the appropriate term is. I'm sorry. But I've heard you've been in the area."

"Yes, ma'am," Heather said. "Investigators will do. We just wanted to ask you a few questions about what's been happening in the neighborhood the last few weeks."

I admired the move. Kate could've never lied about her real job, but by letting Heather take the lead, she was more than welcome to hang back and observe, something she excelled at more than almost anyone I'd ever worked with.

"I don't mean to be curt," Collie said, ushering us into a sitting room that was either one of multiple living areas or what might be considered an extravagant foyer, "but I'm sure you all have a lot of ground to cover. I apologize for not being available the first time you came around."

She looked down at her hands, apparently realizing the admission she'd just made, then quickly recovered. "Tea? Coffee? I just got a shipment of the loveliest beans from Guatemala."

"We're fine," Heather said. "Thank you, though. We just wanted to ask a few questions and we'll be out of your hair. I understand you work from home and I'm sure your time is valuable."

Collie hesitated again. "You do your homework, I see." She laughed, a kind of awkward, uncertain sound. "Maybe you know everything I have to say already."

I settled into a highbacked chair, Heather and Kate taking seats on a couch to my left and Collie perching herself—there was really no other word for it—on the edge of a seat matching my own to the far side of the fireplace.

"We're just trying to get an understanding of what's been happening here," Kate said. Her tone was a little too cop, but at the same time, Collie seemed like a woman who might need firm, straightforward dialogue. If nothing else, it might keep her slipping up.

Collie looked down at her hands again and shook her head. "It's been a bad few weeks, a bad few months, really."

I was surprised to see her wipe an eye with the back of her hand. She was either an amazing con-woman, or sincerely emotional over the thought of what had been happening.

"Beatrice and Hattie," Heather started.

"Lovely girls," Collie said quickly. "Hattie and I hadn't been friends terribly long, but Beatrice..." She looked up. "I suppose you all know, but this isn't an easy place to live. I know that sounds spoiled, like I'm complaining about having what everyone wants, but it can be... isolating. Especially if you're a woman who lives on her own. I know the gossip started flying as soon as my moving vans pulled in, probably before that even. But Beatrice... she was a kind soul. She was the first friend I made when I moved here and the one who actively tried to make me feel welcome." She paused. "I don't know where any of you live, but I assume you wave to your neighbors when you see them?"

Heather nodded.

"Here, that's a thing you have to earn." She sighed, rubbing her palms on her pant legs. "This is a safe place, or at least it used to be. But being here doesn't in any way guarantee that you'll be happy. It's kind of like a beautiful prison."

"We've been hearing that," I said, breaking into the conversation. "So why not get out?"

She sighed, her shoulder sagging. "Because I had Bea, and Hattie. We aren't all terrible people, despite what others might say. We're just... cautious." She thought about the word. "Maybe not cautious. Vulnerable feels more correct. This place," she said and gestured around the room, the house, the neighborhood, "it's built on very fragile egos."

I nodded. "I know the type."

She looked at me, her eyes almost subconsciously going from my jacket to my shirt, my pants, my shoes. It was an assessment that had become almost second nature to her. "I believe you do."

"We just want to know a little more about Hattie," Kate broke in. "We've been hearing varying stories, in particular with regard to her drinking."

Collie nodded again and took her gaze off my shoes. No doubt she'd noted the designer name that was nowhere visible, but obvious to those with the right eye. "Hattie was having a tough time adjusting," she said after a moment. "Her... um, friend. The young man?"

"Mason?" I prompted.

"The plumber, or whatever he was," she said. "He never seemed to want to be a part of her life here. Maybe it was sour grapes. Maybe it was something else entirely. I wouldn't put it past the neighbors to have made him feel unwelcome. But she struggled with sort of... almost living a double life? She drank, yes, but that wasn't entirely because of him. It wasn't entirely because of any of the rest of the folks here." She glanced at the hall door, toward the kitchen. I realized Hattie might not be the only one with a drinking problem.

"Her parents," Collie began again, pulling her eyes back to the room. "They were always the main problem. At least from what she told me. The man..." She looked at me and I almost believed the questioning look on her face.

"Mason?"

"Yes, Mason. He was a stressor, to be sure. But Hattie had so many things. There wasn't really a safe space for the poor thing. Alcohol is an easy way to make yourself feel like you've got things under control."

"To a point," I said. "But it's obviously also an easy way to drown in this neighborhood."

Before she could respond to my tired jab, Kate spoke up again. "Does the name Jacobi Milton mean anything to you?"

"I..." She looked up at the ceiling, a gesture that I never quite trust. Half the time it's genuine thought; the other half it's bad acting. "The man with the motorcycle?"

I shot Kate a glance. I wasn't sure how much she and Heather and the rest of the team had shared. I hadn't even seen the news, though I doubted anyone in the Heights would've wanted a report on how unsafe their little world was becoming.

"That's the one," Kate said, keeping her tone neutral.

"I heard he had climbed over the wall," Collie said. "Causing some kind of ruckus." She glanced at the yellowing bruises on my face. "Oh, my dear. Did you...?"

"We're just trying to put the pieces together," I said. "No need for concern."

"Well, no. I certainly don't know anything about that. I'm terribly sorry for... whatever happened."

"The worst of it's over," Kate said. "Mr. Milton has been spending his evenings in the county jail."

"What?" Collie jerked forward.

243

"We brought him in not long after Mr. Starke was attacked."

"I don't see the point in that."

I let my gaze settle on Collie Newman, completely unconcerned that she could see me watching her.

"I just mean..." She held up her hands. "He's not our type. If you want to arrest him, go right ahead. But I just don't want you thinking that's how we live up here."

I glanced at Heather and could tell by her expression she was soaking up every detail for discussion later. "We wouldn't dream of it," she said. Then, surprising me, Heather stood up. "And we appreciate your time. If we have any more questions, we might follow up with you. If that's okay."

Collie stood, looking equal parts relieved and concerned. "Of course. If you could call beforehand, it might make things easier on all of us, but..." she trailed off. "We all have jobs to do."

I thanked her for her time and Kate shook her hand, and before we knew it, we were back out on the front porch, taking the cobbled walkway down to where we'd parked by the curb.

"Well, *that* was something," Heather started.

I turned, putting a hand on her shoulder as a young lady jogged down the sidewalk toward us. "Not exactly a poker face, was it?"

Kate shook her head. "I... *ow!*" She stumbled forward as the young woman ran into her. Heather and I both reached out to break her fall.

The runner stumbled a few steps, caught her balance, and waved apologetically before picking the pace back up and heading down the sidewalk.

"Not exactly the most welcoming place indeed," Heather said. "You all right?"

Kate gave her an odd look and then walked around to the driver's side of the car, opened the door, and climbed in. Heather looked at me.

"Only one way to find out," I said, realizing that we were both suddenly very curious about whether that had been an accident or not.

"You know who that was, don't you?" she asked, her door open.

I shook my head.

"Book club," was her only response. She climbed in the car and I could see her stare go immediately to Kate. With a twinge in my back, I did the same.

"Fortuitous?" I asked, trying to buckle my seatbelt without making it too obvious how much it hurt.

Kate held up a small bit of paper. A time and place were scribbled across the front. "Fortuitous that she didn't hit me hard; enough for her to drop this," she said. "Apparently, our jogger would like to have a chat."

I nodded. Why not?

35

HEATHER TYPED THE MEETING ADDRESS INTO HER PHONE while Kate nonchalantly pulled out from the curb and headed us out of the neighborhood.

"It's still about an hour till I, or we, or whoever is supposed to meet up," she said. "If it's all the same to you, I wouldn't mind bringing Samson along on this one."

I smiled, looking out the window. "Why not? He's the best partner I've ever come across."

"Hey," she said, glancing at me in the rearview mirror.

"What?" I said, pulling out my phone. "I never saw you sniff out a kidnap victim or latch onto somebody's leg, so..." I shrugged.

"Fair," she replied.

I typed out a text to Amanda, letting her know things had taken an unexpected twist and then settled back in my seat. I knew what was coming before Heather even said it.

"We can run you home." She twisted around in her seat. "I'm not sure if this woman wants all of us there, or just Kate, or what. But..." She looked me up and down. "Maybe you've put in a solid day, all things considered."

"Maybe," I said, "but I'm not done yet." I adjusted myself in the seat, trying to find a position that didn't make more than two parts of my broken body scream at me. "We all can agree that Collie Newman was something out of the ordinary, though, correct?"

I saw Heather take a breath and slowly let it out. She knew I was trying to deflect. In all honesty, she probably knew I needed to deflect. But it didn't make her like it any more than she had to.

"Lots going on there," Kate said, flicking the turn signal and pulling back out onto one of the main, more middle-class roads. "What's your take?"

I shrugged. "Genuine enough at first, then a little shady, then what seemed to be annoyed."

"I got that same feeling," Kate said. "We were all the best of friends until Jacobi came up. Then she couldn't get us out of there fast enough."

"Surely you don't think..." Heather started.

I saw Kate hold out a hand, palm up. "She certainly didn't seem like a person who'd never heard the name. As soon as she found out he was in county, her whole persona changed. If she was wanting a safe neighborhood for her and her ilk, you'd think she'd be doing cartwheels to find out we'd gotten someone who wasn't 'their type' off the streets."

Heather looked out the window for a moment, chewing her bottom lip. "I know I'm being the devil's advocate here, but do you think it could be as simple as that? As in this being a thing about 'their type'? She said she didn't feel welcome there. Maybe she's in a conundrum."

"Meaning?" Kate asked.

"On the one hand, Collie doesn't want a bad element coming into the neighborhood. They've had two at least mildly suspicious deaths and now there are bikers climbing over the walls. She could just be genuinely scared."

"But on the other hand?"

"On the other hand, maybe she realizes she's being just as snippy and cold as the rest of the people were when she moved in. Granted, it's not exactly parallel situations, but it's not entirely outlandish. She said it's hard to have money." She patted her phone on her thigh. "Maybe we're not realizing how much of having money comes down to image. You can be as rich as you want, but it won't make people like you."

"Not all the people, anyway," Kate said. She pulled up to a light and then turned right, heading us toward her house. "But at a certain point, you have to admit that it doesn't matter if people like you or not. You can just buy different friends. Fly to Europe and hang out with folks there. I get where you're coming from, but I don't think I'm too interested in what Collie Newman was trying to sell."

"So you think she knows more than she told us?"

"I think they all do," Kate said. "Maybe though." She held the paper up. "One of them is about to start talking."

Just then, my phone started to buzz in my hand. I saw Kate flick her eyes up to the rearview again.

"Hey, Amanda," I said, my voice sounding tired even to my own ears.

"Hey, honey," her tone was cautious, concerned. "How're you holding up?"

"Oh, been better, been worse." I tried to sound light-hearted, not wanting to put any more worry in her mind than I was sure she already had. "Everything okay at home?"

"Yes, yeah." I could almost see her putting a thumbnail up to her mouth and then pulling it back. It was a nervous habit she'd spent years trying to get rid of, but one that refused to budge. "I talked to the doctor today."

"And?"

"And... well." She sighed. I could tell by the tone in her

voice she was debating on how exactly to phrase what she was about to say. "He didn't say you couldn't be at work. But he said you needed to take it easy. He stressed that. I suppose it won't make a lot of difference to you, but I think he was implying easy like half-days, not easy like only a few foot chases."

I laughed a little, a hand going to my ribs immediately. "I'm with Kate and Heather right now. But if that doesn't reassure you, we're just pulling in to pick up Samson. If anyone needs being chased, I'm sure he can handle it."

I heard a slight laugh from her end of the phone, a reassuring sound. She might not completely believe I'd let Samson take the brunt of the work. I didn't entirely believe it either. But she was at least trying to be on my side. "You're not going to a biker place again, are you?"

"I'm actually not sure."

I leaned forward and tapped Heather on the shoulder, gesturing toward her phone. She held it up so I could see the screen and I shook my head.

"Not a biker place," I said to Amanda. "At least, not one I've ever heard of. Could be better, could be worse. But I promise I'll be safe. The only thing you need to worry about with this meetup is me running out of patience."

She laughed again. The sound was tired. I could hear Jade in the background, banging away on one of her multi-sensory toys. I needed to make this up to Amanda one way or another, and soon. The woman was a rock, but there was also no need to push her farther than I needed to.

"If anything comes up; anything at all," I said. "I give you my word I'll hang back. With any luck, this will be short and sweet."

"Home in time for dinner?"

I glanced at my watch. "Home in time for putting Jade to bed. Let's keep things loose."

"All right." The reluctance in her words was almost palpable. "Be safe."

"I will," I said. "I'll talk to you soon."

We said our goodbyes and I ended the call just as Kate pulled into her driveway. As she went inside to grab Samson, Heather turned around in the seat to look back at me.

"You know she made me promise to keep an eye on you, right?" she asked.

"I would expect nothing less."

"All right." She twisted around again so she was facing forward. "Don't make a liar out of me."

"Wouldn't dream of it."

36

"WELL, SAMSON," KATE SAID AS SHE PARKED HER CAR. "Maybe you'll be on car guard duty." She glanced over at Heather. "This is the place?"

I saw Heather shrug and show her the cell phone screen. "Addresses match."

"Hm."

We were in front of a nondescript downtown business. The sign out front said it was a law office, but the size, and even more so, the empty parking lot, made me wonder as well. "What's the internet say?"

"Nel Modesto," Heather read, scrolling down with a flick of her finger. "Mostly civil suits. Been around here a few years. Hang on..." She tapped the screen. "Okay. Miss Modesto has been around here a few years, but she's been around the courts for a while. Not too shabby, from what I'm seeing." She glanced up at the building. "Although I imagine this place didn't come cheap either."

I reached over and petted the German Shepherd sitting beside me, his tongue lolling out.

"Oh," Heather said. "Now I see."

"What?" Kate asked.

Heather leaned over, holding the phone up again for her to see. "That address ring a bell?"

Kate whistled. "The plot thickens."

"Indeed."

"Care to fill me in?" I asked. But before either could answer, a black Mercedes pulled into the spot beside us. Almost before it had stopped moving, a young, athletic woman stepped out, exuding confidence not just in the jogging attire she was still wearing, but in the very way she held her body. She walked boldly up to the car, making a cranking gesture with her hand. Heather hit the button and rolled her window down.

"We need to make this quick," the woman said, pulling her hair back to adjust her ponytail. "Come on inside."

The three of us climbed out of the car and followed her up to the door. She had a ring of keys in one hand and a swipe card in the other. Without the slightest hesitation, she got us into the building, deactivated the alarm, and led us down the hall to an immaculate office.

"I assume you've already figured out who I am," she said, turning the large leather seat behind the desk to face us. Her posture was ramrod straight and her eyes said there was no place for fooling about in this office.

"Nel Modesto," I said. "Though that doesn't give us a lot to go on."

"I'll save you the research," she said, folding her hands on her desk. "You're Mr. Starke. Miss Stillwell. Captain Gazzara. I apologize for not getting in touch sooner. And I very much apologize for the incident that happened a few nights ago. I trust you're recuperating."

I nodded. Something about her tone made the last few words a statement, not a question. It was as if she didn't have time for me to be doing anything else.

"If I'd foreseen something like that, I would've reached out earlier. But some things are beyond even my reach."

"Your reach being what, exactly?" I asked. "You seem to know us, or at least of us." I glanced around, my hands out. "Forgive me for saying so, but I've never heard of this place. None of us have. Which..." I glanced over at Kate and Heather, "is a bit of an anomaly, considering what we do for a living."

"I do my best to stay out of the way of your kind," she said, steepling her fingers. "It's nothing against what you do. In fact, over the last few years, I imagine our paths have been more similar than either of us realized. But legal cases such as you specialize in can get muddy. They drag on. Clients are... not always prepared to fulfill their end of the agreements."

"And so you prefer...?" Heather started.

"I prefer keeping things moving forward and above board. Civil suits are simpler. We can typically settle things amicably, or if not, we settle them the best way we can. But if there's no threat of handcuffs, I find people seem to keep their cool a little easier."

"So why are we here?" Kate asked. "Obviously this wasn't an accident."

"So very few things are." The woman leaned back and opened a small mini-fridge hidden in the shelving behind her. She cracked open a bottle of water, one of the more expensive brands, I noticed, and took a long swallow. Almost as an afterthought, she gestured toward the others, lined up like soldiers in the little cooler.

"No, thank you," I said, answering for all of us. "You seem to be in a hurry and we aren't keen on wasting our time either. So, as Captain Gazzara asked, why bring us in?"

Nel Modesto held up a finger and took another swallow of her water, then recapped the bottle and set it on a leather coaster on her desk. "One, because things are clearly getting out of hand. Your encounter with the..." she said and waved a hand in the air, "the biker. Jacobi something. That in and of itself makes the severity of the situation clear. Two, because this is getting outside my wheelhouse. As I said, I primarily focus on civil suits, not this type of thing. Once I got a good view of exactly what was happening, I knew I needed to bring law enforcement in. The three of you were just a happy coincidence."

"And what is it that's happening?" Kate asked. She was leaned back in her chair, eyebrows up. It was a posture I knew well. Stories were never hard to come by at the police station; true ones were something of a rare breed.

"Quite a bit, from what I've been able to piece together." Nel leaned back in her chair, the fact that she was in leggings and a sports bra apparently phasing her not in the slightest. "I moved to the Heights about five years ago. I'll be moving out shortly. But I wanted, needed, perhaps, to set a few things straight before I did so. When I saw you heading to Collie Newman's house today, I felt like the time might have presented itself."

"So it is something to do with the book club?" Heather asked, looking over at me.

"The book club?" Nel shook her head. "No. Well, not entirely. The book club is just a book club. I can't promise you they actually read any of the books. Most of the time it seems like an excuse to get a little tipsy in the afternoon."

Heather snapped her fingers. "That's why your name seemed familiar."

"Oh, yes." Nel looked at her. "I've been attending almost since the day I moved in. One has to keep up appearances and such."

"But Collie runs the show there, doesn't she?"

Nel nodded. "Of course. Collie likes to run the show wherever she is. Unfortunately, the one person Collie can't seem to keep in check is herself."

"Back up." Kate held up her hand. "If this is something criminal, I'm going to need it from the beginning."

Miss Modesto turned her gaze to Kate, apparently deciding that, at this juncture, the only person with an actual badge was the one to talk to.

"Given the fact that I am due at said book club shortly, we're going to have to keep this brief," she said. "But this should be sufficient for you to follow up on." She cleared her throat, pulling at her ponytail again. "Collie Newman is nothing more than a con artist. It sounds glitzy, or maybe it sounds ridiculous, whichever way you want to take it. But it should certainly not sound surprising. No matter how good of a CPA she is, no matter how much money her parents left her in their will, she shouldn't logically be living in the Heights. Which begs the logical question; how is she there? The short answer is embezzlement."

I raised an eyebrow. "That's a little more than skimming off the top if you're going to buy a house in your neighborhood."

"It's a tech company." Nel waved a hand in the air. "I'm sure you've been around the type. And don't get me wrong, I've got no problem with the little computer whiz kids. But sometimes their focus seems to shift a bit too far toward creating their programs and not enough toward running their business."

I couldn't help but think of Tim. I wasn't even entirely sure he knew what his yearly salary was. It wouldn't be the hardest thing in the world for someone to dip into his account without him knowing it.

"And how exactly did you come up with this theory?" Kate asked, her tone intrigued but cautious.

Nel laughed. "I didn't. She told us."

"What?" Heather leaned forward.

"A little tipsy in the afternoon isn't always Collie's friend. Like I said, the only person she can't keep in check is herself. I don't know if she didn't eat, if she just had a little more than she intended, but she told us herself. Seemed rather proud. Like it was just a big joke."

Kate looked at me. "That's enough to bring her in."

I nodded. "But it's not what we're after." I turned toward Nel. "You've been there for some time now. What do you know about Beatrice Loftis?"

Nel nodded, a small smile coming to her lips. "I was hoping you were connecting the dots as well. Beatrice and Collie were never the best of friends. Tolerant of one another would probably be the best way to put it. Big personalities, high self-confidence. Imagine two female lions. One of them is always going to be trying to outdo the other. Beatrice unfortunately tipped her hand."

"Meaning?"

"Meaning she made it a little too clear that she remembered what Collie had told us about her income. Meaning she pulled no punches in letting Collie know that all it would take was one anonymous phone call and the cops would be at her door and poring over her financial records."

I thought for a moment. It made sense, at least superficially. "But Beatrice died from diving into the shallow end," I said. "I'm not sure how Collie could convince her to do that, no matter how persuasive she is."

"Dove?" Nel asked, her eyebrows up. "Or got pushed? I assume you saw the tox report. The amount of alcohol in her would've killed a horse. For all we know she could've just fallen. Collie loves to be the bartender when we get together. Who knows what kind of concoction she cooked up for poor Bea."

"And the same thing happened to Hattie?" Heather asked.

Nel sat quietly for a moment. It was a confident gesture, one that conversely instilled my own confidence in her. She was used to thinking things through, speaking only when she'd considered her words. "When it comes to Hattie," she said finally, "I've only heard rumors. Hints of gossip. Most of the women in the book club know Collie's bad news, but Collie's got that golden tongue. You all met her. I'm sure her reactions were practically perfect."

"Almost," I said. "But everyone has their flaws."

She nodded and glanced at her watch. "I'm going to have to go before I'm late for the club. Take all of this with a grain of salt, but it's the theory I've been working on. The whispers are that Collie was trying to get Hattie to help her clean some money. Some of the girls even say Hattie was second choice, and Victoria Blue was initially approached, but both turned Collie down."

"Yet Victoria lived to tell the tale," Heather said, glancing at me.

"Only because that woman is smart enough to plan ahead. She keeps to herself, obviously, but it's gotten even more extreme over the last year or so. If I had to guess, I'd say it's why she's getting out of the Heights."

"So she laid low, reduced the opportunities for Collie to do her usual thing, and then, assuming this is a situation where the longer the money sits, the more likely someone will find out about it, Collie back-burnered Victoria and moved on to Hattie. Unfortunately," Kate concluded, "Hattie didn't have the good sense or wherewithal to keep Collie at arm's length."

"That's where I'm at with it," Nel said. She stood up from her chair, subtly ending the meeting. "As for what happened to you." She looked at me. "I'd say you got a taste. Bringing in an outsider isn't exactly Collie's style. But, like I said, she isn't a stupid woman, and she adapts well. Maybe she knew you were going to be a problem but unlikely to show up at a backyard barbeque."

I nodded. It made sense. As the three of us stood up to leave, Nel opened a lower drawer on her desk and pulled out a manila folder. "This is everything I've gathered so far. I don't know if it will help or not, but it will keep you from reinventing the wheel. And probably save you a lot of doors closing in your faces."

Heather reached over and took the file from her. "Thank you. Sincerely."

Nel gave her a curt nod. "We're all on the same team here. And don't forget, for the time being, I'm only a few houses away from Collie Newman. I have a vested interest in this as well."

37

WHEN WE LEFT NEL MODESTO'S OFFICE, WE HEADED straight for the police department. I called Jacque and told her to bring anyone she could and meet us there as well. Kate was already on the phone with Sergeant Corbin Russell, her partner.

We pulled in a few minutes later, Samson hopping out and tagging along, his tail wagging. The dog was as much a part of the police force as any of the other cops. And it didn't hurt he was constantly lavished with attention when he wandered freely around the station.

Kate led us to a small meeting room, briefing Corbin on what Nel had told us, and just as she was winding up, Jacque and TJ walked in as well.

"Tim was conked out at his desk," Jacque said. "Figured he must need the rest and, well, it wouldn't hurt if we had someone in front of the computer if we need it."

"We may," I said, running quickly through what we had just learned. As I talked, I watched Corbin. The man was one of the most logical I've ever met. It was a hard thing for a person in his position and I appreciated his ability to always make the tough call. The wheels in his mind were clearly already turning and as I finished up, I looked across the table at him.

"You're thinking it's circumstantial, aren't you?"

He sighed, folding his hands on the table in front of him. "You know it is, Harry. And you know what kind of a bind that puts us in. How many times have you been completely sure someone committed a crime, but been unable to prove it beyond the proverbial shadow of a doubt? Everything in here," he said and gestured toward the file, "makes sense to you and me, but we have to think like a jury here. There's no sense in dragging this woman into court only to have her walk back out even more confident than she already is."

Heather started to speak up and then held back. I knew what she was thinking as well, that this case was obvious, that eventually enough coincidences became a kind of proof in themselves. But it was going to be a tall order to sit down with twelve people who've never been to the Heights, probably envied those who did get to live there, that there was anything other than jealousy and glamour surrounding the place. After all, why would a woman as well off as Collie Newman need to kill anyone? She could probably just buy whatever she needed. The fact that one of those purchases was more than likely an attack on me was entirely outlandish, but it was flimsy.

We spent the next hour coming at the case from every angle we could, yet continuously coming up against the fact that, while Nel had done some solid research and had put together a more than intriguing story, at the end of the day, that's all it was. Just a complicated set of intrigues that sounded enticing but could also be nothing more than misunderstandings or smoke and mirrors.

"I know we're all thinking it." Corbin leaned back in his chair, pushing the pages toward the middle of the table. "But I guess I'll be the one to say it. Any lawyer worth his or her salt would rip this thing to shreds in no time. If they were really feeling irritated, we might be looking at a libel suit. This Modesto woman likely knows that as well as we do, which is why she's passing the buck to us, so to speak."

"So we just hang back and wait for Collie Newman to do something else?" Jacque said, her annoyance clear in her voice. "We've got solid reasons to think she's already killed two women. I'm not too keen on waiting for the third, or fourth, or however many it takes before someone basically catches her in the act."

Corbin nodded, his eyes sympathetic. "I understand your frustration. And just because I'm not reacting as strongly, please don't think I'm not feeling the same way. But..." He held his hands out, palms up. "We don't have a lot of choices here. Two rich women got drunk and fell into their pools. I don't know about you, but if that's what a lawyer argues, I'd be tempted to believe it. It's not unreasonable."

Jacque folded her arms and sat back. She knew he was right; we all did. But it didn't take the sting out of it. Just then my phone started to buzz in my pocket. I assumed it was Amanda checking in. The day was winding down already and I should've been in touch with her by now. To my surprise, the caller ID said Mason Willis.

"What can I do for you, Mason?" I asked, stepping to a corner of the small room to try and maintain a bit of privacy.

"I'm not sure..." His voice was strange, a mix of strong emotion tempered with what was maybe concern, or even embarrassment. I knew the tone well. I'd heard it more than enough times when I was on the force and twice as often once I'd opened my own detective agency. He was worried something had happened, but he was equally worried he was making the wrong choice by calling the authorities.

"Tell me what's on your mind," I said. "I'll let you know if we need to do something about it."

He sighed, gathering himself, trying to keep his emotions in check. "All right. I'm at Hattie's right now. I came over to gather up a few of her things and some of the stuff I'd left here. Nothing important really... sentimental things. I don't know what's going to happen with the place, but I figured her folks will eventually sell everything they can."

"Right," I said, unsure of where this was going. "Nothing wrong with that. As long as it's within reason."

"Yeah, no. I mean, I know. It's nothing of any value really. Letters, photos. Stuff you couldn't sell and no one would really want."

"Okay," I tried to coax him forward. My head was starting to hurt again and this day was dragging on much longer than I needed it to.

"The thing is, since I'm here, I opened some of the windows. Kind of bring in some fresh air and... well, it sounds like there's something going on at Collie Newman's place."

"What?" I held up a hand, gesturing for the others in the room to quiet down for a moment. "I'm going to put you on speaker, all right?"

"Sure. Whatever you need to do."

I set the phone in the middle of the table, speaking clearly. "Mason, I have some of my team here, whom you've met. We're also with two members of the Chattanooga PD. That's nothing for you to worry about, but I wanted you to be aware."

"Oh... look, Mr. Starke, I'm not even sure this is anything."

I knew the presence of police made most people second-guess or clam up, but he deserved to know. "Just tell us what's concerning you. I trust everyone in this room, both for intellect and discretion."

"Well..."

For a moment, I thought I was going to lose him.

"Do it for Hattie," Heather spoke up.

Mason sighed again and began speaking. "Well, everyone, I was telling Mr. Starke I came over to Hattie's to get a few things. Nothing important really. But while I was here, I opened the windows. A place like this needs to breathe just like any other home. You'd be surprised how often..." I could practically see him shake his head through the phone, trying to stay on track. "The point is, there's a lot of yelling going on over at Collie Newman's place. I wasn't eavesdropping or anything, but it's kind of hard to not hear it, you know? Anyway." He took a deep breath. "Someone keeps talking about a spiked drink, and I guess maybe I'm jumping to conclusions, but do you think that's what happened to Hattie?"

Before I could even reply, chairs were scooting back from the table as everyone came to the same conclusion.

"Mason," I said. "We don't know anything for sure, but you did the right thing by calling. Stay where you are. Keep your head down. We're on our way."

I got off the phone with him and looked at Jacque. "Maybe we won't have to wait as long as you thought."

"Let's just get there before the next person ends up in the pool," she said.

38

KATE, CORBIN AND SAMSON RAN OUT TO A CRUISER WHILE the rest of my team and I headed for Jacque's car. "I'll call in backup," Kate said, pulling open the door to her vehicle.

"No sirens," I yelled back. "The last thing we need is to tip anybody off."

She nodded, already reaching down for the radio in her car.

As we tore out of the lot, doing our best to keep up with Kate and hopefully avoid a collision on the way, Heather leaned forward between the seats.

"You remember what Nel said?" she asked.

I nodded. "She had to get going to make it to the book club."

"Exactly." Her tone was pensive. "Who knows what we could be walking into?"

"I'm more concerned about what we walk out with," Jacque said, effortlessly navigating the vehicle through the downtown traffic.

It was a quiet ride out to the Heights, each of us thinking his or her own thoughts. Thankfully, the security guard didn't give Kate a moment's flack and she must've told him we were all together, because he waved Jacque through without even having her roll down the window.

"When we get there," I said, "we're going to fan out. I want one of you to hang back and wait for the backup. One of you can go with Corbin and I'll stick with Kate. Don't forget that we're in a police situation now. Kate will give us all the slack she can, but they're running the show, so nobody does anything without an officer at their side."

The team nodded. It was standard operating procedure and I knew it was likely pointless to reiterate it to them, especially to people as field-hardened as they were. But the repetition was what made it work. The more predictable things were, the more we all knew precisely what we needed to do, the less likely it was something would go off the rails. It was especially important when we were racing toward a situation we didn't fully understand.

"And remember, this might be nothing," I said, climbing out of the car and flagging Kate down.

"Doesn't sound like nothing," Jacque said.

She was right. As was Mason. You didn't have to try to eavesdrop to hear what was going on at Collie Newman's house. Understanding the words, though, was an entirely different situation.

"That's Nel," Heather said, looking as if she were about to dart across the lawn.

I held up a hand, both to settle her nerves and in hopes of getting a better idea of the situation by what was being said. Unfortunately, other than the fact that it did indeed sound like the woman we'd met so recently, that was about as clear an understanding as I could get.

"She sounds *hammered*," Heather said, her voice low. "Have we even been gone long enough for someone to get that drunk?"

I could hear a waver in Heather's voice. Something about this case was becoming more and more personal for her, so I pointed to Jacque instead. "You go with Corbin. You two." I motioned to Heather and TJ, specifically pairing them. "Wait for the backup."

Before Heather could protest, I ran across the front lawn to Kate, who had Samson on a short leash. Out of my peripheral vision, I could just see TJ putting a hand on Heather's elbow. The man wasn't much of a talker, and outside of "gruff" I couldn't think of an emotion I'd ever seen him show. But he wasn't holding her back. He was just giving that one touch to keep her grounded. I knew they'd be fine.

"Around back?" I asked as I approached Kate, keeping my voice low, although the odds of anyone hearing a normal conversation over the yelling were pretty low.

She nodded and we slipped around the side of the mansion, making our way quietly along the wooden fence that separated Collie's property from the others. Collie's property, I thought, and Collie's pool. But this would be pure foolishness, committing a crime literally in your own backyard. But, I'd seen more ridiculous things than that.

We crept up toward a gate in the fence and I pressed against it gently, trying to get a view through the small space between the wooden slats. The angle was tight, but I could see what I needed to. It was indeed a very intoxicated Nel Modesto wavering on her feet as she pointed a finger at Collie Newman, apparently trying to both make her incoherent, slurred speech prove a point, and likely, I assumed after my recent encounter with hospital-grade painkillers, just trying to stay conscious.

Collie, for her part, stood with a hand to her chest. Her voice was low, not entirely unsympathetic, but obviously more concerned about the scene Nel was making than anything else.

She wanted Nel quiet; that was her only concern. Collie's eyes were wide, and with the southern belle look of shock she was trying to emote, I couldn't help but dislike the woman. Even down to the hand placement, it was the classic and usually least reliable posture evoked to try and convince someone of your innocence.

I shifted, trying to get a better angle on the scene. There weren't any other voices, but if this was a book club meeting gone awry, it seemed unlikely that there wouldn't be at least a few other people present. I pressed a little harder on the gate, the latch catching on the inside. Just off to the left I could make out three other figures. I wracked my tired brain for the names.

"Five," I whispered to Kate, scooting back so she could look through the gap in the wood. "Collie and Nel and... Franny, Caroline..." I knew the names. Who was the other? "Marilyn," I said finally.

"Last names?" Kate whispered.

"We'll get them later."

Just then, the unmistakable splash of a body hitting water broke through the stillness. Without thinking, without feeling my aching ribs or tired body, the heel of my shoe connected with the gate just above the handle, popping the latch off the other side as if it were connected with nothing more than Styrofoam. I stepped back as Kate and Samson rushed in, then me, the movements so practiced, so automatic that none of us had to think. We were running on pure training and adrenaline.

I knew who was there, at least from what I'd seen through the crack in the gate. Kate was already moving toward the pool's owner, Collie Newman, as my eyes scanned the rest of the yard for threats. There were a hundred places a person could hunker down back there, but in the back of my mind, I knew if there was another assailant, either Kate or Samson would take care of them, or I'd just have to get to it myself. My eyes focused on the only important thing as far as I was concerned. And that was Nel Modesto, still dressed in her jogging clothes and floating face-down in the far side of the almost laughably large pool.

I dove in, just the slightest memory of Beatrice Loftis in my head. I angled myself shallow, skimming the surface so as to protect my own skull and to cover as much ground as possible in the leap. Her arms were out, floating almost lazily just above the surface. The water was clear though. No blood.

With just a few strokes I'd reached her unconscious form and begun pulling her to the edge of the pool. The screeches of the women and the authoritative sound of Kate's voice brought the others running, but I had no concern for that until I saw a familiar hand reach down.

Jacque was at the side of the pool, helping me pull Nel up onto the stamped concrete. Before I could even extricate myself, Jacque was on her knees, breathing into Nel's mouth. It had only been a second, but it doesn't take long to aspirate.

As I pulled myself up out of the water, soaking and feeling a burning in my ribs that I knew would follow me for the next few days, two pairs of hands got me under my arms and jerked me out of the water. Heather and TJ stood over me and, as I heard Nel cough, spit up, and take a deep dragging breath, I was finally able to assess the scene.

Kate had Collie in cuffs already, the woman still bearing her wide-eyed "who, me?" expression. The backup officers, led by Corbin, were separating the other three women from one another, pulling them to different corners of the yard. It was going to be a long night for these ladies, I knew, but odds were, other than witness statements, they'd be back in their plush beds before sunrise.

I lolled my head to the side. Jacque was helping Nel up to

her hands and knees, a few strings of spittle and pool water still clinging to the lawyer's lips. Jacque looked over at me, her gaze saying a thousand things, but the one I knew she wanted to ask was, "Is this enough?"

I lay my head back, even in my adrenaline-rushed stage, still clear-headed to the point of knowing one thing. I wasn't sure.

39

HEATHER DROVE ME BACK TO THE OFFICE SO I COULD GRAB the set of spare clothes I kept there. It was funny in a way, or at least it would've been if my head hadn't been throbbing. I didn't know many jobs where you are so unsure of your day that you make sure a clean outfit is never too far out of reach. Kate had agreed to let us come in and watch as she and Corbin interviewed the women. It was a concession I knew she didn't have to make, but it was also one that I knew had a double use. Kate could save herself a lot of time digging through what my team and I had nailed down; and we got the chance to see this case through to the end.

"You sure you want to be here for this?" Kate asked as she glanced at the door of the interrogation room beside us, the same one where Jacobi Milton had sat not too long ago.

I nodded. "I imagine this is a little different than most of the folks who pass through. They lawyer up yet?"

Kate actually laughed. "You'd think so. But, no. I think this level of wealth convinces you that you can do anything you want, just because you want to. Collie hasn't shut up since we got her in the cruiser. I know you think I'm just out here doing a wellness check on you, which I sort of am, but..." She shook her head. "I needed a break from that woman."

"How so?"

Kate leaned against the wall, her hands in her pockets. "Well, I mean, naturally, 'she didn't do anything.' It's an affront that we would even suggest something so audacious."

"Using her big words, is she?"

"Oh, she's smart," Kate said. "But she's manipulative, just like Nel said. We're lucky this one didn't decide to become a lawyer. We aren't to the 'that depends on what the meaning of is, is' yet, but she's not far from it."

I shook my head. "Good old linguistics."

"And she paid attention in school," Kate continued and held up a finger. "But the embezzlement? She was ready to go on that one. I'm assuming she saw enough TV to figure admitting to one crime will get her out of another."

"Murder and skimming money no one has ever missed are pretty far apart."

She shrugged. "You know what they say. They got Al Capone on tax evasion."

"Right." I thought for a moment, the blood pounding in my temples. I should've just gone home, but I was in it this far. I needed to see it through. "Has anyone talked to the other women?"

"Basic statements," she said, checking her watch. "It hasn't even been an hour yet. They're still likely reeling a bit."

"Then this might be the time to make a move. Let's go see." I paused, running through the list of women, what I knew, as little as it may have been. I snapped my fingers. "D'you mind if I take a shot at them?"

"Sure. Why not? But they're pretty quiet."

"It only takes one. What room is Franny in?"

Kate nodded toward one down the hall across from us. "What's your angle?"

I raised an eyebrow. "If we need a new one, we'll find it. But this woman, out of all of them, she seemed like she actually cared."

"So did Collie Newman."

I sniffed a small laugh. "Then we can't do much worse."

We crossed the hall and I paused outside the door. "You'll follow my lead?"

"Within reason."

"Fair enough."

I stepped into the room, doing my best to hide the ache in my bones as I pulled out a chair and sat down across from the visibly shaken woman.

"We're going to do this quickly," I said. "I don't have the time or the patience for it, and whether I dilly-dally around or not isn't going to save you any grief. You're currently looking at murder charges."

Franny gasped, thankfully loud enough that she didn't seem to notice how Kate's eyes widened at the statement.

"We can put you at the scene of the crimes. I'm sure your book club buddies will be happy to corroborate our findings. So let's make this brief, shall we? One of us would like to get home to a bedroom without bars on the windows."

"You can't..." Her eyes were wide, the same expression I'd seen when Kate and I had just burst through the back gate of Collie Newman's house. For once, I believed it. It wasn't the best feeling in the world to play this game, but I hadn't been entirely false. I was just ready to get home.

"I..." she started again, her hands shaking on the table.

"You," Kate jumped in, "were close friends with two homicide victims. You were within an arm's reach of a woman who almost died today. I know you're used to a pretty pampered life, but most juries aren't entirely sympathetic to the rich."

It wasn't completely false, but Franny was clearly in no position to consider the logic outside of the very real consequences the words held for her.

"But Hattie was my friend!" she pleaded, looking at me for the first time. "I told you that! My husband told you that!"

I considered pointing out the discrepancies in her statements, but it would've been pointless. This woman was about to break, and, like Nel Modesto, she just needed a little nudge in the right direction. "And Beatrice Loftis? You've got a strange kind of friendship with folks."

"No, it..." Her eyes flicked toward the door as if she were waiting for someone, and I thought I knew who, to burst through.

"Collie is currently with one of our officers," Kate said. "If you want to speak, now would be the time to do it."

"Don't I...?" She looked down, and I knew both Kate and I were waiting for the end of the sentence. If this woman lawyered up, it was going to drag out the investigation for weeks.

"No," I said. "You don't need to. If you want to just tell us what happened, maybe you'll be back home by this evening."

I saw her eyes glisten. The tears were a strange mixture of relief, guilt, perhaps fear, but she wiped them with the back of her hand and squared her shoulders. For once I could see the class in this woman after all.

"Collie..." she started, then cleared her throat and tried again. "Collie's going to tell you I'm just throwing her under the bus. She'll probably blame the whole thing on me, for all I know. The others might as well, but I hope not."

"Not quite as close-knit a group as we were led to believe," Kate said.

Franny bobbed her head from side to side. "We were. Or we tried to be. But that was before."

"Before Beatrice?" I asked.

"Before that even. I don't know what all you've heard. Probably not much. And I do apologize for being closed-lipped, but... well, you see what happens if you upset Collie."

"So you all knew?" Kate asked.

Franny looked up at her, for the briefest moment her expression looking like she wanted to feign ignorance. Instead, she shook her head, not in negation, but as if tossing a thought away.

"Collie has some... questionable business practices." She shrugged. "Might be true for more people in the Heights than it isn't. But Collie takes... She handles things differently." Her gaze was heavy on the still visible bruises and cuts on my face. "I guess you know that though."

Kate cut in. "For the record, you're saying that you know personally Miss Newman hired someone to attack Mr. Starke."

"Of course," Franny said, looking down. "I don't think Collie ever intended for any of us to know what she did, but liquor makes for loose lips. Once she'd admitted it, the only options were to try and deny it later, which would've been impossible, or make sure we all knew who was running the show."

"So the book club was more a way to keep you in check than anything?"

The woman nodded.

"What about Hattie and Beatrice?" I asked. "And Nel. I think we all understand what happened here, but we need you to be willing to say it to us and, later on, a jury."

Franny took a slow, shuddering breath.

"Beatrice had a bit of a stubborn streak," she began. "It was something we all knew but didn't take too seriously. Even Collie seemed to think she herself was always running the show and no one else. Bea didn't like that... but until Collie slipped up and outed her financial dealings, no one was too concerned about it. Bea wouldn't stand for it though. It bothered her. She had a lot of pride, and I'm not saying that's a good thing or a bad one, but Bea liked to believe the Heights were a sophisticated, clean, moral place. She believed Collie was tarnishing that image. So, when things got heated between the two of them, and Beatrice was sounding more and more like she was going to be Collie's undoing, there was a book club meeting. A lot like the one you saw today, actually."

"Meaning?" Kate asked.

"Meaning Collie, the ever-dutiful bartender, poured drinks down everyone's gullets till we felt like we were at a frat party. She convinced Bea to dive into the pool, steering her around to the shallow end, making sure we all saw it was a voluntary act, and then..." She took a ragged breath. "Then Beatrice dove."

I shot a glance at Kate. It wasn't exactly murder, but it wasn't exactly innocent either.

"What about Hattie?" Kate asked, her voice softer now, consoling.

Franny shrugged. "Hattie wouldn't dive. I don't know how Hattie was still on her feet at the end. She rarely drank and Collie wasn't taking it easy on the liquor, as usual. It was a lot like Nel, really. Get someone drunk enough, bump a hip when you walk by, and Hattie fell in."

"You saw these things?" I asked. "Or is this what you heard?"

Franny wiped at her eyes again. "No... I was there. I'm so ashamed." She took in a shaky breath, a sob threatening in her words. "I just... who does those things? And once you see them, who's to say you won't be the next?"

"You could've left," Kate said. "Victoria Blue is planning to. Nel as well."

Franny nodded, letting the tears fall now. "And that's what I have to live with. One phone call and I would still have my two friends."

Her shoulders shook as she began to cry and I looked over at Kate. "Thank you, Franny," I said. "We're going to give you a moment."

I led Kate out into the hall and sat in one of the plastic chairs on the near side. "Well, you think she'll keep her word?"

"And talk in court?" Kate said. She looked up at the ceiling for a moment, the drop tiles so pedestrian for the amount of drama that took place in these halls. "I can't imagine she won't. If she thought Collie was a threat before, she has to know she is now." She paused, then said, "They're all accessories to... Murder? Hell, I don't know... something. I'll let the DA figure that one out. If she lawyers up, maybe he'll cut her a deal of some sort. Right now I have to try to figure out what to charge them all with."

I shook my head. "The best and brightest are in the Heights, huh?"

She shrugged. "It's not the cleanest case I've ever seen, but it's done. Get home. Your wife's gotta be looking for you by now."

I stood up slowly, my back throbbing, my head aching, and walked down the hall to find Heather. I needed a ride back and maybe, just maybe, a day off. Or at least a half-day.

40

A FEW MONTHS LATER, AMANDA AND I SAT IN FRONT OF the TV, the late-night news playing at a low volume as we wound down for the evening. Collie Newman's face was in the corner of the screen. No longer were they using the prim and proper professional headshot her lawyer had no doubt given the media when the story had started to blow up. Now it was a haggard, though still defiant, face that looked out at the viewing audience. She appeared tired. She had clearly not fared well through the course of the investigation and trial, but Collie Newman still had a glint in her eye that said she believed she would walk, that her money, regardless of how she came across it, would save her yet again.

"Crazy, isn't it?" Amanda said beside me, yawning and stretching her arms.

"What do you mean?"

"That this is a murder trial. The narrative has changed so much. She flat-out told you all she was committing a white-collar crime, but now half the country thinks she's a murderer too."

I sighed. "There may not be enough to convict her of first or second degree murder for killing Beatrice and Hattie."

"We'll see," she said.

I reached over and rubbed her back. "People like her are slick. But if she gets out of the murder charges, she'll still go to prison for embezzlement. They say no press is bad press, but being accused of two murders isn't great coverage."

The image on the screen changed, this time showing two very flattering photos, one of Nel Modesto, looking like she could hold her own against any lawyer in the country, the other of Franny Cullins. It was an old photo of Franny, and one that I was glad they had used. The woman had been through enough without having her stress broadcast coast to coast. They were the only two who were willing to talk. Nel didn't surprise me, and Franny didn't too much either. She'd been traumatized by the whole thing. It was her way of making up for it, and though we hadn't talked in weeks, I admired her resolve.

"Just the two?" Amanda said.

"Just the two," I said. "Victoria moved out not too long ago. I talked with the DA, Larry Spruce. Franny cut a deal with the DA. She was given immunity for testifying against Collie. As far as I know, that's all they have. None of us saw what happened before we broke through the gate. Nel was already in the pool, face down and drunk as a skunk. Marilyn and Caroline are not talking and doing their best to pretend nothing ever happened. But they've been informed they could be charged with misprision of a felony, and for that, they could get up to three years, but only if Collie's found guilty. If she's not, there's no crime, so no misprision of a felony."

Amanda furrowed her brow. "Misprision of a felony?"

"The short version... Having knowledge of the actual commission of a felony and not reporting it. They were there all three times. They knew what happened. They watched as

Collie got them blind drunk and then engineered Beatrice and Hattie's deaths and the attempt on Nel Modesto, and they did nothing about it. That's a crime."

"What about the attack on you?"

I shook my head. "Collie denies knowing anything about it, and Jacobi's not talking—his biker buddies would kill him if he did." I'd already shared with Amanda that Kate went after Jacobi like a dog after a meaty bone. He didn't stand a chance. He was already in lockup, this time for a long while.

Amanda thought for a moment and then said, "Interesting."

I turned to face her. "What? Are you surprised?"

"Not at all." She stood up, stretching as she always did before we headed upstairs to bed. "But if Victoria Blue moved out, that means there's a very nice, classy castle available in the Heights, just waiting for someone to move in and keep an eye on the place."

I laughed and shook my head, standing up beside her. "I hear their book club needs a new president too."

Amanda leaned in and gave me a kiss on the cheek. "Not in a million years."

I put my arm around her waist and we walked toward the stairs. "I think we've got everything we need right here."

"Maybe even more," she said, leaning her head on my shoulder.

———

It was a week later we learned that, while the jury was out, Collie Newman caved and accepted a plea of the voluntary manslaughter of Hattie Baker and the reckless endangerment—a Class A misdemeanor—of Nel Modesto. There was no evidence to prove that she had anything to do with Beatrice Loftis' death, so she got a pass on that one. She was sentenced to eight years in the state penitentiary for women and, on release, ten years' probation. With good behavior she'd be out in five.

Not what she deserved—I was convinced she murdered them both—but it was something. She took the deal because her defense council told her there was a chance the jury would find her guilty of second-degree murder. If so, she was looking at twenty years. Larry told me he offered her the deal because he was of the opinion the jury would have acquitted her on all counts. She, of course, didn't want to take a chance on twenty years. And she still had to stand trial for the embezzlement charge.

So goes our wonderful justice system. One thing was certain, though. Collie Newman would never again be able to live in Hilden Heights, or anywhere like it, for that matter. She would no longer be "their type."

We'd done the best we could for our client, Mason Willis. He'd hired us to discover the truth about the death of the woman he loved and provide closure. He—and everyone else—now knew that Hattie's death was not an accident, just as he'd suspected. And for that, he was very grateful to the Harry Starke Investigations team.

Thank you for reading **Dead Pool** the twenty-first book in the Harry Starke Novels. I hope you enjoyed it, if you did please help others find Blair Howards Books by leaving a few words about it in the form of a review.

HARRY STARKE WILL BE BACK WITH HIS NEXT CASE!

SIGN UP FOR ANNOUNCEMENTS & GREAT DEALS!

PLUS you'll Unlock 20% Off

Get Exclusive Deals (As Part Of "The Family")

Visit www.BlairHowardBooks.com

If you don't see the pop up to join, just click the blue unlock 20% off icon and enter your details.

Don't forget to confirm your email and whitelist (save as contact)Blair@blairhowardbooks.com to your email system.

CHECK OUT HIS NEW SERIES DEBUT, NEVER SAY DEAD.

YOU'LL FIND A SAMPLE ON THE NEXT FEW PAGES.

Turn the page for sneak peak at Never Say Dead . . .

Chapter One

Monday Evening

Mallory Carver leaned back against the bar counter and stared up at the water stains on the ceiling.

She didn't know how long they'd been there. She'd worked at The Saloon since... she specifically remembered the help wanted sign had appeared in October after she graduated high school, but she didn't apply until after Thanksgiving. And only then because she needed to get out of the house for a few hours each day. But the part-time job turned full-time, and...

Thirteen years later and I'm wondering if I can sell pictures of the ceiling for Rorschach tests, she thought.

She imagined a decade of drunks staring up at them, some seeing their mothers, others seeing their dogs. Maybe some saw a traumatic childhood event; *those would be the drunks that cried into their beer*, she thought.

She'd seen every kind of drunk you could imagine during her thirteen years at The Saloon.

Back in the day, when she was first hired, it had been the Old West Saloon and Cattle Grill. It was a nice place then—fun music, good, inexpensive beer, an attractive menu, and even some coin-op horses out front for the kids to ride. Then the owner died, and it became Mustang Sally's. Sally kept the entire staff, which had been a relief, and she'd been a good boss and had treated everyone well. But then she'd had an emergency and moved out of state. After that it became the Quick Draw, an apt name since people didn't stay long when they found out how much the drinks cost. And now it was The Saloon, where the drinks were cheap because they were cheap drinks. The speaker system was old, dating from Sally's time, but she and the live music were long gone. And Vinnie, who'd owned the place for the last six years, cared more about the pennies he pinched than he did complaining customers.

It's a hole. And I can't dig my way out, she thought gloomily.

She looked at the clock. It was a little before nine PM—what once was peak hour—but the only customers she had was a booth full of bikers drinking the most tasteless domestic beer they had on tap, and Art Peters ensconced at the end of the bar with his sleep apnea.

"If we don't have any business, I guess I might as well start cleaning up," she muttered, slipping an earbud under her long blond hair and starting her favorite podcast.

She felt that familiar thrill at the clanking sound of the clock tower and the bong of the hour as Devin Rudd began his podcast. "Not every terrible tale begins with a terrible event. Many times, the most mundane happenings can lead to the most horrific murders. This, then, is the story of a man who wished to be an art student, and what his desires wrought for those around him. This, then, is another... *Dark Tiding.*"

As the music began, she wondered who it was going to be this time. As Devin Rudd began to describe the idyllic setting in which the killer grew up, she stepped around the end of the bar, collected the bus bin and hauled it off to the dishwasher.

Where could she be? she wondered as she filled the dishwasher and pulled down the hatch. *It was just a routine hike.* As the water began sloshing around inside the washer, she tried to concentrate on the podcast. She'd missed the name of the killer —something mundane, someone she'd never heard of, which was unusual. She thought she knew them all; all those of any note, anyway.

The door buzzer jangled. She hurried back out to see who it was, but it was only the bikers leaving, a half-pitcher of warm beer on the table along with a ten-dollar bill. *At least I don't have to deal with them at closing time.*

Why hasn't she called her mom? It's been six days. Maybe she's lying hurt in a gully somewhere. She pushed the thought away. She had to work.

She grabbed another bus bin and walked over to clear the table, wrinkling her nose at the lingering smell of strong tobacco. *I don't mind the smell of tobacco, but that stuff reeks.* She waved a hand at the invisible odors, but they persisted. She hurriedly scraped the last of the paper trash into the bin and turned to flee the stink, but found herself facing Deputy Kal Cundiff.

"Evening, Mallory," Kal said.

She stopped, startled, the bus bin on her hip. Outside, the sound of motorcycles revving broke the silence.

"Oh, hi, Kal," she said, frowning. "I didn't hear you come in."

"That's because you're filling your ears with garbage," he said and smirked. "Who are you listening to tonight? Ed Gein? Ted Bundy? Or is it a five-part series on Charlie Manson?"

"It's not like that," she lied as she marched past him. But when she dropped the bin out back, she paused the podcast, slipped the bud out of her ear and into her pocket, and returned to her place behind the bar.

"All right," she said. "What brings you in here tonight? And in uniform? Don't tell me your dad has decided to take us seriously."

"Nah," Kal said and pulled a face, unable to look her in the eye. "The Sheriff's office has decided it doesn't qualify as a missing person's case."

"How can that be?" she insisted. "A person just has to be missing for more than forty-eight hours. Julie's been missing for *six days*."

"Mal," he said plaintively, "this isn't one of those podcasts you listen to."

"Screw you, Kal," she snapped back. "Julie is a responsible young woman. She's an experienced hunting guide. She knows the trails like the back of her hand. Ever since Jared got hurt, she's been the dependable rock of the family. She wouldn't just... fly off and disappear without telling someone. It's not in her nature."

"Well, you know... sometimes the pressure builds up," Kal said in his best TV-cop voice. "All that responsibility, helping to run the business and all. And she decides to up and take a crazy vacation. It happens all the time. She'll be back. Mal, we never found her car, not at any of the trailheads. Not everything is some stupid criminal murder conspiracy."

"Is that what you think of me, Kal Cundiff? You think I'm bitching about my missing niece because I listened to a story?" She stepped around the end of the bar and stopped in front of him, using every inch of her five-foot-ten to loom over him. "My sister, Jennifer," she continued, "and my entire family is halfway to mourning because they think she might be lying dead up there in the forest somewhere, and all you can do is make sick remarks."

"Look, Mal, I'm sorry," Kal said, his face turning a rosy hue.

Mallory stepped back behind the bar and slammed down the hatch with a bang.

"Really?" she snapped. "You're sorry. Your dad is sorry. And my sister is at home crying over her missing daughter, and your department doesn't seem to care at all. Was there any other reason you stopped by to see me? If not, I have to close up, so you need to leave."

Kal reached around and pulled out a notebook from his hip pocket. "Okay. I was out of line, and I apologize. As it happens, I'm here to get a few details. Since you fancy yourself an amateur detective, you probably have them all memorized, right?"

She wanted to glare at him, slap the mocking smile off his

face, but there was a sliver of hope: *Is he finally going to take it seriously?*

"Where do you want me to start?" she asked.

"You can gimme the basics first," he replied, his pen poised.

"Her name is Julie Romero. She's twenty-three, five-eight, slim, one-hundred-twenty-two pounds, with blonde, shoulder-length hair. She had her dog, Tobin, with her. Her parents have lived in Chattanooga for the last forty-four years. My sister, Jennifer, her mother, told me that she left last Tuesday morning for a hike on Red Grove Trail, off Highway 64; she didn't know which branch."

"Yeah, I heard," he said. "Red Grove. She oughta know better than to go into the forest up there by herself."

"And why not?" she asked, giving him an annoyed glare. "She's an experienced guide."

She knew that many of the locals had some wild ideas about the mountains and the Cherokee National Forest. And, while there were plenty of real-life dangers associated with walking through forests and mountains, centuries of Native American folklore and campfire stories had convinced half the population that the place was crawling with eldritch deities, dark forces commanded by witches, ghosts, territorial moonshiners, and cannabis and mandrake farmers. Most of it was bunk as far as she was concerned, but Kal didn't look too eager to check out the forbidding forest.

"Look, Julie isn't just some hiker," she said. "She's an experienced hunting guide. She works for her dad, Jared Romero, at his big hunting outlet off 64. She doesn't just get lost in her own backyard."

"Experienced hikers can and do get lost," Kal argued. "Happens all the time."

"Not Julie," she snapped. "If she was going to be late back, she'd have texted her father. What about her Bronco? That wouldn't just get lost, too, would it?"

"We've had an APB out for almost a week," Kal replied. "If nobody's found it, it means it's left the county. And with no evidence to the contrary, it looks like she drove it away."

Mallory opened her mouth to speak, but Kal beat her to it.

"Let me ask you something, Mal. Do you want to be here? In Chattanooga?"

Mallory paused.

"Because you just said she's lived here basically her whole life," he continued. "She's never been anywhere else. Never seen the big cities. Never tasted life outside of town or even outside her own family. How happy was she working for her dad?"

Mallory knew that Julie was frustrated with her dad at times. But she always smiled at everything... but was there pain behind that smile? Longing? Frustration?

How long had Mallory wanted to just pack up and leave? When exactly had *she* decided to stay? She had a sharp mind and a good education, with a 4.0 grade point average. Why did she stay? Why would Julie stay? *Because it's home. That's why.*

"See?" Kal said righteously when she didn't reply. "I knew you'd understand. Just give her another week and she'll come rolling back into town, apologize for being so thoughtless, and then brag about her big adventure in Nashville."

A part of Mallory wanted to believe him. It was an easy out, and it fulfilled all the criteria: Julie was safe. She was having a little reckless fun. Everything would be fine.

But it didn't answer the real questions, the ones her family kept asking. *Why* did she? *How* could she? *Where* is she? Why hasn't she called? And why is her phone off?

"We're not going to agree on this, Kal," Mallory said sadly. "I guess we just don't understand each other. It isn't personal.

No one will listen to us, so Jennifer is going to do something about it herself."

Kal looked alarmed. "You don't mean she's going to go trekking up there her own self? That's insane. She does that, we'll have a real missing person's case on our hands."

"No, she's not going to do that. She's not stupid, Kal. She said she's going into the city tomorrow. Though, I suppose she might have lied to us and planned to run away into the woods instead."

"What's she gonna do, then?" Kal demanded.

"She's going to hire Tucker Randall," Mallory said.

"*What*? That overpriced PI who takes on, what, three or four cases a year? Your family is seriously going to put trust in that hack?"

"We haven't been seeing any results from your department so far, have we?" Mallory said.

"Tucker Randall is a publicity hound," Kal replied. "He'll suck you dry and leave you looking stupid while he parades around on TV."

"Better stupid than useless." Mallory saw that her jibe had hit its mark.

"Well, I've got to get going," Kal said and stuffed the notepad back in his pocket.

"Get it all down, did you?" Mallory asked, smirking, knowing he hadn't written a word.

Kal rolled his shoulders, adjusted his belt, looked at her and said, "Good luck with Randall, but I ain't holding my breath." As he opened the door, he threw one last shot. "If he even takes the case, which I sincerely doubt he will."

Mallory resisted the urge to throw something at the door. Instead, she stomped to the other end of the bar and gave Art a little shove. "Come on, Art. It's closing time. Do I need to call your brother?"

"What?" Art looked at her, then scrunched up his face as he tried to focus. "Nah-uh-uh. I'm good. I'll get home just fine."

I hope Julie gets home just fine, too.

Read More of this Brand New Series
Randall & Carver Mysteries

Find it at https://blairhowardbooks.com/collections/randall-carver-mysteries

Also From Blair Howard

The Harry Starke Genesis Series
The Harry Starke Series
The Lt. Kate Gazzara Murder Files
The Peacemaker Series
The Civil War Series
Randall & Carver Mysteries

From Blair C. Howard

The Sovereign Star Series

ABOUT THE AUTHOR

Blair Howard is a retired journalist turned novelist. He's the author of more than 65 novels including the international best-selling Harry Starke series of crime stories, the Lt. Kate Gazzara series, and the Harry Starke Genesis series. He's also the author of the Peacemaker series of international thrillers and five Civil War/Western novels.

If you enjoy reading Science Fiction thrillers, Mr. Howard has made his debut into the genre with, The Sovereign Stars Series under the name, Blair C. Howard. You can find out more about this series at his website.

Visit www.blairhowardbooks.com.

You can also find Blair Howard on Social Media

facebook.com/bcwhoward

x.com/bcwhoward

bookbub.com/authors/blair-howard